BITTERTHORN

Praise for *Bitterthorn*

'Deliciously Gothic . . . Dunn plays on fairytale conventions to create a lush, atmospheric story of curses, belonging and betrayal with a slow-burn love story at its heart'
Observer

'A stunning meditation on loneliness, with nods to *Jane Eyre*, Angelina Jolie's *Maleficent* and Naomi Novik's *Uprooted*'
Good Housekeeping

'This dazzling YA gem melds a thrilling high-stakes fairytale scenario with suspenseful, slow-burn sapphic romance'
LoveReading

'Kat Dunn has spun a love story both intimate and epic. *Bitterthorn* is a perfect fireside tale, thick with suspense, yearning and wild beauty – I loved every moment of reading it'
SAMANTHA SHANNON, international bestselling author of *The Priory of the Orange Tree*

'A moody and stylish Gothic tale that feels both fresh and timeless – a masterful meditation on grief, loneliness, and terrible love. Gutting and unforgettable'
AVA REID, *Sunday Times* bestselling author of *The Wolf and the Woodsman*

'*Bitterthorn* is beautiful and haunting – the type of story that seeps into your bones and stays with you long after reading. Kat Dunn has spun a deliciously dark fairytale full of the agony and ecstasy of longing and desire, as well as celebrating the power of resilience and inner strength'
KATHERINE WEBBER, *Sunday Times* bestselling author of *Twin Crowns*

'A haunting, atmospheric tale of two lost souls finding each other, and a love that will remake the world. Exquisite'
SHELLEY PARKER-CHAN, *Sunday Times* bestselling author of *She Who Became the Sun*

'Both classic and novel, melancholy and tenderly wrought, *Bitterthorn* crackles with passion and warmth like a fire on a long winter night. With achingly atmospheric prose, Dunn has crafted characters I would die for and a love story as powerful and enduring as a fairytale. A must-read for fans of Gothic romance'
ALLISON SAFT, *New York Times* bestselling author
of *A Far Wilder Magic*

'Girl meets house. Girl meets witch. And oh, does it ever get deliciously interesting from there! Dunn has created a delicately spun cobweb of a fairytale that slowly unwinds a pattern of secrets, curses, love and betrayal – and finally settles around your heart and leaves you glad to have been captured'
FREYA MARSKE, *Sunday Times* bestselling author
of *A Marvellous Light*

'*Bitterthorn* tugged on the threads of my heartstrings until I had nothing left to give it but my soul. Hauntingly beautiful, this Gothic fairytale lingers in the darkest corners of my mind forever more. A triumph'
SAARA EL-ARIFI, *Sunday Times* bestselling author
of *The Final Strife*

'An exquisitely crafted story of love and yearning. *Bitterthorn* drew me in and captured me in its Gothic, fairytale charm. I savoured every word'
JUDY I LIN, *New York Times* bestselling author of
A Magic Steeped in Poison

'This darkly romantic fairytale is a stunning rumination on loneliness, grief, and the aching human desire to love and be loved. Sapphic, Gothic and deeply cathartic – I feel profoundly moved'
LAURA STEVEN, author of *The Society for Soulless Girls*

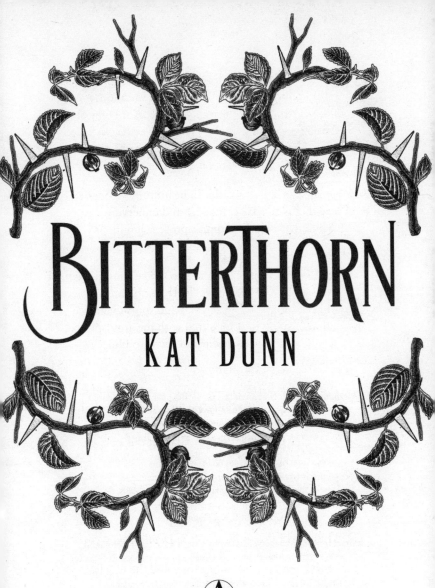

BITTERTHORN

KAT DUNN

ANDERSEN PRESS

First published in 2023 by
Andersen Press Limited
20 Vauxhall Bridge Road, London SW1V 2SA, UK
Vijverlaan 48, 3062 HL Rotterdam, Nederland
www.andersenpress.co.uk

4 6 8 10 9 7 5

Extract from *The Lathe Of Heaven* by Ursula K Le Guin reproduced
with permission of Orion Publishing Group Limited through PLSclear

British Library Cataloguing in Publication Data available.

ISBN 978 1 83913 295 7

Printed and bound in Great Britain by Clays Ltd, Elcograf S.p.A.

To younger me,
I'm so sorry.
It is as bad as you think it is,
but you'll escape

*Love doesn't just sit there,
like a stone, it has to be
made, like bread; remade all
the time, made new.*

Ursula K Le Guin

AUTUMN

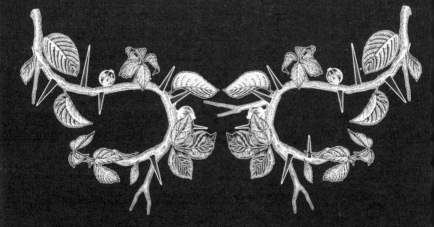

I

I was born from my mother en caul, swaddled in my unbroken amniotic sac like an insect encased in amber, and entirely apart from the world.

I have, in all meaningful ways, been alone ever since.

The doctor grimaced and slit open my cocoon with a knife, spilling fluid and meconium, and like a selkie, I slipped off my first skin to reveal another human one beneath.

My mother was gone in an instant, fainting in shock at this living, squirming thing emerging from inside her.

My father took longer to leave.

I was presented to him, minutes old, in the antechamber to my mother's room, cleaned off and wrapped in lace. I am told he politely enquired after my birth, and had the good grace not to be visibly disappointed that he had no son. A daughter was perfectly adequate, and I had sensibly arrived healthy and whole. My only crime was arriving at all, into the lives of two people who weren't quite sure what to do with a child now it was here. I never doubted they loved me in their own way, but I understood clearly and quickly what I was to them: a problem to be solved.

Who should look after me? Where should I be put? How could things be arranged so neither of them had to change their lives in any real way?

I soon learned my job. A series of nannies and governesses shepherded me from nursery to school room and I saw my parents in slivers like the windows of a zoetrope: Mother dandling me on her knee before a dinner party, my father presenting me to guests as I recited Goethe. Every child is beholden to the gods of their parents, and I augured their meanings from careless words and gestures, made rituals to fit around their whims, and inscribed into my heart the rules they unwittingly handed down. I learned who I was through them.

Mina is a good girl. Mina is a sensible girl. Mina is not demanding.

I was well fed, clean, sheltered by all the protections money and status afforded.

I lacked for nothing, except real love.

My mother would visit me occasionally, when her spirits were on the way up. This interest in me – riding together, a trip to Paris, a painting course – flared up rapidly like a match being struck, and then would be dropped as the flame reached her fingertips, the shrivelled, blackened stick tossed aside before any of the heat could touch her. My mother was delicate, and a child was one burden too many for her to bear – not that she was capable of bearing many burdens at all. She struggled with life as though it wasn't her natural home. The air too thick and syrupy for her to breathe, moving through it like a poor swimmer thrashing amongst the waves.

My mother died the autumn I was twelve.

I didn't understand what it was to need someone, until she was gone.

My father, left with a daughter on the cusp of womanhood, panicked. He did what any prudent man would do and promptly married a respectable widow replete with daughters near enough my age so that someone else could handle *female issues*. As ruler of the small Duchy of Schwartzstein, his time was all accounted for and raising children was not on his schedule.

My mother was tidied away into her grave and my stepmother unpacked her things into her place. I found myself far from home without having travelled a metre. I was living on the outskirts of someone else's family and no matter how many mollifying words my father offered, I knew I was not a necessary star in this new constellation.

My stepmother was not a cruel woman, merely a disinterested one. She had three daughters of her own and no desire to take on another. Johanna, the eldest, Else in the middle, and the youngest, Klara, needed education and good matches to be found, and that was a far greater draw on her attention than a grieving girl child confused by monthly courses and a shape-shifting body.

Still, she didn't throw me into a cellar or make me their servant.

No, she simply turned me into a ghost.

When she and her daughters arrived into our house, in all meaningful ways I ceased to exist. I slipped into my adult woman body in the same way I had been born into the world: cloistered apart from the rest of humanity, shuddering from one skin into a new one, my beating heart a problem to be dealt with.

Already well versed in entertaining myself, in womanhood I never thought to do anything but continue along the same path. If the palace that had been my home was now the domain of my stepmother, I would look beyond for something of my own – and found it in the trees outside each window, the mountains that ringed our capital city of Blumwald, in the pebbly river that churned wild in spring with snowmelt and froze solid enough to skate on in winter. I found home in the crags and branches, in birdsong and my own ragged breath as I walked and walked. I felt power in my independence: far, far safer to be alone than to want and be unwanted.

So I walked, and I walked and walked until my boots were bloody and my face was sunburned, until I became a creature like the foxes and egrets, until I was only motion and pumping heart and nothing human at all. Holding entropy at bay, I heard my father call it once, the constant output of energy to remain in one place. Life was in movement; only dead things were still.

I was a dead thing, in my heart. I knew it like a poison I drank each night and purged each morning. I knew that I was isolated, but I didn't *understand* my loneliness until I knew what I would give to escape it. What I would be willing to do.

Until I knew what it was to love, and be loved.

It was the Witch who taught me that.

II

The news of Bismarck came the day summer died.

The season had stretched long this year, workers sweating in the fields as they brought in the harvest, the last of the radishes, fennel and beetroot flourishing in the shimmering heat until it burst like a blister and a thunderstorm rolled up the valley, bouncing between the mountains to thrash Blumwald with rain and lightning.

I had gone walking early, as I often did. Finally I had woken to a clear sky so I went to my trees to assess the progress of the seasons. I wrapped apples, butterkäse, a piece of smoked sausage, some dark rye bread and a slice of poppy seed cake in a cloth in my knapsack, and put on a stout pair of boots. Dawn cast long shadows across the cobbles. As I wound through the dense knot of forest at the base of the mountain, past logging stations and huntsmen's cottages, I came across a deer carcass, torn open by scavengers. From the bullet wound to its haunch I knew it was a hunter's mistake: a doe targeted then lost. She had come to a quiet hollow to die. Maggots had eaten out the jelly of her eyes and the meat of her swollen tongue. This was the nature of my forest home.

Up on the cleared stubble of the grazing pastures, I sat on a grist outcrop to eat my lunch. Summer: dead and gone. I marked it in the bloom of red smudging the base of the oak leaves, the freckle of gold sweeping the birch. *Quercus robur*, the monstrous oak trees that planted themselves firm with broad branches sweeping the forest canopy, *betula pendula,* the silver birches clustering close with their trunks like peeling skin. They marked time better than any clock or candle or bell in the rings of their trunks and the spread of their branches. All around the forest fanned out like a pack of cards, dense and overlapping, arguing for space. It curved around Blumwald like a cupped hand, across valley to climb hillsides and along riverbanks.

From my vantage point above the city, I saw my father's carriage hurtling along the valley road. At this distance it seemed to move as slowly as an ant, but from the cloud of dust around the wheels and the way the rest of the traffic parted like a ripped seam, I gathered they must have been going at some lick.

I took another bite of my apple and chewed.

He wasn't due back from Berlin for another week; this was either terrible or excellent news. Schwartzstein was a scrap of land as big as the space between my thumb and forefinger when I held my hand out before me, and my father was its ruler. We had slunk around the edges of history while all around countries merged and split and feuded and warred. A nation of sheep and wool and spinning.

No one noticed us, except the Witch.

My father had different plans now: we were to be noticed by someone else. Chancellor Bismarck was unifying Germany and we were to become part of the new Empire. I wanted to know what the news was, but I also knew the best way to be around my father was not to be there at all. This was one of the first laws I learned: if he was in a rare good mood, I was welcome to provide entertainment; if his attention was turned to his duties, I was to pretend I didn't exist at all.

Finding a snag of fleece in my pocket, I plucked two thistles to card it in the old way, watching the carriage draw closer. In a sheep-riddled place like Blumwald, fleece was caught on every fence post, oily and ripe with ovine scent. This was a hunk the size of my palm; cream turned grey with dirt and caught up with burrs and spindly leaf stems and grasses. I brushed it rhythmically like passing over the beads of a rosary, my fingertips waxy with lanolin, to work out the knots and detritus until I had a piece of fibre ready to be washed. A scrap like this would be good for nothing but a drop spindle, spun by hand to add twists to the fibre until it became strong enough for weaving and knitting. I had no spindle of my own to do it, only my mother's, which she had kept more as a toy than a means of creation. I thought of the doe again, her milky teeth bared in a death grin. In a few more years, I would have had a dead mother longer than a living one.

I waited until my father's carriage reached the Summer Palace, then made my way back. I still had one living parent, and the more he withdrew from me, the more I wanted to find a place by his side.

At the tide line where the wheat fields met the bracken and saplings, a spate of shrines were scattered like a warning. A hollow scooped out at the base of an oak, in it a dish of salt and scraps of iron, a twist of yarn and a saint's medallion nestled among it – St Anthony of Padua this time, for protection against evil – a bough of ash to one side and a branch of blackthorn on the other with a cluster of dusty purple sloes still attached. A smear of something red across it all. I thought of the old words: by oak, by ash, by bitterthorn. Half prayer, half invocation. An oath for protection, for binding. All of it a plea against the dark.

In the distance, above the golden canopy of the dying forest, about as far as I could see on a clear, bright day, was the Witch's castle.

The Witch was our curse, the hazy shadow to the bright light of Blumwald. Once a generation, every fifty years or there around, she would descend from her castle to take a companion. One young man plucked out and never seen again. We lived according to the long seasons of her reign: the years directly after her visit like spring, joyous relief and hope. Then, summer as the memory of fear faded. Autumn would come, though, and we could no longer pretend we were safe. Finally, as half a century approached, winter set in, cold and bitter and full of dread.

Dukes rose and fell, wars shifted our borders over centuries, and still we lived tied to the rhythm of her want. It had been a little over fifty years since the Witch had last been seen. We never knew the exact moment she would strike, only that she would, and we lived around the fear of her like a volcano smoking and spitting ash, one eye raised to its fiery summit. An immutable fact that framed the world in salt sprinkled along doorways and windowsills, candles ever-burning on chapel altars, shutters locked tight at the first brush of dusk.

My mother in her worse moods called the Witch a curse on men for their coldness. To be taken from their masterful positions and turned over to the use of a woman. I thought the Witch took them because she could. Because it was a transgression. Who would lose sleep over another *woman* sacrificed?

I thought she took men because she wanted us to know her power.

A candle had been left burning in one shrine. In a flash of anger, I snuffed it out. Salt and iron couldn't protect you from loss. The hurtful truth of death was that it was as mundane as a meal uneaten, a cup knocked over. Exquisite pain that meant nothing. All this was nothing but a hopeful lie.

A twig cracked behind me.

I could see no one, but I felt a prickle along the back of my neck as though I was being watched. As though, in extinguishing the flame, I had opened a door, and something was waiting to come through.

I doused the smouldering candlewick with water from my canteen and hurried on, leaving the shrine in disarray behind me.

*

Shaking off the darkness of the forest, I made for the palace and my father's coach. Past the cathedral, the dry market day in the square, dominated by stalls of cloth and yarn, haberdashery, ironmongery, candles and knives and buckets repaired. Past bakeries already emptied to crumbs and the coffee house, tables outside with waiters fetching small cups of steaming black coffee and soft rolls and pats of creamy butter. I would take breakfast there on a warm morning, with my sketchbook propped before me to outline the rooftops and cobbles, the carriages and water troughs and sprays of clematis shivering up the wooden-framed buildings. I plucked a blossom as I passed, tucking it in my belt.

From the window of my bedroom I could see Blumwald in almost its entirety: at one end was the cathedral with its glistening roof of coloured tiles like the side of a grass snake, at the other, our palace, and between them ran a street like a spine. From it spoked side streets, alleys, squares and wells and market places, tided up by the city walls that were only as tall as the rooftops these days and unmanned for many a generation. Downriver were the tanneries and slaughterhouses turning the water a churning brown with run-off, and the new wool mill with its thundering mechanical loom. My father thought only of railways and factories, but wool and spinning had been the lifeblood of our duchy for centuries before us. In the back alleys and attic rooms of houses, a legion of women still worked at their wheels to bring in a little extra money.

And above us always, the mountain, and the Witch's castle.

My father's horses were being stabled when I arrived, and an unfamiliar man in expensive but travel-stained clothes was directing the unpacking of a series of briefcases and what looked like equipment I'd seen in my geological journals.

My stepmother and stepsisters were in the drawing room, conversation racing along some thread I couldn't catch.

I tried to slip past but was stopped by my stepmother's voice. 'Mina? Is that you?'

I stepped into the doorway. 'Yes.'

A series of menu cards and sheets of notepaper were scattered on the tables between her and her daughters.

'Where were you this morning?'

'I went for a walk.'

She looked over my mud-stained appearance with thinned lips. 'Are you planning to join us once you have made yourself presentable?'

I made a non-committal noise and went to find my father instead.

Soon, I would be the only daughter left at home.

Klara was engaged, Else was already gone to her new husband in Munich, while Johanna had only returned to have her first child. I saw her one day changing muslin squares that she had tucked down the front of her dress. They were stained creamy yellow and smelled strongly of milk. When she spotted me she had shrieked and shooed me from the room with accusations of spying.

I wondered if all my family would change and leave me behind. First my mother had changed into a corpse, now my stepsisters would become wives and mothers, and soon enough my father an old man. It was as though by losing my mother so young, motherhood was a foreign land I had no permission to enter. I had been marked out as different, and the lives my sisters expected for themselves were not available to me.

My father was at his desk in the library, poring over a folder of trade documents he had brought back from Berlin. On a chair beside him was a furl of wool samples, labelled with weight and dye and provenance. The line between his eyes was so deep, it was cast in shadow. One thick groove between his eyebrows, two deep scores either side of his mouth, and a fan of lines across his forehead. My father was not a young man, but I had never seen him look this worn.

I asked after his journey and he waved me into a chair with a dismissive hand. My father would bring me to his side occasionally when he felt like it, and I waited for those moments like drops of rain in a drought. For a moment I would feel like his daughter again, like the loss of my mother hadn't fractured us.

When several minutes had passed without him looking up, I said, 'Perhaps I could help you with your papers? I've said you need a secretary.'

'You were quite right.' He put down a letter and squeezed the bridge of his nose.

I began to gather the mess of papers. I saw a list of names, notes about a railway being built, a conference. 'You have returned so soon. Is everything well?' My eyes lingered on a letter signed by Bismarck himself.

'We are to host a conference for the Chancellor and his cabinet next month. There is much to prepare and little time. If all goes well, I believe we will be looked upon favourably for the location of the new locomotive line.'

A smile broke across my face. 'I am happy for you. I know you have worked a long time for this.'

'I have. We must all put our efforts towards the conference's smooth running.'

'Of course. You will need help.'

I sorted the documents into groups, arranging my father's desk, but he stopped me with a confused smile.

The mistake dawned on us both.

He tried to hide his amusement. 'Oh, no, liebchen. I hired a secretary in Berlin – perhaps you saw him? Klaus Ernhoff, newly graduated from Jena.' He toyed with his pen for a moment then set it to one side. 'You don't want to be stuck in here with me.'

I flushed with humiliation. 'Father—'

He regarded me softly and that was somehow worse. 'Mina, you look to me too much. You must think to your own future.'

I was foolish to think he might want me with him.

My father was a man who managed people like the figures in his account books. After my mother died, I would come to him, deep in grief, looking for someone who might understand what I had lost. Instead he had told me that grief was a physiological process that lasted a year. It had comforted me at first to think there would be a neat end to my pain, but when a year arrived I understood what he had really meant: my allotted time was over and now my grief was not welcome at his door.

'I want you to be happy,' he continued. 'Perhaps we can think again of a husband?'

I could not listen to his words. It was as though the rushing sound of water had risen up about me and numbed my senses.

I had no easy prospect of a husband. The bloom of my youth had barely flowered before it seemed spent; I cannot say I noticed it passing, until I discovered in the way people looked at me that I had wilted and what small expectations there had been were gone.

'I don't think a husband will solve my unhappiness,' I said. 'I don't want to make someone else responsible for that.'

'I feel like you make me responsible.'

You're my father, I wanted to say, *who else is responsible for me, if not you?*

'I fail to understand you, Mina. You're a clever girl, capable, but it feels as though you're waiting for your life to begin.'

'I see.'

His mouth turned down at the corners. 'I've hurt you.'

'No.' Before he could say anything else, I got up, blood loud in my ears. 'Good luck with your work.'

I should have gone somewhere. Back outside, hacking along the field boundaries looking for flints in the tilled soil, or into the forest to sink my boots in mulch, soft and loamy from the rain to pick mushrooms; something that took me out of myself. But the blow had come too hard, felled me too thoroughly.

My room was quiet when I reached it. On the mantel, the clock ticked. Outside the window I could hear the wind in the leaves, the call of birds and the voices of servants ferrying crates to and from the icehouse in preparation for the day's meals. Everything was exactly the same as it had been. And always would be.

I knelt by the ceramic stove that heated my room and folded back my sleeve. The enamel was painted glossy white with gold leaf along the rococo acanthus leaf scrollwork, lifted from the parquet on four ornate legs. It had been recently stoked and the heat rolled off it in waves.

I pressed the milky underbelly of my arm to the surface

and felt an exquisite pain cut a line through me like a spike of lightning.

As though you're waiting for your life to begin.

I turned my father's words over like a newly acquired geological specimen, some shiny square of pyrite or rough wedge of schist, looking for the grain, the structure, the signs of its origin and nature.

I pulled my arm away and inspected the scalded red flesh.

If no one wanted me, then I would make myself disappear.

III

Whispers of a curse filtered through the palace like smoke.

Everything that could go wrong in the preparations for Bismarck, did. Only a matter of weeks separated us from the conference when Cook slipped on a dropped dish towel and put her back out. Then two scullery maids ran off with their gentlemen callers; and due to some poorly labelled bottles, the silverware had been polished with machine oil and all three hundred pieces would need redoing.

It was thought that my father hung us out like bait on the hook. To hold an event like this before the Witch had safely been dispatched with a new companion was considered a terrible risk, an act of hubris. The Witch was a shadow in every room, behind every conversation. Memories were long in Blumwald and people began to shut themselves away; shops closed at dusk, cafe tables fell quiet, spinning wheels stilled. No one wanted to be abroad when she came.

In the cathedral, the cluster of candles at the shrines swelled each day. Not a single companion had ever returned after being chosen by the Witch.

We called them her companions because it was more palatable than her prey.

Perhaps they really did live out a life of service to her – or perhaps she used them for whatever wicked magic she worked. Our ignorance left too much space for horror to harness our imaginations. My father knew his people's fear, but the date was set and he would not be swayed; the opportunity to gain Bismarck's favour was too great to let pass.

While townspeople nailed iron to their lintels, my stepmother ordered farms to slaughter animals, gather eggs, churn butter, mill flour, open beer stores and wine cellars. When fresh flowers were brought into the palace, she followed the maids from vase to vase with her secateurs, snipping off each imperfect bloom. I picked up a rose, one side crushed under her shoe, and brought it to my room where I hung it upside down above the stove to dry. I foraged wildflowers and ferns, gathered in fat armfuls to be arranged in jars and glasses around my room, catkins and thistle as the weather changed, and dried lavender sprinkled on my sheets. I tended plant cuttings lined up on my windowsill: aspidistra, philodendron, hedera helix, neanthe bella palm, each sat in a teacup of water to propagate. The only joy I found left to me was in bringing nature inside.

A few weeks after my father had returned with the news of the conference, I sat outside a coffee house, my sketchbook propped on my knees to work. In my room hung a clumsy drawing I'd made of the forest coiling up the mountainside. Today, I had in mind a different view: the snow-capped peaks cresting over the snakeskin roof of the cathedral. Fingers smudged with charcoal, I worked quietly, taking in the city around me with half an eye. Fewer and fewer men could be seen on the streets of Blumwald; slowly, we had become a colony of only women.

Two passed me now, a broad-shouldered woman of middling age carrying a basket of raw fleece to be spun, and a bent-backed woman well into the twilight of her life. People crossed themselves as they passed and whispered behind cupped hands. I knew them. We all did. Frau Hässler and her daughter Frieda. Mother and sister to the last companion who had been taken fifty years before: Edgar. Oh, we knew all their names, though few dared to speak them aloud, as though mentioning them would draw the Witch down upon them. Like secret saints or the ranks of kings, a history of our curse in seven silent men. Candles were lit to them in every shrine, parcels of food left outside the Hässlers' front door like offerings. As though their suffering could be warded against.

Frau Hässler, at ninety, moved through the world too folded in on herself to notice; Frieda saw all too well. I feared her fate like an omen: a spinster, a left-behind woman society had no use for. Grown steeped in pity and fear, she walked in quiet rage. They were marked by their loss. I thought then of my mother: I was marked too.

The Hässlers turned out of the square and a brief spatter of rain crossed the cobbles, storm clouds rolling slowly down the mountain. A prickle of unease ran through me; I closed my sketchbook and downed the last of my coffee. I would not linger.

At the palace my stepsisters descended into the entrance hall just as I was returning. From their smart hats and freshly brushed jackets it looked as though they meant to take a turn around the estate. I thought they must see me where I sat, tugging off my mud-stained boots, but deep in conversation they swept past me without acknowledgement.

I quieted the pang of humiliation and took myself to my room to tend my plants.

The sash window was open a crack and I heard Klara and Johanna's voices drift up. Their walk had taken them around the back of the palace.

'. . . can you *imagine* her stuck here with Mama. Perhaps she will run away and live in the woods like a wild woman. Like the Witch.'

'It is a sad truth not all women can marry,' said Johanna with a hand on her rounded belly.

'Who would ever want *her*.'

'Hush, that is unkind. If she showed any affinity for the Church I would have thought her a natural for the convent.'

'She's too heathen for that.'

'*Klara.*'

'Sorry. What was it Mama said about a lady's companion?'

'I believe she has made enquiries to find a suitable placement . . .'

They turned the corner and I heard nothing more.

Water overflowed the pot of the parlour palm I had been tending, watering can held fixed as I listened until the soil swam and dirty liquid spilled across the floor. I mopped it up with a cloth on my hands and knees.

I thought of Frieda Hässler, her arms and hands rough from spinning and scrubbing floors, her solitary, grief-marked life. My hands were as rough as hers, my arms as muscled. My grief as ever-present.

No amount of carding could smooth my tangled threads.

Who would ever want her?

My stepsisters never meant any cruelty, but they managed it all the same.

Frieda had lost her brother to the Witch fifty years ago, and now he lived forever in prayers and nightmares.

I wondered then, what fate was worse.

Dead companion – or a living ghost.

Autumn slipped towards winter and ill omens speckled the city: carefully laid woodpiles rotten through, fires dying in the grate, a litter of kittens born with milky, unseeing eyes, a girl slipped through half-formed ice and drowned.

It was less than a week now until the guests arrived, and all the bedrooms had been aired, fresh linens produced and flowers cut. The kitchens took in deliveries of beer and potatoes and flour and eggs and Riesling and vast wheels of cheese and sides of ham and even the Brandenburg Gate in Berlin sculpted from sugar. There was no safe refuge from the planning anywhere. In the mornings I went walking or put on my old skirts to work the apothecary garden outside the kitchens, tending lavender and sage and sorrel and mint while kitchen maids snipped great handfuls off with sharp scissors. When the weather was too bad, I kept to my room, reading and sorting through my geological collection. I borrowed polish and cloth from downstairs to work at each neglected piece of flint and basalt, limestone, dolomite and iron ore, taking the time to consider each in turn: the beauty in their harshness, the impossible compression of time into the palm of my hand. An infinite history that I could hold, and begin to understand.

Klara found me in my room kneeling amongst my samples, smudged glasses perched on the bridge of my nose.

'Mother wants to see you,' she said, casting an eye over my twill skirt and dirty fingernails.

'Why?'

'She's upset. She says you've been rude.'

My brows furrowed. 'When?'

Klara shrugged. 'You're always hiding with a book. And when you come in you don't say hello properly.'

I washed my hands and found my stepmother alone in her solar, a bright room at the back of the house overlooking the lake. It had once been my mother's, and she had filled it with books and replicas of Wallis and Millais paintings: Chatterton sprawled in death on one wall, Ophelia entwined with flowers as she sunk beneath the water on the other. Now the room had been repainted in a dull olive green and hung with placid pastoral scenes.

My stepmother directed me to a seat.

'I apologise if I have offended you,' I said. 'I did not mean to.'

She folded her hands, lips pursed. 'I have tried very hard to accommodate you, Mina, but you throw that in my face when you refuse to participate in this family. I suggest you think a little less highly of yourself. If you mean to spend the rest of your life unmarried and under my roof, then you need to change your ideas. Do you understand me?'

I swallowed and nodded. 'I'm sorry.'

Was there a threat beneath those words? I remembered what Johanna had said. My stepmother had written to try and find me a place as a lady's companion.

'Your father has enough to worry about without you adding to it. He is under an immense deal of pressure that I am not sure you fully grasp.'

'I'm sorry,' I said again.

A spread of menu cards and seating charts covered her desk and I looked to them, feeling as lost as I did at the modiste or with the dancing master.

'Is there anything I can do to help?'

She knew it was a worthless offer as well as I did.

'All I ask of you now is that you do not embarrass me or your father when our guests are here.' She looked at my ink-stained cuffs and dowdy bun. 'At least try to look presentable.'

My cheeks burned but I nodded.

She turned her shoulder to me, pen scratching across notecard like a sharp-beaked bird pecking away at the bark of a tree.

I was too afraid of my stepmother to ignore her admonishment. I was all too aware that as my stepsisters left, there would be less and less of a bulwark between us. My future lay in her hands and she was little motivated to treat it with care.

My sisters joined us shortly after, and I made a point of

standing with Klara at the piano to turn the pages for her, and pouring tea. When Klara tired, I took over; after one sonata, my stepmother held up her hand with a pained expression and said, 'That's enough now. My migraine is bad as it is.'

So I found my embroidery and brought it to sit beside Johanna instead and listen to her discuss names for the baby as she knitted miniature clothes. I stitched the conical bonnet of an inkcap mushroom in fawn-grey silk; a cluster nestled in the rotting crook of an alder branch, a plume of ferns framing growth and decay.

Johanna looked over my shoulder and wrinkled her nose. 'Whatever have you done *that* for?'

I looked at my delicate stitches, the rough texture of the tree bark and the velvety fungi. 'I like it.'

Klara and my stepmother had turned to us, all eyes on my embroidery. Johanna's expression wavered between confusion and concern. 'But what use is it? What is it for?'

I had no answer.

Johanna lost interest in me and Klara brought a stack of sheet music out from its box. 'Did you hear about Jenna Vettel?'

'The poor girl who fell through the ice?' said my stepmother.

I stitched in silence and let the conversation flow around me.

'Drowning must be such an awful way to go. All silent and alone beneath the surface where no one can hear you.' Klara picked up a Chopin sonata. 'Better than the Witch, though, I suppose.'

Johanna stopped, one needle through a stitch purlwise. 'Don't say that. Don't talk about her.'

'Oh don't be so superstitious, Jo. It's not like she'd want any of us. You're not a man, are you.' Klara shivered.

Johanna crossed herself. 'I don't know why she has to come here. Aren't there people where she is?'

My stepmother spoke for the first time. 'And why does the duke bring Bismarck here? This is our capital. She wants to make an impression.'

I thought about this. I had never considered that the Witch could take people from some hamlet near her castle, but of course she wouldn't. She would have no legend if she didn't come as she did, to strike where we should feel safest.

She wanted us afraid.

Klara cut in, 'What do you think happens to them? Does she kill them straight away?'

'That is quite enough of that.' My stepmother clapped her hands together. 'Practise your Schubert, Klara. We will hold a recital for the conference guests.'

I looked to my needlework but my mind was full with thoughts of the Witch. The embroidered mushrooms spread over the rotting log; without realising I had stitched tiny woodlice crawling around the edges, a hundred legs and bodies roiling like a tideline.

An old woman was found frozen to death in her bed the day Bismarck arrived. The clouds gathered around the mountaintops were dark grey and angry. Winter meant to do us harm.

A phalanx of carriages drove through the city gates and up

to the Summer Palace. Wherever I turned there was another minister with his valet and his briefcases, another room with its doors swinging shut on another private conversation. My father moved between them all, smiling and clasping hands in greeting, only the small flicker of the muscle in his jaw betraying any tension, while my stepmother paced the halls and corridors of the palace like a general as she oversaw the installation of an army of staff and visitors.

In his busyness my father had forgotten what else this date meant, and I had not the courage to remind him.

I would commemorate the anniversary of my mother's death alone.

It was hard to wake the next morning when dawn still washed out the sky; the ceramic stoves kept our apartments warm, but too long sitting still and my fingers would become stiff, my toes numb in their boots. A sharp frost had turned the stony pathways icy slick and the lake had nearly frozen over; each day, men tested the edges to see whether it would bear the weight of skaters.

I dressed slowly, anxious to make the right choice with each garment. The furs had been taken down from storage while I was out one day, my stepsisters shaking off the dust and mothballs and divvying them up without me. I had come home to find myself left with a pine green old-fashioned cloak designed to fit over the bell-like crinolines of my mother's youth. With only a bustle to fill it out I had been fair drowning in wool, but I liked the way the cloth billowed around me like a cocoon of my own. Klara had nearly made herself sick laughing at the old-fashioned figure I cut. In her sleek mink coat, vented at the back to accommodate her bustle and frogged from neck to ankle, she had looked like something from a fashion plate.

On this day I was pleased to have the old furs, something my mother would have recognised. It made me feel closer to her in some small, meaningless way.

I swapped my elastic-sided Garibaldi boots for a pair of battered Balmorals and was ready to set off, swathed in scarf and hat against the frost.

I had an appointment to keep.

My maid stopped me with a touch at the crook of my elbow. 'Take care, Your Highness.'

'What for?'

A knowing look crossed her face and I thought of the huddles of women I passed in the streets exchanging stories of eggs with red yolks, blood being drawn from wells, clocks that stuck at midnight.

'She is overdue, Your Highness. When she comes, best none of us draw attention to ourselves.'

I shook my arm free in frustration. The Witch had poisoned every mind but my father's.

The night had been cloudless, dropping the temperature so much my breath clouded before me like mist and the sun crested low over the mountains, a distant pale star in an endless stretch of blue. The town was still cast in shadow from the peaks, but as I made the short journey it retreated like a tideline, uncovering the honey-coloured stone belt of the wall and spires prickling the sky.

Late-autumn forest skirted the flanks of the mountain,

bare-branched deciduous lowland and dense pine-prickled upland, before giving way to scrub and grass in the higher reaches where any trees struggled to survive the raw weather, and a rangy herd of winter-hardened sheep grazed on the last grass before they were brought inside for true winter. In the hazy distance, the Witch's castle rose above it all. I thought about the last leaves falling, the foxes shifting their hunts beneath the earth, the forest floor brittle and frost betraying every move. I wondered what it would be to live in the wild side of the forest. We could see her castle, but it could not be reached. The road would twist like a strand of yarn if ever you set your direction towards her, looping around itself to reach no destination at all. There were stories of grieving parents following after their sons when they were taken, but none ever reached her. Some never made it back to Blumwald at all.

In the far edge of our land was the family chapel. My mother wasn't in the crypt with my father's parents; she had a grave of her own, a chest tomb in white limestone, watched over by an angel, head bowed holding a never-wilting bouquet of flowers. It was extravagant and sometimes I wonder if my father did it as penance for what had come next.

I knelt where her name was carved into the lid. She deserved to be remembered more than any of the men the Witch had taken.

She hadn't been perfect. She hadn't even been easy. But she had been mine.

I traced my fingers over the letters, picking out the moss that was growing there, then laid flowers from the hothouse, a burst of life amongst the desiccated bracken and heaping brown leaves. A memory came to me: my mother waking me in the middle of the night, wild-eyed, pulling me to the open window of her bedroom, the pale cotton of her nightdress flattened against her breasts and stomach by the wind that flooded in. Above us the clouds had eased apart and between their dusty forms the moon floated as fat and round as a coin.

'The mother moon,' she said, wrapping her sinewy arm around my shoulders. 'The maiden waxes into the mother then wanes to the crone. You and me.' She kissed the top of my head and I leaned into her warmth. A rare moment where it felt as though we fit together, mother and daughter.

A month later she was dead.

I thought of us there, maiden and mother, waxing and full. And the Witch in her castle, the crone. The waning moon, swallowed by darkness.

✳

I heard the first whispers of the Witch's arrival as I walked back.

'Soured the milk in the pail with a look,' said a woman carrying a bundle of straw. 'Has the face of a demon, all crooked. You can see the evil in her, our Albert said.'

Another woman crossed herself. 'Set all the cows lowing up at Rottenstedt. And when I set about breakfast, all the boiled eggs peeled blood red.'

In the centre of town it was as though midnight had come at midday. Every shop was shut, every window shuttered and barred. I walked alone past abandoned carts, dropped papers. In the market square, a figure cut across at a run, a boy in his early teens on the verge of tears. A door opened, swallowed him up and the bolt rammed home in a scrape of metal against rust.

I stopped at the only open door: the cathedral. It was empty and my footsteps echoed around the baroque vaulted ceiling. White marble curlicues frothed around the altarpiece and pale murals flowed across the walls and ceiling. Tucked into both sides of the nave were chapels. The saints glowed rosy with votive candles: patron saints of missing people and protection against evil. Each shrine was decked in twists of yarn, raw fleece, undyed rough spun alongside delicate lace weight skeins. Lights bristled like fireflies, like stars, a hundred tiny points of hope, of desperation. Knelt before one altar was Frau Hässler, lace mantilla across her hair.

I shivered. It was the time of the Witch.

At the Summer Palace, fear was ripe in the air. The crush of extra servants hired for the conference, the valets the politicians had brought with them, their wives' maids, who had crowded the palace and its courtyards, had all vanished like dew. Only a few of our own staff remained, exchanging whispers and glancing towards the town beyond the gates. I looked at the girls my age and younger, the older women and the men with white in their hair, and thought so few of us had been alive the last time the Witch visited. For most of us, all we knew was the childhood terror of our parents, passed on to us.

In the kitchens, my father had made a rare appearance below stairs, wild eyed and skin flushed red above his beard.

'You mean to tell me they've *all* gone?'

31

The head butler was a squat man who picked habitually at his cuticles. His fingers twitched as he replied. 'Your Majesty, we cannot force them to work.'

'How the hell am I meant to hold a dinner for the Chancellor of the German Empire with no damned footmen?'

My father's voice, the way he bit his words, roused an instinctive fear in me and I slipped back outside.

Rain had begun to fall, so I stepped into the stables instead. It smelled acutely of manure despite being freshly mucked out, the animal scent of horse and oiled leather. I followed the soft sound of whickering, past my father's Hanoverian stud Gunnar and Klara's dappled mare Lorelei, and a great number of horses belonging, I presumed, to my father's guests. At the end of the row the storm lamps had blown out. The horses were agitated, stamping and snorting and huddled to the right of their stalls. I frowned. It was as though they were all leaning away from the very last stall, where the shadows lay deepest. I could see something moving – human or horse, I could not tell – and there came a long, slow rasping sound.

I stepped into the shadows, and found them occupied. A woman moved between two horses, brushing their glossy black coats. She was taller than me, and still in a travelling cloak, hood shadowing her face. Her dress was black, in some style foreign to me, and all I could see of her was glossy black hair that masked her face, falling loose from a sharp centre parting, inky deep and bright as glass.

'It's rude to sneak up on people.' She spoke without looking at me and I startled.

'I'm sorry,' I said, but I didn't leave.

'What do you want?'

She must be the maid of a politician's wife, who thought little of us backwater people, sent to tend a prize horse. Or a village girl called into to fill a vacancy and unpractised in deference.

'Somewhere to hide,' I said.

At that, the woman glanced up and I caught a flash of eyes as jet-dark as her hair. 'Curious. A princess in hiding.'

'I'm not a princess.'

I wondered how I could speak so plainly to her. My throat was dry, my stomach hollow, and yet the words left my lips without volition.

'But you *are* hiding.' She took a comb and worked it through the knots in one beast's mane. She moved through the shadows like she was one of them, like smoke.

'Yes.'

'Which begs the question, what are you hiding from?'

My stepmother would punish a servant for speaking like this, even to me. Perhaps I should warn this woman before she fell foul of her.

But my words dried up. I remembered, instead, my mother's face peering under tables and behind curtains, looking for me. We had been playing a game, but I had hidden too well. I was hungry and ached from folding myself tightly into the gap between a settle and an armoire and the light had turned cold with dusk. I wanted the game to be over, but my mother had not found me yet. I wanted her to find me more.

She never did. I climbed out at dinner time, and she didn't ask me where I'd been.

'Do I have to have a reason to hide?' I asked, then looked to her horse. 'A beautiful creature.'

'Thank you,' she replied. I caught the glint in her eye, the corner of a smile, and I blushed.

'Excuse me for intruding.'

'Good luck hiding,' she called after me as I hurried past the mounds of saddles and bridles and tack.

I had the acute sensation of walking past the mouth of a cave, smelling the hot, rotting breath of the monster within.

IV

As the sun sunk behind the mountains I dressed for dinner. It was the first in my stepmother's schedule of events. Between negotiations, the men would go hunting for wild boar in the forest; evenings were given over to dinners, cards, and on the final night there would be a grand assembly to which my stepmother had invited half of the German-speaking world. All talk of the Witch was banned within the palace walls. This week my father was a modern German, and we were all ordered to be so too. However risky the timing, this was his opportunity and not even the Witch would be allowed to threaten it.

I decided to make an effort. I had a new evening dress in soft heather-coloured velvet with a three-tiered underskirt, the overskirt drawn up full over the bustle to be held in place by cloth roses and ruffles; the off-the-shoulder neckline exposed my décolletage and I wore only a thin black choker. My hair was piled onto my head, arranged over several rats and hairpieces to make me look something like fashionable. I was not a beauty, I knew that much. Cheeks always red from so much time outdoors, the high dome of my forehead always burned, hair bleached blonde by the sun and so dry it clouded out around my face with each stroke of the brush. There was only one feature I liked – my eyes. Blue like the slices of agate my father had given me on my tenth birthday, sharp and watchful even when hidden behind the little wire-framed glasses I wore when I read.

I caught sight of myself in a mirror as I went downstairs and my heart sank. A beautiful dress on an ugly woman still made an ugly woman.

Drinks were underway and I slipped in, making myself acquainted with a glass of schnapps as soon as possible. A gong sounded, and my stepmother began to bring the pairs together to lead us down to dinner. Klara and my father were paired and positioned, and my stepmother was leading her partner into the line. I chewed the side of my tongue. I had been given no partner. Had I missed some communication earlier telling me who I should be with? I scanned the room but saw no spare man.

I drew up beside my stepmother. 'I'm not sure who I am to escort,' I said quietly. I knew enough not to draw attention to myself.

She turned away from her conversation, brows knitting together in confusion. 'Mina?' She took in the completed line of guests, and me, outside it, and went pink beneath her rouge as her mistake hit her. 'You cannot expect me to keep on top of every minor detail.'

I swallowed against the hot lump in my throat. There was no one for me to go to dinner with, because there was no place for me at the table. She had forgotten me. 'Should I have Cook send me up a tray?'

'Whatever you want to do.' She offered her arm to her partner and turned her back on me.

The guests crossed to the dining room and I did my best to slip away unnoticed. I felt too hot and cold at once. I climbed the stairs two at a time, trying to outrun the shadow that curled around my edges.

I sat halfway up the stairs that curved around either side of the hall, resting my forehead against the bannisters. Above me spread a fresco that covered the whole ceiling, showing the Bounty of Schwartzstein, farmers harvesting sheafs of wheat in one corner, women spinning vast clouds of wool in another, framed by the mountains and the river. On the opposite staircase, the head butler hurried down to the dining room, a notecard held on a silver tray.

I thought about throwing myself over the edge. I could picture it perfectly: the rush of air against my skin, the crunch of bone as I struck the marble. I felt hollow, like a piece of deadwood rotten from the inside out. Perhaps if I jumped, I would only shatter into pieces that could be swept up and tidied away.

Jump, don't jump. None of it mattered. I was done here.

The door to the dining room opened and my father slipped out. He held the notecard scrunched in one hand and took the stairs two at a time. At the landing, he went left towards his study. Something was wrong.

A moment later, I rose, and followed him.

Two voices came from behind the study door – my father's, and a woman's – and a soft yellow light glowed around its edges. There was something familiar about her voice, and I moved closer to listen.

'You must leave at once,' he said.

'I will do as I please.'

'We have *guests*. Most important guests.'

'You do not think me important?'

A beat. 'No, I didn't mean— does it have to be now?'

Through the half open door I could see my father, hands clasped behind his back to stop him gesturing, feet planted firmly and apart – every trick he knew to appear statesmanlike. But the strain in his face was as bad as it had been the day he arrived back from Berlin.

There was something else: fear.

In a large Louis XV chair upholstered in blood red velvet sat a woman dressed head to toe in black. Or not quite toe. She wore a high-necked black dress in shapeless crepe, hands gloved in black silk, and obsidian rounds studded the choker at her neck and the bracelets around her wrist. Her hair was hidden under an old fashioned bonnet, and from its brim hung a heavy black veil that only allowed the slightest suggestion of nose and chin. It would have been the most remarkable thing about her, except for the feet peeking out from under the hem of her dress, completely bare and caked in dirt.

'Pick a companion or I will chose one for myself.'

All the hairs prickled along the back of my neck.

That voice.

The monster had roused from its cave.

The Witch walked among us.

She rose and prowled across the room to my father, tattered skirts dragging on the floor. 'Perhaps I'll go downstairs to meet these charming guests of yours and find one among them?'

I couldn't look away from those bare feet; something so wild and animal juxtaposed with the plush, mundane tread of the rug beneath them.

'I forbid it.'

'You think you hold power to forbid me anything?'

'I will not have half of Germany thinking us backwards simpletons beholden to fairy tales and – and – *witches*.'

'Don't be a fool. You know who and what I am,' she said, voice rising like thunder. 'Give me what I ask for, now, or I will make all the godforsaken souls in this palace tremble with the fearing of me.'

For the first time in my life, I saw my father cowed.

Finally, I understood it. The Witch didn't take a victim: she made us choose. One person in exchange for all our safety. She made us complicit in her cruelty by forcing us to offer a human sacrifice.

I looked at my father in newfound anger. He knew. He had always known.

Who did he plan to offer her? One of the footmen? A stable hand? A farm boy snatched unsuspecting from the evening fields?

Someone was to be plucked from their life and given a new one.

Or perhaps their life would be over the minute they left with the Witch.

I wanted to think if my mother had been here, she would have been braver than my father, but I knew it wasn't true. She would have collapsed under the pressure of the Witch's will, helpless. They had both always pretended to be so helpless, as though their choices were something foisted on them, not the result of their own desires.

I had thought myself helpless, too. At the mercy of my father and stepmother, disposed of as a lady's companion before I became any more of an inconvenience.

I realised I was going to do something extremely stupid. I was going to do it now, before I understood the difference between reckless and brave.

'I'll go,' I said.

It was like stepping off a roof. Slipping under the ice. Drastic. Exhilarating. Destructive.

The Witch and my father turned to me as I pushed the door open.

'Mina, what are you doing here?' My father's face was wide with horror. 'Go downstairs at once.'

I ignored him. I was terrified, but in a numb, distant sort of way. Like I was walking out on stage in my debut role, but at the same time watching myself from some great height. 'I'll be your companion,' I said to the Witch.

I waited for my father to protest again but the guilt was written clear across his face; he was considering my offer. I saw he would do it. He would send me with her if it benefited him. And it would: the problem of the Witch cleared away without another soul involved, and the problem of me. His conference to woo Bismarck could continue undisturbed, and his duchy would be safe another fifty years. I thought of how it would look for him: a noble sacrifice by a selfless ruler to secure a future for everyone.

All it would cost him was his first-born daughter.

Good. I was glad. At least this way I knew where I stood.

'Mina—'

'Father.'

'You don't understand what you're saying.' He looked like an old man, tired and folded in on himself.

Perhaps he did care for me in his own distant way.

It wasn't enough. It would never be enough.

'I know what it is I do.' I turned to the Witch. 'If you will have me.'

'You?' A note of something almost like amusement coloured her voice, and I wanted to know what type of face lay under that veil. One that could still express humour, it seemed. One that was not just cold and commanding.

'Will I not do?'

She cocked her head. 'Leave us,' she said to my father.

'She is my daughter—'

The Witch turned to look at him, veil pleating around her face like the statues in the graveyard forever weeping over tombs.

He stopped talking.

Avoiding my eye, he left me alone with the Witch.

She caught up the edges of her veil and lifted it in one smooth movement, casting it behind her. I drew in a breath sharp with shock. The Witch's face was smooth and pale like chalk, her eyes impossibly dark, lips full and red.

The gloss of black hair, the quirk of her lip – and finally I placed her voice.

The woman in the stables.

I blushed, thinking of what she knew of me: a coward, hiding.

Bare feet silent on the carpet, she circled me, sharp eye looking me over. I felt, suddenly, the weight of my need for her to accept me, the urgency of my desire to flee this place. I would take a life of servitude to her than another moment here.

And if she killed me, I wasn't sure I would mind.

'Perhaps you would offer me a better place to hide than the stables?'

That seemed to amuse her. The corner of her mouth twitched as it had done before, and I felt a moment of recognition.

She raised one hand to my chin, her fingers tilting my head up as she appraised my face. I had expected the Witch to smell of nightmares, of sulphur and blood and fear. Instead, I smelled a confusing mix of moss and earth and rainwater on stone. She was only a few inches taller than me, but moved as though she were a queen and I dirt on her shoe. The silk of the glove was slippery and cool against my skin and a shiver went through me. I felt like an animal on a dissection table, splayed open under the knife.

'I have never been given a woman before.'

'Do I not meet your requirements?'

She gave this some consideration. 'It makes no difference. You come with me willingly?'

'I do.'

'So confident, when you know nothing of me. Nothing of what you are walking towards.'

I met her gaze, the beetle black eyes and blood red lips.

'No. But I know what I am walking away from, and that is enough.'

She held my chin a moment longer, the intensity of her attention like a great pressure bearing down on me, the world reduced to her and I and the thin air we shared between us.

Then she broke contact, lowered her veil and called my father back into the room.

'I will have her.'

I didn't miss the small flash of relief across his face.

I felt strangely light, as though my body were not my own. I had *done* something.

'There must be a binding,' said the Witch. 'Give me your ribbon.'

I pulled the choker from around my neck and handed it to her. She placed one gloved hand over mine, then wrapped the ribbon around both of us, tight enough my fingertips began to tingle from lack of blood. Face to face at the altar of the window frame, a cold light haloed her from behind, casting her into a dark column of black silk. We were joined at the wrist, at the pulse point, the warmth of her body reaching me even through the cloth. My heart was racing, but her heartbeat was slow – so incredibly slow – and steady. This was strength, life. *Power.*

'Swear yourself to me.'

'I swear.'

'No. By the old words.'

My mouth was too dry. For a moment I couldn't work out what she meant, then I thought of the shrine in the woods, the branches laid out on either side of it.

'By oak,' I whispered. 'By ash. By bitterthorn. I swear a bloody oath to you.'

The oldest words in Schwartzstein. Words of the woods and midnight fear.

The words invoked to ward against the Witch, now bound me to her.

I thought she might smile now she had what she came for, but her face was as deathly serious as I felt. Her free hand darted out and something pricked my skin. A dot of red blood appeared on my glove and seeped into hers.

She was speaking but I couldn't hear the words clearly; like voices in a next-door room or when I was sick with a fever, the sounds and shapes were familiar but I couldn't grasp them before they slipped away like water. A pressure clamped around my head and my knees threatened to buckle. All along the skin of my arms, my hand, my fingers, was a soft buttery light, brightest at the ribbon that bound us, like I was a candle and the ribbon the wick.

Just as apprehension was tipping towards dread, she whipped the ribbon away and the pressure cut out. I rubbed my wrist, working feeling back into my fingers.

'It is done. You are bound.' She slipped the ribbon into some pocket concealed in her skirts. 'Come, we leave at once.'

'But it is so late,' I said.

'And?'

'Would you give me a night to – to pack?' I had almost said *to say goodbye*.

My father had remained silent through the binding, standing stiffly with one hand on the back of his chair as if for support. He did not look at me once. If he could not be a good father to me, I felt spiteful pleasure at least to know he was ashamed of being a poor one.

'Very well.'

She swept from the room, pausing only in the doorway to turn back to us, beautiful and terrible. I thought of her dirty feet tracking up the carpets and across the marble, a wild animal loose in our midst.

'We leave at first light tomorrow. I will not wait.'

A shiver passed through me as I realised what I had done.

She was no woman, but a Witch. And I had bound myself into her service.

V

Outside the dining room I found a decanter of claret and tucked it under my arm along with a glass, having abandoned my father to nurse his shame alone. I needed air in order to quiet my hectic thoughts. Climbing up to the roof, I found an old moon waning into its last quarter; from below came the clinking of silverware in the dining room, then after a while, the lilt of voices spreading out to the bedrooms.

It was cold at night in November and I regretted only wrapping a shawl around my shoulders. My view spanned the formal gardens, the lake on one side, then on the other, the city. The summer flowers had long since faded, and now the frost had killed all but the hardiest of the bright pinks and greens and oranges of the autumn-blooming chrysanthemums and dahlias. Soon snow would swallow the last of the leaves that painted Blumwald in gold and red, and my home would become a charcoal sketch of white and grey.

I would not see it happen.

This was the last night wrapped in its protective wall, its mosaic of roofs and streets and squares all in brown and yellow. My mother's city. The home of her bones. Cupped around us, the mountains towered silent and black in outline against the starred sky. Somewhere in the dark was the Witch's castle. I wondered if that was how she saw us, a boil of stone and thatch and tile rupturing the ever-spreading green of her forest.

I downed my glass and poured the next.

Would there be anything familiar in the Witch's world? Would the same flowers bloom there? The same birds call? I had thrown everything I had away in a moment of despair and spite. I had thrown away my life.

Somehow, that was the thought that brought just what I had done into focus.

My stomach heaved. I made it to the gutter in time to bring the wine back up, acrid and dark. Shaking, I sunk back on my heels.

I would live the rest of my life with a monster.

Or perhaps I wouldn't live to see the moon wax full.

The sour smell of vomit filled my nostrils and my teeth felt tacky and coarse. I thought I might be sick again.

I was terrified, but I would not back down.

I was going somewhere no one in Blumwald dared go. I alone would know what it was to be the Witch's companion.

My family might think little of me, but none of them would ever do what I was about to.

Unsteady with drink, I went back to my room to pack. I would not sleep that night.

A team of maids were already at work, folding away my clothes and stowing my dressing table contents into boxes. In a nest of tissue paper, my geological samples were buried like bulbs in winter.

Was I this easy to evict?

With help I stripped off the heather evening gown while directing the final stages: my winter clothes, layers of warm underthings, thick woollen socks, flannel petticoats, tweed skirts and a large, coarse mariner's jumper my father had brought back for me from a trip to Denmark, all stuffed together in a trunk. I left behind all the pretty dresses and flimsy evening things; I needed sturdy, hardwearing clothes. I had to be prepared.

In a carpetbag I packed a change of clothes for the journey, my notebook and roll of pencils. I wanted something of my mother's, but I was at a loss for what to bring. The night was creeping on. I had little time to linger.

I took a fragile book from the shelf: a slim volume of stories for children that had been hers as a girl. She had never read to me from it; that had been beyond the amount of mothering she had been willing to give. But I had liked to turn the pages and imagine myself as her, making the shape of the words with my lips as she had done, conjuring the same images in both our minds.

I folded it up in silk, secured it with a length of twine and stowed it with my books. Then, in a moment of impulse, I added her drop spindle and the ragged length of fleece I had yet to spin into yarn.

My father came to my door an hour before dawn, holding a cup of coffee.

'Here.' He placed it beside me where I sat in my travelling clothes. 'Do you have everything you need?'

I looked at the trunk, the carpetbag by my feet. I didn't know how to answer.

'Did you ever love me?' The question surprised me as much as it did him.

Confusion, fear, the faintest glimmer of embarrassment. He closed his eyes. 'Of course. You are my daughter.'

Even now, he couldn't say the words. That was all the answer I needed.

'What will you tell them?' I hadn't seen my stepmother or stepsisters since the Witch.

'I can raise them and you can tell them yourself.'

I shook my head. 'Explain it however you want.' I didn't owe them anything any more. 'You said I was waiting for my life to begin. Well, it's begun now, don't you think?'

'Mina—' He stopped me as I stood to leave. After a moment of struggle, all he could offer was, 'It had to be done.'

The twenty years of life together, and he ended them like that.

I said nothing, but drained my coffee cup and left my father to carry my bag downstairs. As we passed the bedrooms, I caught a sliver of each tableau through the half-open doors: my stepmother wrapping her dressing gown over her nightdress, Klara knelt at the foot of her bed in morning prayers, Johanna with her eyes shut and her hands clasped around her stomach.

It was over. It was all over.

Only the Witch was waiting for me at the palace doors. She wore the same outfit as the night before – black dress, veil and gloves. So still and unnatural, she seemed to radiate the chill of stone.

I wondered if she slept.

I could not imagine her doing anything so human.

My trunks were lashed to the roof of the carriage as I waited in the blustery wind. Dawn was feeble, thick cloud cover keeping us half in night. I felt strangely clarified, like a shard of crystal through which sunlight poured and split into the colours of the spectrum. Whatever tension had been boiling inside me had dissipated; I had done something drastic and snapped it like a piano string tuned too tight.

The pain had lifted.

For now.

The snow held off as we travelled, a lowering black blanket of cloud that stalked us up the valley. The Witch's carriage was large, a glossy black plush interior that smelled like damp and mould and upholstered in black velvet so cold it felt wet. It put me in mind of a coffin.

My experience of long carriage journeys was to be wedged in against Klara, bustles and skirts taking up too much room. In contrast, the Witch's carriage was impossibly large, space between us almost for another person. The two horses I had seen hitched at the front could never pull something like this and yet we seemed to move at the speed of a locomotive. I did not understand how that was possible, but I decided not to think about it. For a while I looked out of the window, watching the horses swallow up the earth beneath their hooves, but I began to feel sick and confused, so I closed the blind and confined myself to the musty interior. The storm that threatened never quite came, only speckling handfuls of rain against the windows.

Through it all, the Witch sat silent. Still.

Closed up with her, I felt more frighteningly aware of her than before. I was entirely at her mercy; my death could come at any moment. Perhaps she would wait until I turned away, strike like a viper and I would never know it. Or perhaps she would toy with me, cultivate my fear, like fattening a pig.

I had thought I could welcome death, but now it faced me I found myself a liar.

I thought perhaps she slept, but when my skirts brushed against hers she twitched them away in distaste; when a rut in the road jolted me towards her, she leaned away at once. At all times, she sat perfectly upright, gloved hands folded in her lap and heavy veil hanging over her face. Was it stuffy under the veil? Did she find it hard to breathe? Did she feel trapped? Or was it armour, making her feel safe? Mercifully her feet were hidden under the hem of her dress. I don't think I could have stood it, being trapped for hours only centimetres away from those hideous, filthy feet.

I shuddered, and turning back to the window, I began thinking again about that pale, porcelain face beneath the veil. Why did she hide it? The townspeople thought her a monster, a beast of a woman as outwardly ugly as she was inside. Was she happy to let them think it? And the question I dared not ask: what did she want with me?

I realised I knew nothing true about her at all. I had a set of assumptions, the scraps of scattered legend passed down by my mother, and the deep sense of unease that roiled in my gut. I felt like a rabbit in the woods, knowing that it would never understand the mind of a fox.

Somewhere along the way, I had lost track of our progress. I knew we could only be further up the valley or into the next river-lined furrow in the mountains, but I couldn't quite place myself from the shape of the peaks. It was the single most disconcerting feeling, like missing a step going down stairs, expecting solid ground and encountering only a lurching void. Following the river, it would eventually take you north to Nuremberg or south to Munich. All travellers took that road, the post riders and the farmers bringing food in to market and the merchants shipping huge bales of wool on barges along the water – and the railway would follow it too, eventually. But we didn't. At some point when the blind had been down, we must have taken a fork, though I had not noticed the carriage shifting direction. We still moved impossibly fast but now the road was narrow and rocky, the tree line creeping closer on either side. And slowly, steadily, we climbed.

Dusk swept in between one bend in the road and the next. Trees became an impenetrable thatch of black and grey; no lanterns hung from the posts of the coach. How could we manage such incredible speed without seeing clearly? Just as I worried that the Witch intended to carry on through the night, we came to an inn nestled at the side of the road, half-timbered with a sharply gabled thatched roof that overhung the ground floor, ready to stand the weight of snowfall. It was a modest place with only two storeys and no sign outside, but lights were blazing in all the windows, and I was relieved at the thought of one more night between myself and my fate.

The Witch barely waited for the carriage to stop before letting herself out. Could she really so little stand to be around me? No innkeeper was waiting for us but the Witch went inside, so I followed.

An empty room with tables and a broad fireplace. Stairs up.

The Witch began to climb and again I followed; she snapped round and I felt the intensity of her glare through the veil. It was the first time she had acknowledged me in hours.

'If I had required a dog to cling to my heels, I would have bought one. I trust you can look after yourself for one night?'

Not waiting for an answer, she stalked upstairs, long skirts trailing behind her. I stood at the bottom, dazed.

Outside, the carriage had disappeared, and there was no sign of our driver. The inn seemed to be empty, but on further investigation I found a table laid for one by the fireplace, a plate of boiled potato dumplings and thick slices of pork in a watery sauce waiting alongside a stein of beer. I thought at first it must have been meant for the Witch, but when she made no further appearance, I sat down and began to eat. I was tired, and in the space of a day I had torn my life into little pieces; suddenly I didn't care about how the Witch might react or what I was expected to do. There was food and I was hungry.

Upstairs was a series of doors that were all locked save one, which opened onto a room freshly made up for a guest. Behind one of the other doors must be the Witch, but I did not know which one and I doubted she would respond to me if I went looking. My trunks waited for me at the foot of the bed so I went in. I locked the door behind me, ill at ease. Perhaps it was not so strange that there were no other travellers staying in such a remote inn at this time of year, but surely strange to hear no servants moving in the corridors, tending fires or delivering food and bags.

That night I lay like a still column under the bedding, one tallow candle burning as I could not bear the total dark. I listened for the familiar noises of the forest outside, but I heard nothing. Only a heavy, dull silence, as though I had been plucked out of time and lay in stasis while, somewhere beyond, the world continued without me.

I must have slept because I woke with the shutters open and a cold autumn sunlight filtering in. Fresh water was on the washstand, and a set of simple travelling clothes had been taken from my trunks and laid out ready for me.

A cold prickling sensation. Someone had been in my room while I slept.

In the corridor, I thought I saw the edge of skirts disappearing around a corner, the whisper of hushed voices. Perhaps the servants here were just as afraid of the Witch as they were in Blumwald.

Downstairs, breakfast was waiting, and so was she, sprawled on a chair by the stove, chin resting on her fist, face hidden behind her veil.

A pang of fear hit me. I pinched the inside of my arm until my thoughts quieted, then I made a bargain with myself: one action at a time.

All I had to think about was the present moment.

Walk across the room. Pull out the chair. Sit at the table.

Keep myself in the Witch's favour, if such a thing existed.

I picked up my knife and fork and said, 'Good morning. I see the snows have held off another day.'

She didn't reply but I hadn't expected her to.

I chewed mechanically, barely aware of what I was eating. The fear was worse this morning. The flashes of excitement I had felt at leaving home, being let into the secret of the Witch, had dissipated. Now all I could think was that I had given myself over to the monster that had stalked my home for centuries, and like a fool thought I was doing something brave.

Under the table I pinched my arm again.

Logic, that was the only way I could get through this. If she meant to kill me quickly, surely she would have done so already.

Fifty years. That was how often the Witch took people.

Perhaps we really were her companions, and when our lives ran out, she was lonely enough to take another.

In that light the Witch, slumped by the fireplace, seemed quite a different figure.

I tried again.

'Do we travel much longer?'

'No. I would have left already but it seems you sleep in.'

I considered the veil she still wore, despite the fact I had seen her face when we were bound. She didn't want to be seen, yet she had a whole duchy ensnared in fear of her.

'If you would rather not wear that any more, we could ride with the carriage blinds drawn,' I offered. 'Perhaps the journey would be more comfortable without it.'

I saw my mistake as soon as I made it.

She stiffened, a wave of anger rolled off her.

'Do not dare tell me what to do. I do not dress for *you*, and I owe no one my face, least of all some pampered nobleman's daughter who knows a world so small it could fit on a thumbnail.'

She left me at the table and I burned with shame and fear. She was right. I knew nothing of this world. I was out of my depth. She had assessed me, and dismissed me, and was completely correct in it.

Outside the air was brittle. I could taste the snow poised to fall. The carriage and horses were drawn up outside and it seemed so normal in daylight. I walked around it once, trying to make sense of its strange dimensions, the uncanny speed with which we had moved. Nothing but an ordinary coach, only a little old fashioned and heavy on its vast wheels. The Witch mounted the step and disappeared inside. I felt a moment of panic at that threshold waiting before me. The inside of my arm was still sore from where I'd pinched it.

I focused on the pain, and climbed into the carriage.

We departed. In daylight I could see now that the building was not quite as swallowed by the forest as I had thought. A slender river ran around the back and on through a village; we mounted the hummock of a bridge and drove through the centre, where I saw faces at windows, a flash of pale skin and hollow eyes before they vanished. A few scrawny chickens pecked through the dirt, and in one place, I saw a bucket freshly abandoned, the ground around it stained a richer black with spilled water, as though someone had heard the approaching carriage and fled. An uneasy knot grew in the pit of my stomach.

We turned another bend, climbing sharply upwards through the forest so that now the hamlet was laid out in full like a map. Beyond, the road switchbacked up the mountainside, bordered by craggy overhangs of raw rock face, and spindly trees, barren for winter. I could see why we stopped; traversing this road without daylight to show our path would be far too perilous.

And above us all, lowering over the forest, was the Witch's schloss.

A castle, medieval in foundation, with generations of additions mounded up into a monstrous, looming thing, perched on a spur of rock that jutted out from the mountainside. On three sides a drop, one sheer to the river winding hundreds of metres below, the other two far enough to break your neck; the final side rose up to the peaks above. The road wound around the base of the spur, almost lost amongst the rambling thicket of blackthorn, spikes prickling along its branches like claws. Mist cast the world in an unreal milky pall; I could hear the river thundering below, but it was lost to the veil. Above us, the castle was inhumanly large. Great stone fortifications made up its base, slick with moss and weeds, and above it, jumbled walls rose up to a confusion of angled grooves and spiked turrets. The more I looked at it the less it made sense. I could see windows, squares that must make up rooms and rounded places I thought would hold spiral staircases.

Our path made a final curve to a bridge that spanned the chasm between the rest of the mountain and the castle. Lowering my window, I looked out as far as I could. The world was washed out, even the trees had lost their lustre, and the sky was a low frost waiting to fall. Ahead, the bridge reached a gatehouse, a blank portal through which I could see no more.

I longed for a kite to cry, a fox to bark. Something natural to tell me I was still in the world I knew. Instead, silence.

The carriage slowed as we crossed the bridge and the metal shoes of the horses rang loud on the cobbles. The great iron-barred doors creaked open, and we passed through to a courtyard.

As at the inn, the Witch didn't wait for anyone to help her out. She flung herself out onto the flagstones and near flew to double doors set into the vast bulk of the castle. They swung open before her like a swarm of fish parting around a shark, and then she was swallowed up by the dark interior.

I paused a moment, pulling my cloak more tightly around me, to take in my new home. There were weeds growing between the cobbles and a number of the outbuildings had fallen into disrepair. Our driver led the horses not towards the stables – grand things that had once had space for countless animals, now scuttled like wreckage – but back through the gate, the doors clanging shut behind him. I had wanted to speak to our driver, our strange silent attendant of the journey, but he had hurried away. I had never even seen his face.

I could not go back, so I had to go forward. I climbed the steps to the great hall, and before I had time to think about what I was doing, stepped inside.

A vast, vaulted ceiling spanned above us, beneath my feet flagstones spread out, chipped and dirty and unloved. Two great fireplaces ruptured the walls at either end, both empty and cold. Wood panelling had once covered the stone of the walls up to shoulder height, but it was half rotted away, planks shearing off like dead skin. A wooden staircase swept up two floors above, and reaching to the ceiling was a dense thicket of tapestries, lost to smoke damage and gloom.

Struck through the middle of it like a split wound, a gash of limestone mountain, bedrock thrusting up to cleave the hall in half. It was as high as my shoulder and entirely wild.

This was not a home.

The Witch was halfway up the hall when she ripped the veil from her face and flung it to the floor. She kept marching onwards and I hurried to keep up, hesitating a moment at the pooled swathe of lace, debating whether to pick it up. Was that sort of thing part of my duties as companion? I left it, and caught up as she reached the staircase.

As before she stopped, blocking my way. Her face was unreadable. Not blank – it was anything but. That beautiful face, its sharp cheekbones and wide, storming eyes, had an expression too complicated for me to understand. The disdain for me, the anger I had seen before was there still, but also something of sadness about her eyes, exhaustion, and was that – fear? Then the expression closed off in a snap and there was only a sneer twisting her perfect mouth.

'Go wherever you want, but stay out of my way.'

'Where should I—'

'I don't care. The Tower is off limits.'

Before I could say anything else, she stalked up the stairs without looking back. The doors at the top slammed behind her.

Alone in the vast hall, I went back to the veil and picked it up for something to do. Then I turned slowly around, taking it all in. This mausoleum, these withered remains of some past, glorious world. This grave that I was to live out my life in.

For the first time since offering myself, I let myself stand still and look at the thing I had done.

I knew there was no steel in my spine. I was a soft, stupid girl who had sent herself into exile for want of a little attention.

Now I was trapped in a prison of my own foolish making.

WINTER

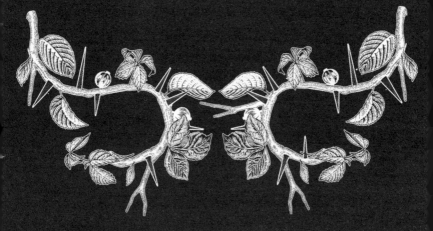

VI

Clutching the Witch's abandoned veil, I walked the dungeon-like halls and staircases of the castle until I opened a door on the first floor to find a bed made up and my own trunks sitting at its foot, just as at the inn.

It was a spacious room with bright windows set deep into the thick outer walls, and a person-sized fireplace stoked high. The bed itself was something strange and small, raised up on a plinth with a series of steps going up to it, and heavy drapes hanging all around. But the most remarkable thing was that all the walls had been painted with an interlacing pattern of vines and leaves and flowers. Faded green on whitewash, the branches swept up the walls and onto the beams in bursts of rose and peony and mugwort blossom to nestle in between the timbers. Set amongst them were knights and women in medieval dress, shields and swords in hand.

I went around in wonder, touching the faded paint, looking at the tiny brushstrokes still fixed in the plaster, the mark of a hand that had been dead and withered for centuries gone. It wavered on the line between beautiful and terrifying. No different, I told myself, than my mother's painted silk wall hangings, or the vast battle scenes displayed in our formal dining room. But it unsettled me. The tangling vines, the strange flat eyes of these ancient people.

Only the swatch of plaster over the fireplace was bare – then I realised it was not undecorated, but rather the decorations had been chipped away, just as protestants had hacked the saints off church walls. From what remained of the paint, it looked to have once been a coat of arms; only the curl of a fleur-de-lys and the lost angle of a chevron left their mark. I touched a finger to the coarse plaster. Bristles of horsehair sprouted from the raw surface.

'Will you be wanting a meal, my lady?'

I turned to find a woman in the centre of the room, from where she had come I could not say. Average height, average build, everything about her seemed entirely calculated to be unremarkable. She wore the apron and shoes of a servant – the housekeeper perhaps? The great ring of keys the size of my hand hanging from her waist confirmed it.

'Oh – yes, if it's no bother.'

'Doesn't come into it, my lady. I will bring up a tray.'

She began to leave and I called out without meaning to. 'Wait – don't go –'

Turning back to me, her face was placid and indifferent.

'What I meant to say is, you have not told me your name.'

'Wolf.'

'Wolf?'

'Ursula Wolf, my lady.'

I misliked that answer as much as I misliked her name.

'Do you live in the castle?'

A small smile at that.

'Oh no, my lady. The staff live in the village. It is only yourself and the mistress who will stay here overnight.'

'And where is the village? I couldn't follow our route here.'

Wolf considered her words. 'You are right, it is quite an out of the way place.'

'Perhaps if I could see a map.'

'There are no maps. If you are wanted here, you are likely to find your way. If not . . .'

Her vagueness unsettled me. I chewed over the question I had wanted to ask the Witch the whole journey here but had not had the courage to. I leaned towards her, lowering my voice as though confessing to a priest. 'Please tell me, what exactly am I to do? What did my predecessors—'

'Meals will be brought to your room three times a day,' said Wolf as though I hadn't spoken. 'You're free to leave the castle – the doors are never locked – but beware, the forest around these parts is treacherous.'

'I know my way around the forest quite well, thank you.'

Her cold eyes held no humour in them. 'Things are different here, my lady. You'd do well to take care.'

I shivered.

'Would you like me to bring more wood for the fire?'

'Just something to eat. Thank you.'

She left, with no curtsey, though I reminded myself I didn't care about such things.

I could run now. The castle was an empty horror; no one would see me if I simply left and took my chances on foot.

Then I thought of the twisting holloway that climbed the mountain, the close-gathered trees meeting over the sunken road. The confusing geography that made me feel strange and dizzy if I tried to hold it in my mind.

No, I must take my chances here.

I wasn't sure if Wolf would act as lady's maid and expect to unpack my clothes herself, so I left them for the time being and started with my books and papers and carefully wrapped specimens. There was no bookshelf, but a handsome writing desk was pushed up against the wall beneath the windows so I lined up my volumes there and organised my research papers alongside. I had begun reading on the new techniques used to track time in soil strata and I thought to continue my study without my stepmother's disapproving looks.

My specimens I took special care unpacking. I had insisted on bringing the large, grid-like piece of storage my mother had commissioned for my twelfth birthday. That year before she died, she had begun to take notice of my interests, as though I was a curious spectacle in her own home she could pass the time with. Worked out of polished beech, backed in green baize, the case took the shape of a large square, about two metres by two metres, and split up by means of horizontal and vertical partitions into four hundred individual squares of space. Modelled after a pharmacists' cabinet, each slot was home to a different specimen of rock. I had arranged them into columns of igneous, sedimentary and metamorphic, marking out the strange birth and life of each piece. Matte panes of grey slate shot through with threads of white, a polished square of granite, freckled amber, a lump of diorite dappled like a Dalmatian, snags of pyrite as gold and shiny as a pfennig. At the centre of it all, a geode the size of both palms together, a smooth egg of rock split open and the two halves displayed side by side to show the crystalline hollow within. White at the outside, bleeding to blue and purple, I had always thought the crystals looked like teeth. A beautiful maw waiting to clamp shut.

My father had first gifted me a sharp flake of flint when I was seven. But he had given me more than that: it was somewhere to belong. The earth spread out from my feet to the feet of every other living thing on earth, one endless rocky blanket fathoms deep and centuries old. I was at home where it ruptured out of the ground into mountains and cliffs, raw, rippled insides on display, rock packed tight in striations, crumbling like cheese or glossy like water. Out there it didn't matter if I was wanted or not. Out there, I would always be enough.

When I was finished I stretched my back and went to the windows to let in a breeze. A good half-metre in depth, they felt like tunnels between the underworld of the castle and the bright day outside. I thought about pulling some of the pillows and blankets from the bed and making myself a reading nook. It would feel better to be only a breath away from nature. The view was beautiful: straight down the valley, the planes of forest-top flanking the hillsides, and in the distance, the shape of peaks. I wondered where the village we had stopped at was from here. Down the valley, surely, but I could see no smoke rising from fires or any opening in the trees.

It was like the wildwood had swallowed up the rest of the

world, and I was stranded, an anchorite in the most remote wilderness.

✳

The meal was simple, far plainer than what I was used to in Blumwald, but it was hot and filling and I was grateful for it. While I ate, Wolf looked over my clothes trunk and tutted, before declaring she would find a girl in the village who could 'do' for me. I wondered if Wolf worked alone or whether a girl from the village 'did' for the washing and scouring. I almost protested that I was quite capable of dressing myself, then I thought about rejecting another chance for company and stayed quiet and let Wolf make her plans instead.

There was plenty of the day still left, so I set myself exploring; first retreading my route back to the dank, echoing cave of the hall and then in careful loops to trace the flow of corridor and staircase. I began to draw the outline of a map on a piece of scrap paper but the castle seemed to defy geometry. From the outside it was clearly square, but inside I found myself turning five corners to complete a loop of the building. When I tried to order the lines and angles, I felt sick, a pressure building in my temples. I had always found my way walking from the ground beneath my feet, the touch of the tree bark, the smell of moss or the sound of birdsong; I would do the same here.

The hall was cold: that was the first landmark I fixed in my mind. Cold as the icehouse set into the grounds of the Summer Palace, it was the frozen heart of the castle from which everything radiated – the closer you were to it, the colder you felt. The closer to the walls, the more sunshine soaked in. Though it made no sense – the thick stone walls of the castle should have been the coldest thing. At one end were the doors we had entered through, two storeys high and as thick as my body; at the other a grand staircase sweeping up to the double doors that the Witch had disappeared through on our arrival. On closer inspection, the staircase was rickety and eaten through by woodworm. Several steps were so badly rotted that they crumbled under my weight. I do not know how the Witch dared mount them, but I avoided them entirely, finding my way up by the spiral staircases and servants' stairs.

And all around the hall's high walls, the rotting tapestries. When I looked closer, I saw they depicted battles, great hordes of soldiers in armour, dragons rearing over mountaintops and all of it drenched in blood, limbs mangled, heads rolling on the ground. The red thread had darkened to rust and was wet with damp. I touched my fingers to it and they came away stained claret.

I found myself avoiding the hall if I could.

The next landmark was the Tower. Standing at the western corner of the schloss, the Witch's Tower was the void in my internal map. Like the coat of arms hacked off my chimney breast, the Tower could only be known from the edges it left behind: a bulging wall that disturbed the dimensions of the other rooms, corridors that ended in smooth walls. A mystery whose solution was carefully guarded from my sight.

The rest of the castle I picked off piece by piece: rooms stuffed with junk and broken furniture, collapsing walls and smashed windows, moss growing between the stones and always a dripping sound I could never quite find. I never saw another living soul save the rats that scurried in the dark corners, and the pigeons roosting in the vaulted roof of the hall. I assumed – I hoped – that Wolf and the other servants were in the kitchens, keeping to themselves. In one grand room I thought might have been a dining hall, I found a portrait that had been slashed through with a knife so badly it was impossible to pull it back together. Like the shattered coat of arms in my room, I traced my finger over the remains of oil paint so old it fractured like mosaic.

Everywhere, shadows. Pools of ink gathering at the edges of rooms, encroaching from the corner of my eye, darker than any shadow had the right to be.

There was something wrong with the castle.

The room next to my own was the only door I could not force: the handle simply did not turn and no amount of wrenching moved it. I knelt and looked through the keyhole and saw a space much like my own, a sliver of bed and perhaps something that could be a desk. I gave the handle one last rattle then gave up and continued along the corridor.

I stopped in one room populated by travelling cases of varying ages. Seven in total, ranging from a smartly painted trunk like the one my mother had kept her winter clothes in to something so solid and ancient, it looked like a fallen tree trunk, studded with pointed metal rivets and bound in iron. I frowned, thinking of the age of some of the trunks and who they could have belonged to, and shut the door.

I came across the Witch's apartments quite by accident. Set in an unassuming swatch of second floor corridor to the west, where the windows faced the thick hatch of trees on the mountainside and the light never really reached, there was a study, like to my father's as the oak was to the acorn. It was vast, a palace of books and rugs and chairs, a huge globe in one corner so old half the world was missing, a fireplace blazing and a chaotic desk the size of my bed covered in broken quills, crumpled blotting paper, spilled ink, yellowing newspapers and a large paperweight in the shape of a clawed foot clutching a nub of bone. There was no sign of the Witch, but surely these must be her rooms. Through a connecting door I spied a bedroom, but knew better than to pry that far. Wolf arrived holding a small bundle of letters and I bolted with an apology.

But my curiosity had been lit. The Witch was something like human, there was proof. She slept and spilled her ink and got cold without a fire. That thought comforted me. She could not be so completely alien, and if only I could find the right way in, there might be a way to live together.

If only my curiosity had stopped there.

Some secrets aren't worth the pain of knowing.

I slept poorly, kept awake by the howling of wolves, the groan and creak of the old building shifting. I had still not been summoned by the Witch and Wolf had said precisely three words to me when bringing a tray of breakfast to my room, so I was acting entirely on my own initiative as I presented myself at the Witch's study the next morning, hoping to make a good impression.

I was mistaken.

The door was open when I arrived, so I knocked on the doorframe and waited on the threshold. The Witch started at the noise, and on seeing my presence, her beautiful face fell into its habitual sneer. I arranged myself into a smile in return.

'What are you doing here?' she snapped.

'Good morning. I thought to present myself early and see how I could be of use to you.'

'Of use to me?'

'Yes.' I had trapped myself with her and I was determined this would be a different life than the one I had with my family. I pressed on: 'You were insistent on taking a companion, so surely there are things you want from one. I trust you don't mind my speaking frankly. We were bound, and now I am yours. Is that not so?'

'It is.' She looked pale, and that note of fear had returned to her disposition. It baffled me. What could she have to fear in me? I almost felt angry. How dare she be afraid when I was the one so vulnerable.

'It would make things easier if you gave me your name,' I said. We had always spoken of her as the Witch but if we were to live together I needed to make her something different than the legend who kept us bound by fear.

Her lip curled. 'Of course it would. That's the most important thing to girls like you, isn't it, etiquette and *niceness*.'

I shrivelled. If I were at home I would have slithered away by now, disappeared into the trees or shut myself away with my collection. But I was far from home and my old self felt distant. 'I see nothing wrong with wanting to be thoughtful and considerate in my dealings with others. Perhaps that is an alien idea to you. But so be it, if you will not tell me your name then I shall call you Witch.'

The Witch said nothing. Her lip was still curled, but now in amusement not contempt. 'Very well, that can be my name to you,' she said and went back to the letter she was writing.

A moment of silence passed and I realised she meant to dismiss me. At this point my irritation with her was passing into genuine confusion. What *was* I doing here?

I gestured at the chaos of papers on her desk and thought of that stinging moment of miscommunication with my father. 'Can I help you with your accounts?'

She didn't look up. 'No.'

'Then perhaps I could play you music.' I looked around but saw no piano, the only instrument I had any acquaintance with.

'That will not be necessary.'

With the last of my courage, I entered the room and placed myself before her desk.

'You bound me, you brought me here, and now you ignore me. Why? If you don't tell me what I'm here for, how am I ever meant to help you achieve it? Tell me, what did your previous companions do?'

I thought she might rage at me. Anger snapped through her like wind in a flag, and her fingers clenched around her pen. 'You are here because I require you to be here. That is all you need to know.' Her voice was calm and cold, frighteningly so. 'Any further curiosity on your part is of no interest to me.

Do not think to pry into my business behind my back because I assure you I will know, and if I find out, I will make my displeasure known swiftly and with no remorse. Do I make myself clear?'

For the first time, I saw something old behind her eyes. I saw the ancient Witch of the wildwood looking out at me from behind a pretty porcelain mask. An instinct deep within me sensed danger, just as I had in my father's study when she had first come to us. It felt as though my guilt was writ clear on my face. I had already snuck through the castle exploring. Did she know? My own death hung on the horizon, pricklingly close.

I swallowed, and stepped back, making it all the way to the door without turning my back on her.

'Very well. I won't bother you again.'

I should have fled then.

Instead I lingered in the corridor, at a loss for what to do next. Without the Witch, I had no purpose here and that thought loomed before me like a cliff edge. If I fell, surely I would die.

The door to her study opened and I hastily concealed myself in an alcove housing a grandfather clock. The Witch emerged, brows furrowed in thought, and drew a key on a length of cord from beneath her bodice, and unlocked a plain door beside hers. I caught the flash of spiral stairs and then the door swung shut and she was gone, the sound of a lock turning like the final punctuation at the end of our altercation.

Cautiously, I crossed to the door and placed my hand against the wood. The Witch's Tower. The only place she had forbidden me to enter.

I took the stairs to my room, thinking about the words that had caused her to lash out. She didn't want me to know about my predecessors.

She had been furious, but I thought perhaps I had seen something more.

She felt guilty.

I feared what would come if I found out why.

✳

Living in the schloss was like going back in time. Like picking through the layers of striated cliff-side, marking earthquake and landslide and drought and flood, the schloss was an archaeological dig through decades – *centuries* – of domestic life. I found Wolf in the kitchen cooking over an open fire, no range in sight, and a thatch of copper pots hung from the ceiling between the foliage of drying herbs and ropes of sausage and garlic and paprika peppers and swags of thyme and rosemary and basil and mint. It was beautiful, but it was like something out of a woodblock carving in a children's book. The woodsman's cottage, the fairy-tale kitchen. Wolf waved me out with the same lack of interest she would wafting out a fly. Two village girls assisted her and neither acknowledged my presence.

The rest of the castle was the same. Of course I had expected the schloss not to be on the gas or have a flush toilet – but this was something else. My bed, on inspection, was a proper tester, with layers of mattress ranging from pea shuck at the base, to straw, to horsehair and then the newest layer of feather. Below, it was roped with pegs to tighten. The bath when it was brought to me was a vast wooden thing like a barrel split open, tarred and held together by ornately wrought metal bands, and filled with buckets of water heated in the kitchens. Rush lights lined the hallways and wood smoke came from my fireplace. And yet, I saw servants rarely. There were the maids in the kitchen, and the girls who came to help me dress most mornings, but I never saw the same face twice and too often when I spoke to them they drifted past as though I were the unseen ghost haunting the castle, their eyes glassy and vacant.

The more I thought about my situation, replaying the scenes in my mind like a magic lantern show – The Witch Arrives, The Daughter's Sacrifice, The Offer Accepted, The Women Bound – the more questions I had. I had seen the Witch from my window on occasion drifting down the road that led back to the village, veil over her face and long skirts dragging. It should not have shocked me so to see that she was no real monster, but I confess it did. She looked young, yes, but not quite as young as me. Perhaps Johanna's age. That brought strangeness with it again: a woman unmarried, without children. Living alone, riding where she wished in her carriage and making demands of my father. It did not fit with the world I knew, but to look for answers would be to risk more than I could afford to lose.

I ventured outside instead, following the path from the castle I believed must lead to the village. It was strange, from Blumwald the Witch's castle was always visible on the horizon, jutting out from the trees like a snapped bone, but now I was here, Blumwald was nowhere to be seen. Perhaps it was some odd trick of perspective but I could catch no glimpse of my old home. There were only the mountains, and the pines, and the river.

The snow still held off, but it loomed in the heavy, brittle clouds as an ever-present threat, and the air was so sharp it felt like pins against my face and in my throat. I relished it. Something truly alive, distractingly so. The more time I spent alone in the castle, the more I felt like one of the dusty, cobwebbed pieces of furniture abandoned decades past. I longed to be back in my forest, to feel the cold and wind and rain like a second skin.

I followed the track that twisted around the spur of rock the castle sat on down into the valley. At one bend, I caught sight of the Tower and its window, and saw a face. The Witch was watching me.

At first I thought I had taken the wrong path. There was no sign of life, only the trees weaving together overhead in a barren winter canopy, and then a few steps on the forest broke apart and I found myself in the village. Sunlight prickled through the mist, the horizon lost in the dense mesh of forest. I knew the maps of Schwartzstein in more detail than most, and the Witch's castle was marked on none of them; no surprise then that neither was this lost village. Wolf had told me that unwanted visitors could not find their way to it, and I had no struggle to believe it.

I threaded along the packed dirt street, passing tightly nestled houses with gabled roofs and fronts painted in blues and pinks and yellows, metal hanging signs marking the baker and butcher, the ironmonger and seamstress. The road opened out into a square with a horse trough in the centre, the squat church on one side, and on the other, I recognised the inn that the Witch and I had stayed in the night before our arrival. On the far side, the road we had come from disappeared into a blur, slipping in and out of focus. I thought of the stories of grieving mothers and abandoned fiancées trying to follow their men taken by the Witch, how every road would bend away from her castle, and they found themselves back where they started.

Today the village was not quite so completely as empty as the inn had been, but I seemed to be the only person walking the street. Instead, life seemed to be behind rapidly closing shutters, children snatched back from doorways. I went to the church, thinking of the candles lit at the saints' altars, and my mother's stone casket. The doors were locked, so I walked around the graveyard looking for the names of the past companions: Hässler fifty years before me, Hülkenburg before that, Frentzen, Danner, Lotterer, Rosberg, Sauber. But there were no graves bearing their names. Brow furrowed in confusion, I walked the stones anyway, reading the names and dates. Beloved mothers, devoted daughters.

My predecessors had not simply disappeared. I had found seven trunks in that room, stretching four hundred years into the past. I left the churchyard for the bakery. Seven men at least had reached the castle.

I had a purse of coins with me so I opened the door of Bäckerei Walther and joined the women buying their morning bread; it was the only place that seemed occupied. A narrow space with racks of dense pumpernickel, rounds of farm bread, small pebbles of milk rolls, and slabs of rye; at the back, a discard basket of burned loaves.

'Good morning.'

Several nervous glances were exchanged before the woman behind the counter said, 'Good morning. Can I help you?'

'Please, finish serving.' I gestured to the women who had arrived before me.

Another flurry of glances.

'That's not a problem. Let me get you what you want and you can be on your way.'

I ordered a piece of poppy seed cake, not knowing what else to do. 'Do you supply bread to the castle?' I asked.

'No.' The woman took my money and handed me the cake.

'I arrived only last week; there are many things I'm not yet familiar with.'

'We know who you are, Fräulein.'

'You know I am – the companion?' I changed my mind at the last moment from mentioning the Witch.

'Is there anything else I can help you with?' she said firmly, ignoring my question.

'Not from the bakery, thank you, but I would be grateful if you could help me with a few questions I have. If you know who I am, perhaps you knew those who came before me?'

Another customer interrupted at this point, putting herself between me and the baker.

'We don't have anything to do with the castle if we can help it. Young people go up there to work, and you think you've been there a day but you come back and a whole month of your life has been gobbled up. You've made your purchase, so you'll be glad to be on your way,' she said, an instruction not a suggestion.

'Quite right you are.' A hand touched my arm and it was Wolf steering me out. 'We'll be off now, thank you, Frau Walther.'

She didn't let go until we'd cleared the village and were climbing the road to the castle. Wolf looked distracted, eyes darting behind us. I felt the sense of more scurried movement somewhere out of sight, and a fleck of irritation marred my mood.

'Should you be so far from the castle, my lady?' said Wolf.

'Am I not allowed to walk where I please?'

'Indeed you are. But the path can be treacherous, the weather changes quickly.'

'I haven't seen the village since I first passed through it. If this is to be my new home, I thought I should get to know it a little better.'

'Of course, my lady.'

I didn't know how to ask what I wanted to. The moment in the bakery made three times I had asked about the previous companions and three times I had been rebuffed. 'How long have you served at the schloss?' I asked as we curved the final bend in the road and the castle came into view.

'Many years, now.'

'Did you know the Witch as a girl?'

A trick question, and Wolf skirted around answering.

'I have been here most my life.'

'Who lived in the castle before the Witch? It seems a grand place for one person.'

'Things don't change so much around here, you'll find.'

'I thought there might be a family mausoleum connected to the church but I didn't see anything. Does the Witch's family have their own chapel in the castle?'

Wolf didn't reply.

My mind snagged on thoughts of the Witch: the burned loaves in the bakery had reminded me of her awful unshod feet. Dirt-encrusted and bare to the world. Like an animal. Something beyond the boundaries of society.

A mist had rolled in, half obscuring the bridge over to the spur of rock and we walked on in faith alone. I tried one more time.

'I thought I might see the names of the previous companions,' I pressed my question.

'They have no grave, my lady.'

A crow burst from the tree line in a flurry of glossy black feathers and claws.

Wolf continued. 'Will you be wanting something to warm you up? I will have tea sent to your room.'

'I am quite warm, I only want to know what I'm doing here,' I snapped. I was shocked at my own boldness. Day by day I had felt myself changing; being snatched from familiar surroundings had left my outline ragged and unformed, as though I could unravel into someone entirely different. 'The Witch won't tell me, you won't either and the people in the village think I'm some bad omen come to curse them. The Witch doesn't even seem to *want* me here, so I don't understand why she was so insistent on bringing someone. Is it me? Am I doing something wrong?' My voice faltered.

Curls of mist lingered on the cobbles of the courtyard and the castle rose up above me, silent and cold and impossible.

'The mistress will make it clear to you when you're needed.' For a fraction of a second, Wolf softened, something human came into her face. 'Take my advice, stop rushing for something that will come soon enough. Enjoy your time.'

She went inside and I lingered by the door. Wolf had given me a series of frustrating non-answers, but the more she spoke the more an idea had coalesced: something dark lurked in that castle, beyond the darkness of the Witch. I had suspected it from the strangeness of the building, the decay, the shadows deep despite the midday sun, and the Witch's own peculiar behaviour, fossilised in years alone under some great pressure of which she would not speak.

Perhaps I should do as both Wolf and the Witch had said, and leave the past alone. I had no interest in digging into my own, so perhaps I had to leave the Witch's alone too.

But something else had stayed with me.

Wolf had said: *enjoy your time.*

My mind supplied the rest of the sentence: *while you can.*

VII

I learned to avoid the Witch like scenting an oncoming storm. She swept around the castle, barefoot and brutal, a cloud of poison staining the walls black. The door to her Tower remained locked, and she launched out of it at unexpected moments, wood slamming against stone. Her clothes were always black: black silk, bombazine, crepe and cotton, a confused mixture of modern and ancient. For three days straight she wore a flimsy dress with an empire waist that looked so like the gown my grandmother wore in a youthful portrait, I was struck dumb with shock; that ghost arising here, the perfect memory of my grandmother who had died many years since. Was the Witch in mourning? I wondered. I dared not ask her.

I slept poorly. Wolves came down from the mountain each night to howl a protest beyond the castle walls and I woke often to check the oil lamp by my bedside had not gone out. In the dark I felt unmoored, a castaway in the middle of a vast, cruel ocean. In the days I kept myself to the castle grounds instead; the Witch was rarely found too far from her Tower. There was the cliff edge, falling away to the fast-moving river below, the path winding down to the village, a well. When I drew water from it, the water was mineral-stained, spilling over my hands red like blood and I recoiled in horror. Whatever was wrong with this place, it had spread its poison. The forest was as strange as the rest; ancient wildwood, untouched by people. Below was a stretch of deciduous beech, above, a conifer forest weaved a deep thicket of branches and needles so dense that at times I had to walk backwards to force myself through their prickling barriers. Vast tangles of bramble clogged the clearings, snaring my skirts and forcing me to move slow and stork-like, lifting each foot high before lowering it slowly to flatten the thorns. And everywhere, wildness. I saw fox and wildcat tracks in the dirt, great badgers' sets, birds' nests and spiderwebs, and bark alive with insects, woodpeckers gathered to pick out grubs. Wolf had been right, at least in part. This was a forest too old and alien for me to find my place.

But there was so much beauty too: frost turning webs to filigree, ragged blooms of fungus on the underside of fallen trees, frills of moss like lace. It was a palace, a fairyland, a solitary kingdom I moved through like an awe-struck traveller.

Tucked in a sunny patch of ground abutting the Witch's Tower I discovered an overgrown kitchen garden. At first I thought it was nothing but a weed-strewn patch of ground, then I recognised the shape of planting beds, of a low, crumbled wall ringing them and here and there wild sproutings of herbs that had been tended once.

I asked Wolf about it when she brought me my dinner.

'Not in use for many years, Fräulein.'

'Does no one have the inclination for the work?'

'We can bring up all that's needful from the village.'

I meant to ask Wolf something more, to extend a hand of friendship to the only other person who shared my world. But she left swiftly, keeping her back to me as though I was an ugly sight she didn't want to be reminded of.

I let the rejection sting for only a moment, and then I turned my thoughts back to the garden. Of course. It would be a waste of time to tend a whole garden for one person, but the thought of it lying there neglected and unloved was too much. I had my geological study, but I needed something more to give myself a purpose. For now, I started with separating the weeds from the remnants of the old garden, making notes of rosemary and basil and mint and thyme. Even here, I was ill at ease; I found mugwort and foxglove and other more deadly things planted purposefully alongside the kitchen herbs. I made careful note of where the danger lay.

Once spring came I could set about restoring the garden properly.

If I lasted here that long.

I lived, and moved, and breathed alone. It was as the Witch had ordered. I kept out of her way, skirting the Tower like a bruise, and asked no more questions of her. I had never been quite so completely alone and at the start I did not know what to make of it. I was afraid of it at the same time as feeling exhilarated. The freedom to wander, unimpeded, with no one ringing the bell for dinner or waiting for me at the breakfast table, had a great pleasure in it. I lived exactly according to my own peculiarities. I tied up my skirts and wore my hair plainly, I ate whatever I felt like and carried apples in my pockets so I could disregard the meals Wolf brought to my room.

In the silent evenings I would sit at my window and take out my mother's drop spindle and the ragged scrap of fleece. No matter how I tried to hook the fleece or how I twisted the strand, the thread always broke, the fibre frayed. I could not do what my mother had. She was lost to me in a hundred little griefs I found anew each year.

Was this the freedom I had longed for? It was certainly the peace. No Klara chattering inanely every time I tried to read. No stepmother hovering, wondering what I was doing and if I should not be doing something more improving and less damaging to my eyesight. Not even Wolf gave me any indication of her opinion on me. I felt like in some way I had become the untamed beast in the castle that Blumwald was so frightened of, Wolf was bidden to come feed me three times a day like an offering laid at a pagan monument. I roamed wild and uncontrolled.

And miserable.

No, not at first. Misery was a creeping thing, like the dew settling on grass or the cold fingers of frost meeting me in my bed at night and crackling the insides of my windows. I had longed to be left alone, to escape the lie of my family, only to discover this was a different kind of poison. Slow acting, but lethal. At first it numbed me, pleasure leaching from my days like a summer leaf draining of sap to greet the autumn. Then loneliness came, a creeping oily stain that stopped me from enjoying it at all.

I lay sleepless in my bed canopy one night, when I had not seen the Witch, or Wolf, or even a servant for three whole days, my nails to the soft, fleshy insides of my arm. I let them dig in one by one. A sharp bright pain that felt like clarity in a fog, like an answer. It had been – God, how long had I been at the castle? A matter of weeks, and I had unravelled. The potential for newness, a different life, turned brittle and sloughed away like rust. Any drive I had felt, even to find out what happened to the previous companions, dissipated like ash. Perhaps they had suffered as I did, drowning slowly in their own misery, far from the sight of any living thing. A human being was not meant to be totally alone. I understood it now as I never had before; like a plant needed light, a human needed company.

A floorboard creaked outside my door.

I froze.

The boards creaked again.

The pain in my arm fled from my mind. There was something outside my door.

Someone.

I held my breath and waited for the sound to come, but it didn't. There was a spatter of rain against the window, the sound of wind in the chimney. Nothing more.

Had I dreamed it?

The longer I listened and heard nothing, the more I began to doubt myself. It could have been anything. The castle was strange enough, I knew that. And who could be outside my door?

My arm throbbed, and I felt suddenly foolish and ashamed of resorting to my childish violence against myself.

I did not need to invent horrors in the night. My life was enough of a horror already.

✳

The next morning I made sure the oil lamp by my bed was freshly filled, its wick trimmed and glass wiped free of soot.

Still, sleep abandoned me.

The nights were dark and slow like tar; I was a human offering thrown into a peat bog to drown by degrees. I stumbled through my days, clumsy and stifling my yawns, and found myself looking for faces everywhere, straining to hear voices. More often than not, there were none. The reed lights smoked where no servants trimmed the wicks, cobwebs fanned over doorframes unswept.

In the great, echoing halls and dead spaces time flowed so slowly that I began to lose track of myself. Some days I could read a whole book and come out to find the sun in the exact same place in the sky; other times I would wind around a loop or two of staircase to climb a floor and suddenly half the day was gone. The clocks, few that there were, told different times in their different places. I thought I had explored the castle thoroughly in my first week, but still found myself walking down corridors that led to somewhere I hadn't expected. I mistrusted my own mind.

Perhaps a half week after I thought I heard something outside my room, I took what I thought was the route from my bedroom to a room of books, uncut direct from the binder's, but found myself in a corridor I didn't recognise. Through an arrow slit by the spiral stairs I could see I was on the far east side, in the lower half of the castle that overlooked the sheer drop to the river. My rooms were above, and the Witch's quarters by the Tower were in the west wing near the mountainside.

I opened a door at random.

It was only a door, a human-sized, plain wooden door like all the others I'd encountered.

It opened into the Witch's study.

I stepped back and shut it, blinking.

I had seen strange things but this – *this* – was impossible. Had my mind slipped so far from sanity? I opened it again, but the room was still there. Colours muted with early morning light, it was warmer than the corridor I stood in, a fire stoked at the other end of the study. I touched the side table within reach, sliding my fingertips over the polished grain of the wood.

It was real. Which meant it wasn't impossible. The sign of a rational mind was to change one's belief in what was possible when presented with evidence. Evolution was impossible until we saw evidence in fossils. It was impossible that the earth was more than the six thousand years as the Bible taught, until the study of rock told us otherwise.

I hesitated on the threshold.

The Witch said she would know if I pried. The back of my neck prickled. Was she watching me now?

I knew to go through this door would be to cross a line, but in that moment my fear of the Witch was eclipsed by my curiosity.

I stepped inside.

It was quiet. Softly, a clock ticked and somewhere outside the window trilled a woodlark. In this room it was early morning, the day just easing into motion. In the castle I'd left behind it was some time after lunch. I walked around the room once, finding details in the scrollwork or wallpaper I couldn't have dreamed up. On the Witch's desk was the scatter of papers I'd seen before; with the tip of a finger I lifted a few sheets of handwriting. There seemed to be two hands – one in Kurrent, the fluid hand I had been taught by my governess, the other in blackletter, a square and sharp-edged Gothic script I had only seen in old Schwartzstein legal documents. Most of the desk was taken up by several stout ledgers all opened to pages tightly filled with columns of numbers and dates that struck me as odd. They bore no resemblance to my father's account books. What could the Witch be recording so diligently?

There was an unfinished letter in the one clear space, dated Tuesday last. Curious. Had it been left unfinished so long? No . . . the pen that lay beside it was still charged with ink. That this room occupied a different pocket of time and space to the rest of the castle, I had already grasped. But I had not thought it might occupy an entirely different *day*.

Before I could start reading, a voice came from beyond the main door. The Witch. She barked an order, I presumed at Wolf, then the doorknob turned.

I shot back across the room and pulled my door shut just as the Witch entered. For a breathless moment I stood on the other side, palm flat against the wood. Did she see me? Would she follow? I didn't dare open the door again to check.

Nothing happened: I had escaped unnoticed.

But now everything had changed. I knew I was not losing my mind.

And I knew my sneering mistress truly was what everyone had accused her of being.

A *Witch*.

As my maddening, solitary days passed, I stopped avoiding the Witch. I was drawn to her like a drowning woman grasping at another body. I was sinking, and I didn't care if I dragged her down with me.

If I heard her down a corridor, I stood my ground and waited for her to pass, savouring her disdainful sneer or irritation. Even her rage failed to move me. I was a tree in a storm, lashed by wind and pelted with rain, but it only nourished.

The less I avoided her that following week, the more I noticed her. At a window watching me as I walked in the yard. In the shadows of the great hall as I made drawings of the ragged tapestries. Always watching me. For someone who had insisted so forcefully to detest my presence, she sought it out just as much as I.

I risked visiting her study through the secret door at least once a day, and each time it spilled me out into that same Tuesday morning, wet ink and dawning sunrise. I only stayed a moment or two to confirm it truly was what it seemed. A scientific experiment, repeating the same action under different circumstances to elucidate the forces at work. I had discovered something far beyond anything I might have expected, but I had no one to ask about it. No books to consult, no theories to assess. As in all things now, I was alone.

So instead I took to waiting outside the door to the Tower in which she was so often cloistered, to ambush her with suggestions to tidy the place up: send the tapestries in the great hall to be cleaned, fix the broken windows, sweep the blocked chimneys. She stormed past with a glare, or snarled at me to stop cluttering her hallways like litter. This only encouraged me. I took to complimenting her hair, asking after her night's sleep, tagging along behind her to ask about the history of the castle and the local geography and whatever else was at the top of my mind.

'Did you know that the oldest spiral staircase still standing is in Trajan's column in Rome?' I said, following her down a set of steps. 'It's nearly two thousand years old but the Old Testament possibly mentioned spiral staircases in the Temple of Solomon so they could be even three thousand years old as an architectural feature.'

She stared at me, haggard, deep bruises under her eyes from lack of sleep. 'Why are you saying this? What is wrong with you?'

I smiled to hide the pang of hurt. 'I think my family had the same question. If I knew how to be whatever it is you all want from me, I would, but I don't.'

'Try harder.'

I turned into her own personal demon, haunting her doggedly until she started peering round corners or pelting out of her study door to avoid me. I was so lonely even these fleeting encounters were better than nothing. And the fact that it bothered her so clearly, pleased me. I might not be wanted but at least she couldn't overlook me.

A storm blew in by the end of the week, trapping me indoors. I paced outside the normal entrance to the Witch's study, wondering if I had annoyed her so much she wouldn't come out while I was there, when the door banged open and the Witch appeared. Or rather, a stack of books higher than her head appeared. The stack dipped to get under the lintel but not enough; the top tome was dislodged and a curse came from somewhere behind. I caught the book – an edition of Goethe's *The Sorrows of Young Werther* so old the spine was brittle and loose – steadying her and placing it back on top. Her waist was hot under my hand. She emerged, hair tangled and falling in her eyes, cheeks hollow. I waited for her to snap at me for breathing too loudly.

Instead, reluctantly, she said, 'Thank you.'

My face blazed hot immediately and I said a quick, 'You're welcome.'

She lingered, lips parted so I could see a flash of white teeth and red mouth, and looked at me as though she would say something more. Then she barged past me, stepping on my foot.

I held the hand that had touched her to my chest.

It had been nothing, but that sliver of contact lit a flame in me that burned for hours after.

*

When the storm finally passed, I did as I always had done when I felt alone and sinking: I walked. The forest might be strange and ancient and unwelcoming, but to walk amongst the trees, feel my thighs and lungs burn, my cheeks redden from wind and my feet blister, I felt at home in some small way. I had lost my early caution the longer I spent completely alone. I was no longer afraid for my safety, as I set little store by it. I had more to fear in the Witch than I did from the trees and wildlife.

The forest in winter was beautiful. Bare branches wove and swayed together as brittle as hay and heavy as stone. The ice groaned and cracked under its ancient weight, and sharp, flinty air sliced my throat. Dim light fell fractal, a half-world between the death of winter and the waiting spring seeded within it.

I left early one morning, lunch packed in a knapsack and a block of sugar cake in my pocket, and started walking. While the clear weather held I wanted to scale far enough up the mountain to get a view of the castle in its setting. The horizon had been confined to walls and ceilings for too long; I needed an ocean of sky above me.

The weather turned halfway there. I had begun to lose my grip upon the passage of time, but I thought we must be where November slipped into December, and winter truly claimed us. Clouds rolled up the valley, grey and heavy with snow. Frustration bit. Finally, I had felt the stretch in my limbs, the weight of loneliness lifting off me – but it was not to be. I turned for home, but soon enough I lost my way. The sky grew darker, a mind-slowing cold began to build and I became clumsy as my toes numbed in my boots. I walked and walked but still the castle did not appear. Had I gone too far? I didn't know the landmarks of this forest yet and it would be all too easy for me not to recognise home.

The first few flakes of snow fell lightly, but its gentleness didn't last. Soon great handfuls shuddered down between the bare treetops, no canopy to stop them. I picked up speed – and regretted it a moment later when my foot caught on a root and I plunged into the leaf mulch. The shock made me lose myself for a moment, then come back in spikes of pain – barked shins and palms, root-bruised rib. My ankle flared so bright I thought I would throw up. A sprain, and a nasty one at that. I had fallen enough times before to have twisted my ankle more than once.

But never like this. And never so far from help.

Using the trunk of a springy young elm, I tried to stand, but my ankle was a white-hot point of agony with even the slightest weight. I found a stout stick to help me hobble into the lee of an oak.

My mother had often been afraid when I went walking in the snow. She told me stories of woodcutters who had frozen to death minutes from their warm hearths, lost in the fury of a blizzard. She had been too afraid to go with me. Too afraid to leave her bedroom half the days, snow or sun. Turned inwards, wrapped in a shawl amongst ripe sheets and scattered books, she had been so easily overwhelmed by the world, and so unable to escape her own sadness.

I thought of her now, her heart-shaped face and glittering blue eyes as she told me of frostbite, of falling asleep to be buried alive in snow.

The snow came down harder and harder, making my

fingers clumsy as I pulled my cloak closer. Threat gathered all around, in the snow and the dark, and the pain.

This was a mistake I would not survive.

The snow settled and the cold came biting. I tried to keep moving as best I could to maintain body heat, hobbling from tree to tree. But I knew it was pointless. I was too far from the castle; already the light was fading as the short winter day lapsed into night. I found another tree to shelter under and dug myself into its roots, packing leaf mulch and snow around me. Anything to keep warm.

At least the cold had numbed the pain in my ankle.

I couldn't sleep, not if I ever wanted to wake up again. The twilight forest provided more than enough distraction in snuffling rodents and flitting moths, boughs groaning under their weight, and all around me the deathly fall of snow. I ate the crumbs of the sugar cake and let a little ice melt in my mouth.

Then, the soft crunch of footfall, muffled.

My breath caught.

There – it came again – the sound of something moving closer.

I held perfectly still.

A bear? Rare, but possible. A wolf? Most likely, but it wouldn't come alone.

No option heralded a pleasant future.

Wolves didn't hunt people, I reminded myself, that was a fairy tale. They were far more interested in deer and rabbits and other easy prey.

But too many myths had come true for me. I lived with the Witch in a castle where magic was real.

And right now I was easy prey.

A shape separated itself from the trees and I screwed my eyes shut. *I am small and quiet and nothing, I am not here, you will not see me.*

The crunch of footfall so close, I could feel the snow shifting. Warm breath on my cheek.

'You are terrible at hiding.'

My eyes flew open.

The Witch crouched in front of me, pale face frowning. A shadow made flesh, black dress, black cloak, black hair streaming behind her and gem-studded with snowflakes.

I blinked in drowsy confusion. A hallucination? Had I fallen asleep and was dreaming?

I reached out a numb finger and traced the plane of her porcelain cheek. Real.

'It's you.' I broke into a delirious smile. 'I'm terrible at lots of things.'

'I see the cold has addled your mind no further than before.'

I looked at her bare feet, almost as pale as the snow. 'Aren't you freezing?'

Her lip curled. 'Am I not a Witch?'

It was no sort of answer at all, but then she hooked an arm under my shoulders and hauled me up; unthinking, I let my weight fall on my bad ankle, and cried out.

'I cannot carry you,' she said.

After a moment with my eyes closed to let the nausea and pain wash back like the tide pulling out, I said, 'I can manage.'

The Witch led us to the foot of a fallen oak, its trunk the

height of a woodsman's cottage. When it fell the root ball had ripped out of the earth, a tangle of grasping arms knotted and frozen in the air, and beneath it was a tree-cave, a temporary hollow with a root-roof waiting for us. The Witch lowered me in then made quick work of stacking branches around the hole to create a wall, packing it tight with snow. Night had almost swallowed us, and in the shelter it was darker still. Already, I felt a little warmer.

The Witch crawled in beside me and closed up the gap with more branches and snow until we were sealed in like babes in the womb. It was close quarters, so close I could feel the jig and jostle of her elbow as she worked, her bare foot rucked up against my calf and her skirts draped across my knees.

My initial happiness at seeing her had faded and now I realised the situation I was in. The Witch had *found* me. Which meant she had been looking. Out in the dark and cold, for someone she despised so much she had ordered me out of her way. I had thought to make a nuisance of myself, but not like *this*.

In the dark, she was little more than shifting body weight, the rustle of skirts and those glittering black eyes like beetles. I held my breath, waiting to see what was going to happen.

She slumped beside me, the line of her arm hot against mine, heavy and human; only her bare feet stood out, ice-pale flashes in the darkness. How she survived the cold I did not understand, but there was very little about her I *did* understand so I left that thought along with all the other impossible things.

Something brushed against my fingers – at first I thought

it was a spider, something long and sinuous – then I realised it was just her hand, falling limp at her side.

'How did you find me?' I whispered. 'I didn't think you'd notice me gone.'

No response, only the shallow rise and fall of breath. Then those eyes, flint-sparks in the darkness.

'I notice you.'

I swallowed, mouth suddenly dry. A thread of tension drew taut between us; I felt every mote of air in the gap between our bodies, the radiating heat of her, the weight and shape of her so close we breathed the same air.

I flushed and turned away first.

The Witch threw her cloak around us. 'It is a freezing night. We must share our warmth or you may not survive.'

Her arm snaked around my waist and tucked me against her, and I could hardly make my thoughts line up with any sense. The soft swell of her breasts pressed against my back, the line of her thigh matched up with mine. I became more acutely aware of my body than I had ever been in my life.

She hated me so thoroughly, found every moment of my company unbearable, every glance met with contempt. And yet she saved me. I couldn't understand it.

Tentatively, I let my hand fall over hers, cold fingers slotting together.

She had bound us together that night in my father's study.

To what end, I did not know.

VIII

I had little memory of how we came out of the forest and back to the schloss. I woke in the white heat of fever, the world glittering and wild. Wolf tended to me; I was dimly aware of her comings and goings with wet cloths and willow-bark teas. Sitting always in the corner, never speaking, was a figure all in black. A month before this would have frightened me: an omen of something deathly. But now it was a comfort. My silent sentinel watching over me.

The morning my fever broke I opened my eyes to find the Witch sitting at my bedside. A large rocking chair had been pulled up close and beside it was a console table with a basin of water and a wrung-out cloth. The Witch was slouched low, brows furrowed as she read from a small volume with a cheap binding debossed with the title in English: *The Woman in White* – a novel, I realised, in groggy confusion. Her black outfit today was a loose Aesthetic gown with briar embroidery running down the front.

As I blinked myself awake, she quietly marked her place and set the book down.

'Wolf said you would be back with us today.'

I could just about manage to turn my head to her, blinking, my body little more than a lump of lead from my neck down. The dreamy, delirious state had passed and now I felt as though I had been run over by a cart.

I wondered at her sitting vigil. Perhaps she needed the company as much as I did.

'Here. Drink this.' The Witch passed out of view for a moment, then came back with a tin mug of water. Perching on the edge of my bed, she held the cup to my lips, then settled me back down.

I felt every place where her skin touched mine like an iron brand.

An effect of my illness, I was sure.

We hung there for a long moment: me collapsed on the pillows, hair fanned out around my face, her leaning over me, expression intent and watchful. I remembered curling against her in the forest, the rapid rise and fall of her breath and her strong arm clamped around my waist.

'I notice you too.' My voice was hoarse and cracked.

She tensed, drew back to her chair and turned her head so the dark sheet of her hair fell over her face.

But I had spoken now, and it could not be taken back. 'Tell me the truth. Why am I here?'

Her hands twitched on the arms of the chair, and I thought she might tell me. But I should have read her better: her body was a taut line, all rigid muscle and fleeing energy. I had been wrong before. She wasn't annoyed by me.

Without a muttered excuse, she picked up her book and fled.

She was *scared*.

*

It took me several days to recover from the chill I had caught in the forest, and another few after that for my ankle to comfortably bear my weight. It was the first time I'd slept soundly since arriving; whatever Wolf was giving me for the pain knocked me out and I almost began to forget about the horrors that haunted me.

All things considered, I had been extremely lucky – no, not lucky – *fortunate*. Fortunate that the Witch knew how to survive a night in the snow, fortunate she had noticed me missing, fortunate she had decided it worth her time to come after me. I had plenty of time laid up in bed to think about these things. The Witch said one thing and did another; she claimed to loathe my presence, but she risked her own safety to protect me. I thought perhaps for once I might have understood something about her: she was proud, too proud to admit she needed someone. A companion.

But she did need someone. She needed me.

I thought about my predecessors again. Had she told them she was afraid to be alone, or had she treated them as she had treated me? Had she started out open and grown closed? What had hurt her so badly she saw no other way than to tell me I was nothing to her?

When I was able to leave my rooms again it was like seeing the castle through new eyes. The dank, mouldering hallways, crumbling masonry and rotted panelling no longer felt frightening; now it only felt unbearably sad.

To keep my weight off my battered ankle, I used a carved walking stick that I had found in a coat stand amongst moth-eaten astrakhans, silk umbrellas and one impossibly heavy Russian winter coat trimmed in fur. The Witch herself seemed to have vanished into her Tower for good. I no longer caught her watching me from windows or lurking in shadows. I waited outside her door for hours and it never opened. She was simply *gone*. I looped the castle twice a day hoping for some hint of her, but it was like I was a ghost haunting an empty house.

So I retreated to the window seat I had created in my room, wrapped in my winter cloak, looking out of the frosted window panes over the snow-covered treetops. I didn't dare go walking on my own again in this weather; the snowy forest floor offered a hundred unseen obstacles and it would only take one misstep to leave me injured and stranded again.

I wasn't sure the Witch would come for me a second time.

My spirits sunk lower and lower. I was so lonely I felt physically cold. Every room was too chill, too big, too quiet; there wasn't enough flame burning in me alone to warm them. Sometimes I would break something just to feel the violence of it, snip off locks of hair or smack a bruise into my leg. I clung to that night in the forest, thinking it meant something, that something in my relationship with the Witch would change, but I was a hopeful fool.

The first night I went without Wolf's medications, I woke softly with a clock somewhere chiming three o'clock. The night was inky black with cloud cover. I lay still, waiting to understand what had roused me.

Then I heard it: the creak of the floorboards outside my room.

This time it seemed more deliberate, as though someone was shifting their weight while completing a task. Then – clear footsteps pacing outside.

Fear gripped me. The heart-pounding horror of something unknown prowling closer at my most vulnerable moment. For a breath I was struck by the thought that I would not be allowed rest; that I was being punished for wanting more than my lot.

I held my breath.

Silence.

Time stretched out unbearably. If I breathed again I was sure the footsteps would come again. My chest burned. My head swam.

With a gasp I sucked in a breath.

Still, silence.

Was my mind playing tricks on me?

Then, softly, footsteps retreating down the corridor.

I woke sick and confused and with no memory of falling asleep. It was horribly cold, my blankets had slipped to the floor in the night and my feet were near blue. Patience worn threadbare, I dressed and stalked across the castle to the main door to her study.

I knocked. A dull sound muffled by a thick layer of dense wood.

Nothing happened.

I knocked again but no one answered, so I crouched down with difficulty to peer through the keyhole. All I could see was the thick curtain to keep the cold out. I pressed my ear to the door and heard nothing.

I rattled the handle. Locked.

If she wouldn't talk to me, I would find answers another way.

I went to the other side of the castle, ankle sore and mood growing ever more sour. The door to the past stood before me, as plain and unremarkable as before. Weeks of isolation and a brush with death had worn away my fear of the Witch's threats. I was already trapped in a living death, and I no longer cared much what happened to me if I was caught.

I went inside.

The study was different. I stood on the threshold, brows furrowed as I counted off all the little things that were wrong. For one, it was mid-afternoon, judging from the way the shadows fell, not the early morning it always had been. There was a fire in the grate, and there was a new scatter of books across the table under the window. The ledgers had all been folded shut and stacked to one side.

On the desk, the half-written letter was gone. Instead, there was a newspaper dated Tuesday last.

I fell back, almost laughing with the realisation. It wasn't just a door to *one* specific Tuesday – it was a door to always the *last* Tuesday.

I had come for answers, but had stumbled on something quite different.

I circled the room, taking in this new portrait of her life, looking for any sign that my arrival had changed things for her. What did I want to see? Proof I was right, and that she needed me? If that was the case, I was sorely disappointed. Things were moved round, a discarded scarf, an empty coffee cup, but nothing more.

I was looking at a taxidermy crow when the main door was flung open. In a heartbeat I dropped down behind the settle. The bravery I had felt before entering her room vanished. The door slammed and the floorboards creaked as she paced in front of the empty fire grate, black skirts trailing behind bare, dirt-encrusted feet.

Inching behind the barrier of furniture, I paused at a gap, feeling every inch the deer alert to the hunter.

Then I saw her.

The Witch from a week ago, in that loose Aesthetic dress, hair streaming free around her face. The Witch was *distraught*. She moved staccato from desk to doorway, unshed tears glittering in her eyes. A black-edged envelope was twisted in her hands. She stopped by the fireplace, and for a moment I thought she might throw the letter in and burn it – perhaps she thought it too – but instead she snatched up a piece of glassware from the mantel and smashed it into the grate. Then another, and another, as rage consumed her and she systematically destroyed everything in reach. She tore flowers, shattered china, flung the ticking clock to the ground so it crumpled, hands falling still.

I held my breath throughout the whole explosion, frozen in fear. I knew I should use this moment to flee. But I couldn't.

My need to know held me fixed. And all I could think was: she had bare feet, someone needed to clean up the glass shards before she stood on them.

With everything in ruins, she collapsed into a chair, chest heaving and hair stuck to her cheeks. I had never seen her cry before.

Slowly, she eased the letter open, and read. The paper was black rimmed like the envelope – black for mourning. Black for death. My heart ached for her. Last Tuesday she had learned someone had died, and it had hurt her this badly.

And I added to her pain now by intruding on something private.

I took my chance as she wept and slunk towards the door – and I almost made it. My weak ankle betrayed me and I knocked against a console table carrying a heavy vase of dried flowers. The vase rocked in an arch of momentum that sent it toppling to smash in a shower of china shards.

The Witch's head snapped up.

I emerged from behind the table and her expression turned from shock to fury. She lunged, snarling, as I flung myself at the hidden door. Her face was mere centimetres from mine, I saw the betrayal and anger and shame – and then I slammed the door closed in her face.

I leaned against it, eyes shut for a moment as I caught my breath. She didn't follow. Perhaps she couldn't. I understood so little about how the magic in the castle worked, or if there were any logic to it at all.

I opened my eyes, and went cold.

The Witch – *my* Witch – stood waiting for me.

The anguish I had seen was gone. Now her anger was honed like a fine blade, cold steel sharpened and oiled until she could cut me with just a whisper.

'I'm sorry.' I didn't know what else I could say.

Her eyes narrowed, a dangerous brightness there, like a cat that, having cornered its prey, knows it can take a moment to play.

'*Sorry*?' she hissed.

'I intruded into your space, but I didn't mean to hurt you.'

She came alive at that, eyes flashing and lips pulling back in a snarl. '*You* could never hurt *me*.'

I had never been any good at arguments. I avoided them if I could. If someone hurt me I ignored it, or ignored them. Stay apart, stay quiet, and send myself into exile to the trees. It was easier that way.

My back was pressed up against the door like the bulk of the castle could lend me support. I had landed my full weight on my ankle in my flight and it sang in pain.

There was no way I could escape this.

I could only go through it.

'I saw the letter you were reading,' I said.

'You read it?'

'No, but I saw the black border. I know you lost someone. I'm so sorry.'

'Do you think I *care* what you think just because I stopped you freezing to death like an idiot?' she spat. For a moment I thought about scrambling back through the door to last Tuesday and throwing myself on the mercy of the past Witch. I would find no quarter here. 'Do you think I want to tell you my feelings as we braid our hair? You were a problem, and I solved it. That is *all*.'

The blow landed better than she could have imagined.

'If I am a problem it is only because you brought me here,' I said and thought of all the times I should have said it to my father but hadn't been brave enough. 'Why does it matter to you what I do if you think so little of me?'

'Because my business is *mine* and mine alone. You have a whole damn castle to yourself and yet you insist on trampling through the one space you are kept out of. Do you understand the word "private" or are stupid little rich girls like you incapable of conceiving of the notion that their presence isn't wanted absolutely everywhere they go?'

If only she knew how well I understood what it was to be not wanted.

I fell silent and she met it with a sneer.

A bubble of panic swelled. With me duly reprimanded, I could see her readying to leave, her attention drifting. She would leave me entirely alone again and I *could not bear it*.

'Wait.'

'Excuse me?' Fresh unfamiliar shock of being spoken back to.

'You can be as mean to me as you like,' I continued, 'but I won't stay out of your way.' The fear of that loneliness had broken me open. I felt again the desperation I had the night the Witch had come to my father. I was going to do something rash, because it was better than carrying the pain.

'For God's sake, why?'

I looked her direct in the eye, the truth plain between us. And I told her: 'Because I am *lonely*.'

And there it was. The truth of the matter.

'I will make you an offer.'

She scoffed. 'It is laughable you think you are in a position to be making offers to *me*—'

'I promise I won't pry into your business again, but I need something in return.'

'You have a whole castle and half a mountain, what else could you need?'

'Company.'

Of course I wanted to find out the reason she took me. Of course I wanted to know what happened to the men before me. But I would throw all of that aside not to be alone.

Her face fell. 'No.'

'Not all the time. Perhaps a few hours a day.'

'Absolutely not.'

'You brought me here as a companion. Let me keep you company.'

She folded her arms. 'You will get in my way.'

'I won't. I might even be helpful.'

'I doubt that.'

'Wouldn't you prefer to keep an eye on me so I can't pry?'

Her eyes narrowed. 'You try to goad me. I do not like it.' She tapped her foot, considering, bare sole slapping against the flagstones. 'I will take breakfast with you.'

'And then I will join you in your study in the evenings.'

'No—'

'Yes. I will keep myself occupied and you can do whatever it is you do.'

The Witch did not look happy. But nor was she flying into a rage again. I had been right: she was as lonely as I was.

'And you will stop your prying?'

I offered my hand with a nod.

Reluctantly, she took it. 'Very well. I agree to this bargain.'

Palm to palm, fingers twined, we bound ourselves to each other again.

But this time, I felt something very different.

Hope.

IX

Breakfast had never seemed so loaded a meal as it did that next morning. I woke well before dawn and dressed myself in the dark, fingers fumbling over buttons and ties, too early for any maid to assist me. I had proposed this new plan and if it ended badly it would be on my head.

I had informed Wolf the night before of the change in arrangements and, as I had requested, an empty room on the ground floor had been turned into a breakfast parlour for the Witch and me. I had chosen the room due to its windows facing south-east, framing one swathe of the valley and mountainside. The castle was undoubtedly well positioned with the bulk of the mountain to the north and the river valley snaking south. From this vantage point perched above the tree line, we would see the best of both dawn and dusk, and even the short winter days could flood the right room with light.

There was a round table made of rosy cherry wood in the centre and two chairs with plump cushions pulled up on either side. Wolf had set places for two and was delivering plates of cheese and ham and butter as I came in. I adjusted forks and inspected the cups for chips or stains. I was almost entirely sure the Witch wouldn't notice a damn thing, but I wanted to make our fresh start a good one. My mother, when she had been at her best, had insisted on breakfast every morning, the two of us together at a table in the bay window of her apartment. My father was always away on business, or tied up in meetings, so we made what family we could together, sharing honey from the hives in the palace grounds, jam made from fruit we had gathered. When her mood slipped again, I would sit at the same breakfast table, set out the same jars and plates and wait for her. She wouldn't come, but I waited for her all the same. There had been nothing else to do. She was my mother, and even the dim, tenuous love she offered was better than nothing at all.

I had none of the richness of the Summer Palace at my disposal now, but I wanted to show the Witch that company was a gift, not a burden.

As Wolf set down a steaming pot of coffee, I realised what was missing. From the kitchen I plucked up dried herbs and flowers – sage for wisdom, rosemary for remembrance, dandelion for happiness and chamomile for patience – and brought them back to the breakfast room to arrange in a jar in the middle of the table. It was only a little snatch of the garden brought inside, but it made my heart calmer to see it.

Then came the wait. I sat in one chair, watching the butter soften and the fresh rolls cool. What if she did not come? We had shaken on our new agreement, but that did not mean she could not change her mind. Perhaps she had spent the night brooding on my selfish intrusion and would call the arrangement off; perhaps she was still angry and wanted to punish me. Or perhaps she was so unused to the idea of breakfasting with someone, she had simply forgotten.

I was playing out scenarios in my mind for how to casually remind her, when the Witch emerged. Chivvied along by Wolf, she was even more chaotically dressed than usual in a petticoat, an ornate stomacher from a sixteenth century dress and over it a too-big frock coat with frayed cuffs that hung halfway down her palms. Without a word, she climbed into the empty chair, one leg drawn up to her chest, the other folded across the seat, and eased the mass of her tangled hair out of her face, blinking owlishly at the spread of food before her.

'Coffee,' she growled.

I pointed to the coffee pot. She looked back at me expectantly.

'You have to pour it into a cup,' I explained.

Glancing heavenward in exasperation, she gave in, and sloshed steaming hot coffee into a cup that she downed and immediately refilled.

I had made a joke and she hadn't bitten my head off. Promising.

I took a roll onto my plate, tore it in half and began to apply butter, watching the Witch out of the corner of my eye. I was determined to act naturally, but somehow I was more anxious this morning than I had been when we were fighting. At least then I'd known where I stood; now I had set foot in a new country where I did not speak the language or know the customs, but I was determined to make it my home.

'Are you planning to have any bread with that butter?'

'What?' I startled and looked down at the roll in my hand

that was now plastered with a solid inch of melting butter that dripped onto the tablecloth. 'Oh.'

I scraped off a layer and spread it on the other half of the roll. The Witch had slowed her coffee intake and was now looking fractionally less like a walking corpse. Her plate was still empty, and I watched her prod the different cuts of meat, the boiled eggs, salamis, slabs of cheese and bowls of winter fruit with curiosity.

'So what does one do at . . . breakfast? What is it for?'

I laughed. 'Haven't you had breakfast before?'

She looked uncomfortable. 'I am aware of the concept.'

'We eat something together. Prepare ourselves for the day. Wake up.'

The Witch took an apple and began to slice it neatly into eighths. 'The last time I ate breakfast, peasants still took a flagon of fermented oats into the fields while they worked.'

I opened my mouth to ask another question, but she pointedly arched a brow and I closed it.

No prying, I had promised.

Afterwards, we parted, and true to my word I paid no attention to the Witch in her Tower until evening came, when I gathered up my books and a rock sample and carried them over to the Witch's study. It seemed like she had been waiting for me. The desk had been meticulously cleared of any trace of personal identity, all letters disappeared into the drawers, ledgers stacked innocently on a shelf, and not even an open book to give me any suggestion as to what was on her mind.

Very well.

I gave her a smile, turned my back and flopped down in front of the crackling fire to spread my books and samples and tools around me. My heart raced and I could feel her eyes following me, but resolutely I ignored her and began to flip through a text on igneous rock formation.

That first evening we didn't say a word. I studied my books and took absolutely nothing in, and repeated the exercise the next night and the next night, and the night after that. It was a strange echo of evenings spent with my stepmother and stepsisters with our needlework and piano; a different vein of tension ran through these nights. Instead of slipping into the background, I felt all too visible. The Witch sat at her own books, quill in hand. She was careful to only keep one ledger or piece of correspondence on her desk at a time so she could guard it. All I could catch were ranks of figures scratching down columns, copied from a small notebook. Did it have something to do with all the time she spent locked in the Tower? I had the impression of something being measured, monitored. I wanted to ask her what it was she worked at, but my promise not to pry was fresh in my mind.

At the end of the first week, a shadow fell across the page as I read. The Witch had come out from behind her desk and was hovering behind me, squinting at the typeface.

'Are you really reading about rocks?' she asked.

'I am,' I said without looking up.

A moment passed. 'What *for*?'

I closed the book. 'Because it's interesting.'

She looked at me in blank incomprehension. 'It's rock.'

She seemed at war with herself, torn between her curiosity and her stubborn desire to deny me any value.

Curiosity won out. She folded herself onto the rug and picked up the piece of basalt I had been examining earlier with my magnifying glass, turning it over, running her thumb over the coarse grain.

'And what exactly is it about this rock that is interesting to you?'

I searched for the words. Usually it was my family asking me to *stop* talking about geology.

'Because it's all of history folded up into something you can hold in the palm of your hand. This rock could be older than almost anything else on the planet.' I took it from her hand and turned it over to show her the pockmarked texture on the back. 'These formed in magma then cooled so quickly the bubbles froze at once. The eruption that created this could have happened thousands of years ago, or even more, but we can touch these bubbles and for an instant, travel in time.' I stroked my thumb over the rippled, honeycomb formation, then handed it back to the Witch. 'It's like magic.'

She examined it in silence, a troubled expression marring her face. I was growing used to the way her brows puckered together in deep thought or concern, the downward tug at the edges of her mouth when she was about to snap at me, or the faint lines at her eyes that only appeared when she was trying not to smile.

'The rock is time,' she said. 'And time has value to you.'

'It makes me feel better to remember that time is so much

bigger and older than I am. I am not alone because I am a part of it.' I thought of my mother, who lived only in memory. Who would never join my future. 'Our histories are still with us, if only in this way.'

She was watching me again, that intense, glittering gaze that had skewered me in place in our forest shelter. Heat rose to my cheeks. The Witch leaned forward, her skirts rustling and I felt the brush of her arm against mine. For a heated second, I thought she was going to touch me.

But then she gently placed the basalt back in place and drew away, leaving me suddenly colder despite the glowing fire.

'Some things,' she said, 'are better left in the past.'

Despite her insistence that my interest in geology was peculiar, the Witch continued to humour me, and over time asked about each of my samples as I brought them to her study. I took over a sideboard for myself, evicting spiders and mouldering documents to create a store for my rocks and equipment. Most nights she stayed behind her desk or in a large wingback armchair half in shadow, curled up with her knees to her chest, reading or writing or simply staring out of the dark window. Though her days were still mostly occupied with her work in the Tower – and whatever it was that generated an unending stream of numbers for her to enter in the ledgers – I began to find her more often around the castle, always at a distance, but now she seemed unbothered about sharing space with me.

I was making drawings of the rotting tapestries in the great hall one day when she came up behind me so quietly I half jumped out of my skin.

'Don't startle me.' I had carved a jagged black line across my drawing, ruining it.

'You should pay more attention,' she snapped, then caught herself, and said in more measured tones, 'I have something for you.' From a pocket she pulled a piece of rock, about the size of my fist and pale butter yellow, scored deeply on one side. 'You like rocks.'

She held out the piece of sandstone expectantly. I took it from her and examined it. It looked like a piece of masonry; the scored side had been exposed to the elements for years, rain and snow wearing down the crumbling surface into the pattern I now saw.

I looked up to thank her – but she had already gone.

I put the rock gently into my bag to take back to my room.

When I was ten, before my mother died, I had rescued a puppy from the kennels, a runt, scabby and bony and snapping at anyone who came near. My father had been furious. But what angered him brought my mother back to life. By those days she was a living ghost, drifting between bed and armchair by the window in her nightgown. When I brought the dog to her, she was present in the room for the first time in months. I wondered later if she felt it a kindred spirit, something discarded and damaged. I wondered if that was how she thought about herself.

With patience, she showed me how to leave the dog in peace to adjust to its new home, to move with soft confidence. The dog had not known kindness, she explained, guiding me to the welts on its back and the glassy fear in its eyes, and it would not know how to recognise it at first. So I must be patient. I must be trustworthy and consistent.

Slowly the dog had let me come close enough to treat its injuries and even pet its head. A year on and it was a happy, healthy thing that bounded around the house scratching the parquet floor and sleeping at the end of my bed every night. When my mother died, my father told me it had gone missing during her funeral, but he usually said whatever was most convenient for him. My stepmother, when she arrived a few months later, was terribly allergic to dogs and I lay awake at night, turning these events over in my mind.

But the lesson still stood: change was possible. It just took patience. Care. Love.

Far easier to offer that to the Witch, than to think why I might need it myself.

*

The footsteps outside my door left me in peace for a week after our bargain was struck. I began to think of them as some passing madness, a manifestation of my loneliness and regret for coming to the castle that had been banished by my new-found connection with the Witch.

I was wrong.

I woke in confusion one night, when the cloud cover was absolute and the wolves came low and howling. Something had roused me but I could not remember what.

The bed was freezing. I felt around with my foot for the fire-warmed brick Wolf had placed beneath the covers but found nothing. Only a cold, hostile expanse. I tucked my legs up into a ball and opened my eyes.

The storm lamp had gone out.

My breath clouded like milk in the air, like I was drowning in the cold.

The floorboards creaked.

Fear gripped me at once: I was alone in the dark and the footsteps had come back.

I lay as cold and still as snow, paralysed. I could not escape. No matter what I did, I could not escape this darkness that followed me.

The thought sparked a new one: if I could not escape, then perhaps I should stop running.

Perhaps I should face whatever I was running from.

Silently, I slipped from my bed and padded softly across the room. I thought to surprise the pacer, but it was as though the sound was woven to my own movements; as I advanced, the footsteps retreated. When I opened the door a fraction, all I caught was a whisper of black skirts disappearing around the corner.

The Witch.

I gripped the doorknob tighter.

The Witch paced outside my door and I did not know why.

Hot with sudden anger, I followed her. How dare she torment me like this. We had made our bargain, she had no right to frighten me so.

As I turned the corner, a flash of deeper black amongst the shadows showed me her path. With my lamp gone out, I stumbled after her as best I could, but it wasn't long before I was lost. One part of the castle looked much the same as another in the dark; I could not have come far from my room but I found myself entirely turned around.

The first door I tried opened onto a storeroom so unremarkable it did little to help me orientate myself. The next was a bedroom, just as indistinct. The third door was cold to the touch, and I stepped inside hesitantly.

I had not come to this room before. The wall facing me held a series of magnificent windows with pointed arches, but each had caved in, the stone crumbling and worn to expose the room to the night sky and prickle of pine trees on the hills beyond. A blanket of snow drifted through the open wall, banking in corners and glittering like felled stars.

The wrongness sat heavy in my stomach; the longer I stood in the room, the more I felt consumed by dread. This was not right. I did not belong here.

I left as silently as I had entered and searched my way back to my room huddled into the shadows, as though the castle was a creature that could sense my movement and I did not want to wake it. At last I came to the locked door beside mine, and once inside my room I barricaded myself in.

Perhaps the Witch was right: it was better not to pry.

I might not like what I would find.

The snow that had started when I was stranded in the forest had not stopped since. Every part of the castle was freezing, and my nights of poor sleep meant it was an effort to drag myself out of bed each morning. A thick snowpack swallowed the forest over a metre deep, the surface rippled and puckered by the wind. The castle had been closed down, windows shuttered and outbuildings locked up, with only the rooms we used regularly kept open and warmed. I found myself dashing between my bedroom and the study wrapped up in my winter cloak, breath clouding in the stone corridors glittering with hoarfrost. I thought then of my mother's grave, of the stone angel looking over it and how it would look draped in a cloak of ice. My mother had loved the bite of winter as though it was the only thing that could bring her to life.

This was the longest I had ever spent without visiting her.

Sometimes I wondered who I might have been if my mother had lived. I grieved over a figment, a ghost of something that never was and never could be. An echo of another girl I would not know.

Some vast, yawning space opened up beneath me. I would never visit my mother again. We were truly parted forever.

I worked to keep those thoughts far from me.

Naturally, my mind turned to the Witch. I tried to keep my promise not to pry, though it was not easy, shut in for days against the snow that piled against the windows. I wanted to know why the Witch had been outside my room. I wanted to know what it was she wrote in her ledgers. And behind it all, was a low hum of ill-ease about my predecessors.

But our agreement was all I had to keep me from my loneliness, so for now, I would bite my tongue, and stay my hand.

Instead, wrapped in my cloak, I raided the three different libraries in the castle, gathering books on garden planting, guides to herbs and edible wildflowers, medicinal plants and useful shrubbery and brought them to the study with an eye to making a plan for the kitchen garden once we reached the other side of winter. There might be seedlings lying dormant that I could salvage, but I wanted to have a list prepared for Wolf to send for cuttings and seeds of anything else I wanted to cultivate. My rocks lay neglected, while my botanical readings grew in tottering stacks around the floor. The Witch, bit by bit, was moving out from behind her desk or the shadowy armchair, and closer to me. The knowledge warmed me: something, at least, was growing in this frightening place.

There was a room I knew that was well stocked with gardening tools, though they were all in a state of disrepair. It lay near the kitchens and I could reliably find my way to it most days. One morning around the middle of December I had gone hunting for a better trowel as the handle of the one I had taken first was rotten through with woodworm. At the bottom of a cupboard stuffed with twine and pegs and cracked pots, I thought I saw the flash of metal. When I crouched down I saw that I was right – but it was a tin of keys, not the blade of a tool.

I thought of the key to the Tower that hung around the Witch's neck. Temptation called me. Would one of these fit that lock?

No. I must not. The risk was not worth it. The Witch had begun to trust me, I could not squander it.

Then another idea struck me.

The Witch's Tower was not the only locked door.

The room beside my own was a far less risky venture.

The Witch, as ever, was shut up in her Tower, and I heard the sound of Wolf in the kitchens ordering around the maids undertaking the castle's laundry. Curiosity got the better of me, and I wrapped the tin of keys in an old cloth to hide it as I returned.

With sweating palms, I knelt at the door. There were tens of keys in the tin, some as large as my hand, half rusted and coarse. I considered the lock and selected a key that seemed likely. Of course, it did not turn, so I tried another, and another. As the pile of incorrect keys grew, I felt foolish, and afraid. If the Witch caught me, surely this would be considered prying – and for what? To find another room full of broken chairs or rotting carpets?

I should stop.

And yet, I kept working through the tin.

Until at last, one turned.

The lock was stiff and heavy, but it gave under my ministrations, and the door swung open.

Inside was a bedroom much like my own, the bed made up, but otherwise stripped empty. Every surface was covered in a thick layer of dust. In one corner was an escritoire, its lid drawn down, but I caught a flash of white feather where it had not been properly closed. It was stiff, and took a little effort to open, but when it lifted, it revealed a desk scattered with quills and dried-up bottles of ink.

And an unfinished letter, dated a little over fifty years ago.

I pulled back as though I had been burned.

I recognised the Witch's hand well enough by now and this was not it.

Edgar Hässler.

How many times had I heard his name? Seen his mother knelt before the shrine to St Anthony? This letter had been written by the man who had lived here before me.

My fingers hovered over the paper. There was no point pretending I did not mean to pry now, and if anyone had any right to know the business of a previous companion, surely it was me.

Before my fear could get the better of me I took up the letter and read it.

It was the work of a few moments. Edgar had only written a handful of lines before he had been interrupted, seemingly never to return.

Dearest Mother,

I write in the hope of this letter reaching you, though I do not know how, or when it will. This place is strange, in a way I cannot begin to explain. Correspondence does reach us — the Witch has newspapers from all over the continent — but the way for a man seems much harder to navigate. If this is the only letter that reaches you, then the thing I most desire to tell you is that I love you, and Frieda, and miss you. But I am proud to do my duty, though I would wish to better understand what it is. The Witch has told me

And there it stopped.

I threw the paper down in frustration. What had the Witch told Edgar? What did he know of our role here?

I searched the desk but found nothing. The rest of the room had been stripped. The clothes press and chest of drawers were empty, the sheets rumpled but nothing left beneath the pillow or under the mattress. If this had been Edgar's room, any trace of him had been tidied away save the desk that had been protected by its tricky lid. Perhaps he had sat down on his first night here, frightened and lonely as I had been, to write to his family. Perhaps the Witch had told him the secret of his role here, and that had caused him to abandon his correspondence. Or perhaps he had struck his own bargain with her.

Looking at the dropped quill, the splash of ink, the sentence stopped dead, I had misgivings.

The Witch's secrets piled up, and I had not a single answer at hand.

∗

Unease sat with me for the rest of the day, like a stone I carried beneath my breastbone. No matter how busy I kept myself, I felt the weight of it, caught its shadows moving in the corner of my eyes. I had made a promise I did not know if I could keep.

I hid it as best I could from the Witch as we sat together that evening. Snow fell softly outside the window and the fire crackled; I closed my notebook and turned to the Witch.

'Thank you.'

'For what?'

'For spending time with me.'

'I am only keeping to the terms of our agreement.' The Witch turned a page in the little clothbound novel that had arrived in the post. The title was something in English I couldn't quite understand – I could see that it translated to something like 'moonstone' but I wasn't sure what it could be about. 'As I hope you are keeping to yours.'

I thought of the footsteps and the hidden room, the unsent letter, and said, 'Yes.'

'Good. Then my evenings are yours.'

I was on the rug before the fire and she sat in a chair with her bare feet tucked beneath her, so that I had to tilt my head to speak to her. Her eyes were shut and I allowed myself a moment to take her in. The smooth, icy plane of her pale cheek, the dark flush of lashes against her skin, the full lower lip as red as blood and hair a glossy, coal-like black hanging heavy over her shoulders in tangled waves. I remembered seeing her for the first time, and being so shocked to see someone so unearthly beautiful when we feared her so. Now all I saw was someone so acutely human. In the chapped skin of her lips, the lines beside her eyes, the bitten quicks of her nails and the rapid rise and fall of her chest as she breathed.

She had gone from *Witch* to *my* Witch, and I didn't quite know when.

A soft knock announced Wolf at the door. She held a letter in her hands, small and battered. The Witch held out her hand for it but Wolf shook her head and looked to me instead.

I took it, slow with surprise. I had not expected any letters to reach me, and thought of what Edgar had said in his. Correspondence reached the castle irregularly. I broke the seal with trembling fingers. I knew the paper – it was from the palace in Blumwald.

From Klara. It was dated a week previous and lasted only a few lines.

'My father has had an accident.' Panic and dread flushed hot and cold through me. 'He fell from his horse. They don't know if he . . .' The letter dropped into my lap.

The Witch sat ramrod straight, uncertain. I looked at her, words unformed on my lips, the silent question strung between us.

'No.'

'No?'

'No. You cannot leave.'

'My father—'

'I heard what you said.'

I felt then my heart break. '*Why*?'

A storm crossed her face. 'Because you bound yourself and I will not allow you to break that vow.'

I folded the letter into a bullet of paper and ink, turned the nub between my fingers. I remembered the Witch that day in her study when she had received her letter limned in black. How she had cried. I wondered again what she had lost by being here; perhaps my father wasn't so big a sacrifice in comparison.

Whatever tenderness had been between us before had turned brittle like frost. I didn't mean to cry, but I did. As soon as I felt the wetness against my skin I made quick work to excuse myself.

I had thought my life so terrible I had put myself into the

Witch's hand, severing myself from my family forever and until now I hadn't let myself think about what that meant. The love between my father and I had been stretched so thin, but it was still there, a filigree strand as fine and ephemeral as a spiderweb. If he was alive, even if I never saw him again, that thread remained intact.

I carried the fear of it snapping like a wound in my heart.

X

Wolf and the Witch were together at the kitchen table the next morning.

I had wondered where the Witch went after our breakfasts together, but had not expected to find her somewhere so domestic. I had borrowed a thimble and thread from Wolf to mend my stockings the day before and had come to return it. My mind was foggy with worry for my father and I had darned the stocking to my skirt and my sleeve and my own finger before I gave up on the task.

Outside the kitchen I stopped short when I saw the two women. It was a conversation I knew wasn't for my ears; yet I lingered. Their voices rolled and danced together in the easy rhythm of long acquaintance, a familiarity I was not yet a part of. I stepped sideways into a shadow and listened.

Wolf stood, lifted the tea kettle from the fire and poured it over a pot of nettles. 'That is out of the question and has never been done before.'

'I was not asking your permission,' said the Witch.

'You will not gain my forgiveness either.'

The Witch held out her cup and Wolf filled it. 'It might surprise you that I seek neither.'

'Then why tell me if your mind is made up?'

'You would rather find out when her bed is empty one morning?'

A rock plunged in my stomach. What did the Witch have planned for me?

'I only think of you,' said Wolf. Despite the gruffness of her tone she brought a plate of lightly sugared biscuits to the table and pushed them in front of the Witch. 'You really think she'll return?'

I swallowed my shock.

'Does it matter?' snapped the Witch. Wolf began to speak but the Witch held up a hand. 'I know. I know it matters.' She sunk her head in her hands.

Wolf drank her tea. Snow fell outside the kitchen window, a blue wash of light fractured as it crossed the table.

'If she doesn't, we'll find another way,' said the Witch. 'Someone else. Wolf, if I could have seen my father one more time, just once . . . I can't say no to her.'

'She's not your friend.'

'I know that.'

'Do you?' A moment passed. Something light swelled in my heart. 'You only make it harder on yourself when you get attached to them.'

The Witch rose, dashed her cup in the sink. 'Don't you think I know that? It's not you who has to—'

The thimble in my hand slipped, clinked on the flagstones.

A small noise, but enough for the Witch to stop, for the both of them to turn towards the door.

My time was up. I had heard too much, and my flash of pleasure at finding out the Witch meant to let me go to my father had been quickly replaced by that prickle of dread every time I thought about her previous companions. I left, thinking to pack a bag for my journey to Blumwald. The more I tried to focus on the problem of my predecessors, the more it slipped out of view, like a phenomenon I could only see from the corner of my eye.

A little later, Wolf came to my room with my official permission to leave. I tried my best to look surprised, and it was no effort to show my gratitude. Wolf was stiff, mouth tight with disapproval but she said nothing to me and I wondered again what it was she knew about the Witch that I didn't. Before I finished packing, I slipped back into the abandoned bedroom and took Edgar's half-finished letter. Perhaps I could do some good by delivering it, fifty years late.

The carriage was waiting in the courtyard when I descended, carpetbag in hand. Its smoky dimensions stood out like ink against the fresh snow and the steam of the horses' nostrils coiled above them so they looked like red-eyed devils. The Witch detached from a nest of shadows in the great hall. I had wondered why she hadn't come to tell me herself of her change of heart but I understood it when I saw the raw misery and confusion in her. She looked tense enough to splinter from a single touch, the dark smudges under her eyes pronounced; for the first time I felt the balance of power shift between us.

She needed me, and in letting me leave she was trusting that I needed her too.

'Thank you.' I held my bag before me, a barrier between us.

'You complained too much. I knew you wouldn't shut up if I didn't relent.' The words were sharp but there was no bite to her tone.

Before I could go, she darted forward, clasped my hand in hers. Her skin was warm – it still surprised me – her fingers rough like the women who worked the spinning wheels and the looms. 'I hope your father lives.'

Awkward, a step sideways from the right words, but I was touched.

'Thank you,' I said, words thick in my mouth. 'For everything.'

I squeezed her hand in return, then took my bag to the carriage; she followed me to the door to watch me go. Snow had begun to fall again. The flakes caught in her hair, a scatter of stars against black waves.

I mounted the steps into the carriage and we drew around to face the open gate. My world had become anchored to the Witch, and I felt it shift as we drove over the bridge and into the snow-covered forest; a new tethering thread spooled out.

Home lay just as much behind me as it did ahead.

We drove into Blumwald in a flurry of snow and lamplight.

I had tried to mark our way, but something in the jolt of the carriage and how the trees slid past in a blur like oil swirling through water made me sicken. The more I tried to concentrate on our route, the worse I felt. In the end I drew the blind and shut my eyes against my dizziness, turning my mother's drop spindle between my fingers as a talisman against my fear. The Witch's castle did not want to be found. Without her carriage, I would be alone between those fearful trees, in the gloom and the rot and the mist.

It was a relief, then, to see the walls of Blumwald rise from the snow-covered valley, when I finally summoned the strength to look out of the window again. Christmas had consumed the city; the square was full of market stalls and advent lights shone in every window. The salt and iron that had marked homes before had gone; the Witch had visited her terror and all who remained were marked safe. I had taken their fear away from them, and as my carriage passed through the streets I brought it back. Heads turned, mouths clenched, but I paid them no heed. My worry had built over the long journey back; it had been over a week since the letter had been sent. What if I were too late?

The palace was shut up and dark and I feared the worst. The servants were as bad as the townsfolk, twitching and whispering at my arrival, but I was led upstairs to my father's bedroom by the light of a candlestick. Our apartments were as cold and hushed as the winter forest; it was as though the grave had spread its icy embrace around my home in preparation. I thought then of the weeks before and after my mother's death. The stopped clocks and the muffled bells, all the warmth and colour drained from the world, and the waiting, the long, smothering nothingness. I pressed my hand to my father's bedroom door, stiff with fear. I could not bear to go through all that again.

Before I could open the door, my stepmother came out, looking harried and holding a bowl of water and dirtied cloth. At the sight of me, they tumbled from her hands, splashing across the parquet.

'Mina!' Her face was ashen. 'How is this possible?'

I tried to peer behind her into the dark sanctum of my father's bedroom. All I could see was the heavy drape of the bed curtains and the dim shape of a body. 'Klara wrote to me. Is he –' I couldn't bring myself to finish the thought.

'The doctor is with him now. He has been . . . we will know more tomorrow.' She struggled to gather her words and stared at me as though the dead had risen and walked before her. 'Why are you here?'

I felt an old familiar tension settle onto my bones. 'He is my father. Of course I came.'

'If the Witch finds out you ran away . . .'

'I didn't run. She let me go.'

My stepmother did not seem convinced. She stepped closer. 'Mina.'

'I swear.' Before she could say anything else, I asked, 'May I see him?'

Her mouth was a tight line. 'You'll be in the way.'

It was too easy to fall back into the patterns of the girl I used to be here, but they fit badly, like a shoe outgrown. 'I'll do as the doctor says. I'm sure you can use an extra pair of hands.'

A maid came round the corner carrying a fresh cloth and water, and stopped in shock at my presence. I took them from her with a smile.

'There's been a spill.' I indicated the dropped bowl and

towel at my stepmother's feet, and with their attention diverted, I stepped past her and into the sick room.

A hush fell.

My footsteps were muffled by the heavy carpet and curtains hung by the door and windows against the cold.

The doctor was by the bed, bent over the slack body of my father. A moment of horror gripped me: another corpse-parent. Then I saw the shallow rise and fall of his chest and it gave me freedom to breathe too. I set the bowl down by the table and dipped the cloth in the water. My father was stretched out on his bed under bulky covers that were pulled back at one corner to expose a leg bound tightly to a splint. His skin was waxy, drawn taut over his cheekbones and jaw. Gently, I pressed the cloth against his sweat-stained forehead.

'Tell me.' My voice trembled. 'Will he live?'

The doctor knocked my hand away. 'Less of that, unless you mean to bathe him.'

I listened, numb, as the doctor explained to me the fall, the fracture, a fever that had plagued him since. I had read so much and yet had nothing of medicine, nothing of any use in the world. I only understood as much as my stepmother had suggested: a crisis gripped him. If he sickened further, the outlook was grave, but if he passed the night and the fever broke then there was hope. I felt my cheeks wet with tears: relief I had reached his side, and fear of the hours to come.

My stepmother returned and we passed a painful night in vigil. I had hoped to be of some use but I was only underfoot, closing windows when they were to be opened and speaking when the doctor wanted silence. I felt as though I should tidy myself away and sit the night alone, but that voice had waned in power since living with the Witch and I warred with it through that agonising night. Change had begun its work on me but I was not yet loosed from the yoke of my past.

Dawn broke with the fever, a healthy colour coming to my father's face as light lined the curtain edges. He did not wake, but the tension lifted from the doctor's expression and for the first time since Klara's letter had arrived I felt the world solid beneath me. I turned to the window to hide my face. Relief was a sweet drug and I cried freely in that tiny moment of privacy, shoulders trembling. I had weathered one more storm and come through safe.

✳

I fell into a deep sleep until midday, but woke uneasy. My father was out of danger, but memories of my last night in the palace came to me. The Witch with my father. A thought I had been ignoring for too long: he knew about the Witch. He might know what she planned for me. When I came to my father's rooms I was shooed away by my stepmother, but she softened enough to tell me he had woken and taken a little soup, and perhaps he would be well enough to see me that evening or the next day.

I took my chance to walk through my old home one more time instead. In daylight, I could see the palace was not quite as abandoned as I'd thought. My stepmother's preparations for Christmas were well under way; I passed deliveries of claret and schnapps and salted hams and boxes of candles and candied fruit and nuts and cloves and an order of half a dozen geese to be stored in the icehouse. Memories lay everywhere: choosing and felling a tree with my mother and father, in the years they still spoke to each other. Cutting swags of ivy and holly, evergreen branches and fir cones to make decorations, until my mother grew overwhelmed by the world and retreated to her room, leaving me alone with a forest of scraps. And after she died, walking through the snowfall alone, sighting snow hares, the deer creeping closer to the town as the mountains became impossible for all but the hardiest creatures.

I wanted to stay within the fantasy of those memories. Every lonely, difficult moment turned sweet with age.

Reality met me sharp and clear in town. The whispers and looks of the night before had swelled into people hovering at the edge of my vision, slipping close to ask snatched questions, about the Witch, the castle, what had happened to me, to touch the edge of my sleeve in wonder. I was a creature of myth. Rare and unreal and unnerving.

At the edge of town, work was under way to mark out the foundations of a new station for the railway. My father had got what he wanted. Sacrificing me to the Witch had been worth it. I thought of her alone in her study, marooned in that collapsing wreck of a castle. The line between us pulled taut and I realised, with a flush of confusion, that I missed her. The Witch had let me in, even if only a little, and that warmed me in the coldest moments.

Here, I had no one.

As fresh snow fell after lunch I stopped at the cathedral, slipping between its monstrous iron-studded door; I was not the demon they thought me, iron could not hold me back. The interior was dressed in violet for advent, and the witch-cursed saint-shrines burned dim – there was no need for protection now the Witch had visited her doom on me. Only one figure sat before the shrine of St Anthony of Padua, hunched in a black lace mantilla, rosary bead clicking between her gnarled fingers. I saw a strange echo of the Witch in her black veil, before the woman rose to leave and I saw it was Frau Hässler. I slipped behind a pillar, debating what to do. Edgar's letter was still in my pocket where I had slipped it before I left.

Frau Hässler shuffled from the cathedral and I followed. She went to a small, respectable cottage showing signs of lost money – a cracked pane in an upper window, rotten wood around the frame. Snow caught in my hair and clung to my cheeks. Despite my cloak and muffler I was freezing. I knelt at the step, and edged the paper under the door. Even this far away, I feared the Witch discovering me. Those who had been taken before me were as much my business as hers, but I feared her fury if she found out what I had done.

As I still knelt, the door was answered by a middle-aged woman as hard as a bar of iron, tall and stiff-backed with chestnut hair shot through with grey like dirty ice melt. Frieda.

I looked up at her, awkward in my winter cloak and muffler dangling from one hand.

'Yes?' She was brusque, then her eyes widened as she recognised me. 'How is it possible you are here?'

'Who is it?' a voice came from behind her, thin and frail. Frau Hässler.

Frieda's hand closed around my arm and I was drawn inside before I could speak.

'It is her. The new companion.'

Frau Hässler peered at me through rheumy eyes, crossed herself in shock. 'Is it true?' She reached a hand to test my flesh. 'You came back.'

'Yes.'

'How can it be?'

I did not know how to answer why I alone had been granted such a privilege, so instead held out my hand, and the letter in it. 'I came to bring you this. It is from Edgar.'

She gave an involuntary moan and sat down heavily by the fireplace. 'Is he well? Why did he not come too?'

A new horror filled me.

She thought Edgar could still be alive.

My cheeks felt hot with shame. I should have done this differently.

'I have not met him. He is not . . . this is all I found.'

I held the letter out and Frieda took it from me.

While Frieda read the letter I looked about me at their home. I couldn't bear to watch Frau Hässler's face. The room was small and bare, showing the same decline as the exterior. Enough wood burned in the fire, but the walls needed whitewashing, and the rug across the boards was threadbare. It looked as though their life had been jammed into the only room that they could afford to heat, a bed in one corner and a table in another, and taking up much of the space a great spinning wheel with a fistful of fine ivory wool wound around the bobbin. In a place as backward as Blumwald many women still hand-spun when they had no other way to bring in money. I wondered whether Frieda or Frau Hässler was the spinster here, or both. Of all their possessions, this was the one in best condition. A basket of fleece sat at its side, a hunk speared on the needle of the distaff, from where the fibres were drawn down into a thread that looped the hooks of the flyer and onto the bobbin. Operated by means of a foot pedal, the great wheel turned, spinning the bobbin to put a twist into the thread, the twist that transformed raw wool into yarn. A simple, household magic I had never learned.

Frieda finished, and said, 'So, Edgar is dead.'

'Don't say that.' Frau Hässler reached for the letter, running her fingers over the faded ink. 'See, it says here, Edgar is thinking of us.'

'He never finished writing.' Frieda shot me a sour look. 'He never got to leave that place.'

'I'm sorry,' I said. My presence here felt like an insult.

Frau Hässler hunched over the paper, rereading her son's last words to her.

'Losing Edgar broke her heart, and our family,' said Frieda. She turned her back to me, settling herself at the wheel to spin. 'We don't need you coming here stirring up the past. You escaped the Witch, well, good for you. My brother didn't. Thank God for watching over you, and leave the rest of us alone.'

'I'm sorry,' I said again.

I knew I should go, but too many questions crowded on my tongue. My father and the Witch, conspiring together in his study . . .

'What do you remember of when your brother was taken?' I asked. 'Do you know why he was chosen?'

'He was chosen because he was no one important.' Frieda's words were underscored by the rhythmic hum of the wheel, the clack of the flyer. 'One day we were happy, the next the Witch came down from her castle and Edgar never came home. We had a letter from the old duke telling us that he had been taken by the Witch and offering us compensation.'

I frowned. 'Compensation?'

'Money. As though we were farmers who'd lost sheep to the wolves. Money for a life. A life buying everyone peace from the Witch.'

I thought of my Witch hunched over her ledgers, or reading English novels, or picking out the chives from her eggs at breakfast. I could not understand how that woman could be the monster they all feared.

'I saw him,' said Frau Hässler. She had begun to pray, holding onto her rosary beads like they were the hand of the son she had lost. 'I saw Edgar in that carriage of hers – his face in the window – and I saw that awful creature, like a demon in black rags. She had her hand on him, but when he saw me too he smiled.' Her voice broke. 'He told me all would be well. He told me he would write.' Glassy tears spilled down the deep furrows in her cheeks.

Edgar had gone to the Witch, and disappeared, like all the companions.

Save for me.

'Mother. Stop this.' Frieda brought the wheel to a halt and turned to me with eyes like fire. 'What good does it do you to come here? What do you want from us?'

I blanched. 'I only wanted to understand why the Witch

143

takes us. I don't know what it is for and no one will talk to me.'

'What does it matter? You escaped. Only a fool would go back.'

I bit my tongue. I did not think they would welcome knowing that the Witch had let me go of her own accord. I rose and thrust my hands into my muffler to stop them from trembling. 'I apologise for intruding.'

Frau Hässler's bent fingers closed around my wrist. 'How *did* you escape? Why are you the only one? What did you do?'

I backed against the door. 'I don't know.'

'Please. There must be something. What about the Witch? Tell me, what did she do to my son?'

'I don't know,' I said again.

I was a worthless substitute for what she had lost. It would have been better if I had never brought the letter, I saw that now. It would have been better if I had never come back to Blumwald at all.

'Please – don't go –' Frau Hässler scrabbled at my wrist but I slipped from her grasp.

I was not proud of it, but I fled.

*

Fear and suspicion chased me back to the palace. People crossed the road to avoid me, bolted their doors shut and I even saw lines of salt crusting windows. I was marked by the Witch and now I carried her curse with me. This deep into winter, day was only a suggestion, a few hours of lighter sky before night returned. The snow had stopped but heavy, low clouds covered the moon, promising more. The mountains rose vast and blank. I moved through the streets unthinking, no longer afraid of being a woman out alone after dark. Now I was the frightening thing that moved in the shadows.

I don't know what I had expected from that meeting, but the pain of Frau Hässler's loss was too close to my own buried grief for my mother. There was nothing meaningful I could learn about the Witch from people who saw her only through the lens of their own heartache.

Still, I could not shake the image of the unfinished letter. I could think of countless explanations but all felt flimsy in the face of what I knew: no companion had ever returned from the Witch's castle, except me. Why? What had happened to them? And what made me different?

The Witch had not made me promise to return, and in truth I feared doing so. Some dark secret lurked within the walls of the castle, within the heart of my Witch, something more than anyone in Blumwald could begin to imagine. Frieda was right. I would be a fool to go back.

And yet.

Could I see a life for myself here?

I had known the answer to that when the Witch had come before.

For better or worse, I had caught the Witch's eye, and after a lifetime of being unwanted, that was too precious a thing to lose. Whatever had happened to the previous companions, perhaps it could be different for me. It already was: I was here, free, with the Witch's blessing. She needed me to return, and however pathetic it might be, I so desperately *wanted* to be needed. Perhaps I could be the one to solve the mystery of the Witch if I lived long enough in it. If that was the cost of having a place to belong, maybe I was willing to pay it.

There was only one thing still holding me here.

✳

I found my father attended only by a maid sitting by the door darning a sock. The deathly pall that had shrouded the room the night before had gone and the curtains had been drawn back to showcase the faded sunset. Before my stepmother could evict me again, I excused the maid and closed the curtains against the night.

The Witch demanding a companion from my father played over and over in my head. He knew something. Wolf knew something. They all knew something about the Witch and no one would tell me the truth.

'Papa?' I drew a chair to his bedside as his eyelids fluttered open.

'Mina?' His mouth made the shape of my name.

'I am here.' I clasped his hand between mine; his skin was paper-thin and felt as though it could tear if I wasn't gentle. Though the colour had returned to his face, his ordeal showed in the hollows of his cheeks and deep shadows around his eyes. In the turn of a season he had become an old man.

'Mina?' A light of recognition crossed his face and he struggled up. 'You can't be here, the Witch—'

I pressed him back into his pillows. 'All is well. She permitted me to travel.'

'You do not understand . . . she must have a companion.'

He drifted in and out of the present moment, looking about him in confusion.

'Papa, calm yourself. Are you in pain?' I refilled the glass of water by his bed, checked the bottle of laudanum. 'We have been so worried for you. The doctor says you will recover, though it may take time.'

I fed him a small glass of diluted laudanum and dabbed his mouth with a napkin. When he was settled I considered my words. He was the only person here who knew something of the Witch's secret and I could not leave without taking this chance to ask him – but now, sitting before him, I remembered the way he could sew my lips shut with a look.

'Why are you here?' he asked again.

'I received a letter from Klara about your fall. Of course I came.'

'I see my daughters all defy my orders.'

That stilled my hand. 'You ordered her not to write to me?'

'It is too dangerous. If you left the Witch . . .'

'I thought you would be happy to see me,' I said to cover my hurt. 'Don't you want to know how I am? What my life is like there?'

His gaze landed on me and I realised he looked at me in the same way the townspeople did. Caution, and fear. I thought again of Wolf and the Witch talking in the kitchen, of her strangled, animal tenseness as she watched me go.

'You know why she takes us,' I said slowly. 'You don't care what I could tell you, because you already know.'

Fear leeched into his face. 'If she does not have you she will need somebody else. If you have tried to *escape*, then the scope of her anger frightens me to think about.'

'I told you. She let me go. She trusts me to come back.'

He gave a hoarse laugh. 'She *trusts* you? I thought you understood how serious this was, the duty you took on. You must return at once.'

'If I don't?'

'Mina.'

'If it is so desperate a situation, then why not simply tell me what is at stake? *Why*, Papa?'

He took my hand and at first I thought he meant to comfort me, but his grip was too tight and I felt my bones grind against each other. 'Mina, you do not understand what you risk by being here. Do not force me to say, because it is better for you that I remain silent. But listen to me. You cannot. Stay.'

I wrenched my hand back, cradled it against my chest.

'I am not yours to command any more,' I said. 'You ended that when you gave me over to the Witch.'

'Then I ask you not as your father, but as your duke. You must go back.'

The relief I had felt at seeing him well had soured, and now all I felt was an extreme exhaustion. I had already made up my mind to go, but his rejection was the hand at the small of my back, ushering me out of the door.

'Very well,' I said. 'I will go at dawn.'

By the light of my candle, I passed through the darkened hallways to my room. The dustsheets had been hastily folded away and fresh bedding put out; my carpetbag was set on the dresser. Another last night at home, so different from the first. I thought of my Witch in her castle, terrified I would leave her, and my father on his sick bed, frightened I would stay.

I lay awake a long time watching the flame burn down the wax.

The Witch's carriage still waited in the stables when I checked the yard the next morning, the horses in their harnesses and the driver perched in his seat, as though they'd known my decision before me.

My carpetbag took ten minutes to pack.

Leaving my father would take a little longer.

I waited around a corner until I heard my stepmother leave, then went to my father's bedside once more.

'I'm going back, as you asked.'

He tried to hide it, but I saw the flicker of relief in his face.

'I know the Witch hides something in that tower.' My hands were twisted into the skirt of my travelling dress. 'If you insist my place is there, at least tell me the truth. Please. This is my last chance.'

I saw the possibility unfurl; his lips parted, his eyes intense and as troubled as the Witch had been. Then the cloud passed and he looked away.

'Let people keep their secrets, Mina. They may have good reason.'

It took a great effort to keep my composure. My father was a coward, and I could no longer deny it. He looked so very small and human in his nightshirt; a man who loved me, but didn't want the demands that came with love.

'My girl.' He reached for my hand and I let him clasp it. I must learn not to want more from him than he was able to give. But for all the tension between us, he was my father and I wanted to believe he would tell me if I truly was in danger.

'Be well.'

As I left, I felt the certainty of it this time. I had come back, against all odds, and he had made it clear he would rather me gone.

I put on my travelling cloak and went down to the carriage.

The driver waited wordless as my bag was loaded and I arranged my skirts on the bench inside. Lamps were lit at the four corners against the winter gloom and we set out.

I left Blumwald for the second time, but this time I was running towards, not away. Sleep came to me in fits and bursts as we thundered through the forest, and as the sun crested the mountaintops the castle emerged from the trees.

I smiled.

The village, the bridge, the gates. The great hall with its breeching wall of limestone. The rotting tapestries, the worn steps of the staircases.

I had made an oath. I was the Witch's companion now. I had a place, and it was here.

I was waiting in our breakfast room still in my travel-stained clothes when she came in, and was rewarded by the flood of emotions over her beautiful face. Confusion, relief, and then the thing that lit a warmth within me as my own heart echoed hers – hope.

'You came back,' she said, half question, half thanks.

'I came back.'

The distance between us closed one step more. Just as my father had, she reached out a hand for mine and this time I let it be taken, and drew her to sit by me, hip against hip, shoulder against shoulder, head against head.

I was home.

XI

The Witch's welcome shut all thought of Blumwald from my mind so swiftly.

She complained vociferously about being abandoned and of the mess I had left behind me in her study. Every noise I made was too loud, I chewed egregiously at breakfast and my clothing was an insult to her eyes.

I loved every moment of it: I had been missed.

A few nights after my return, I had my courses and was in too much pain to have any interest in dinner, so I went to her study, planning to make a quick apology for my unavailability and retreat. I found the Witch in the middle of the room, eyes closed and viola raised to her chin, one hand dancing over the fingerboard, the other bowing lazily, drawing out a slow, melancholy tune. She moved with grace – I already knew she was capable of that – but the open vulnerability in her face, the sadness that drew her hand and the bow so movingly across the strings was mesmerising.

I never wanted to stop watching.

The wall between us was as glass and I could truly see her. I could see pain and longing and regret, desire and passion and beauty, the distance shrunk until I could think her thoughts, feel her fingers brush across my arm, her sigh shudder through my body. In that moment, I thought I could love her.

I shifted my weight, and a creaking board betrayed me. She stopped short with a sharp screech of the strings and glared.

'I didn't mean to interrupt.'

'You never do mean anything, do you,' she snapped, vanishing the viola back into its case, 'and yet you always manage to do the least desirable thing.'

Once those words would have hurt me, I would have snapped back and the day would sour. But now I knew it was nothing but the spikes on the shell of a conker, a little defence easily discarded.

'Who taught you to play?' I asked without thinking.

To my surprise, she answered.

'One of your predecessors.' She went on blithely, as though she had not set flame to the tinder of my curiosity: 'What is wrong with you, why are you wearing a bedsheet?'

I swallowed the questions that lay on my tongue, and looked down at the counterpane I had wrapped around me. 'I came to say sorry but I won't be joining you this evening.'

'What?' She stopped what she was doing and frowned. 'Why?'

'I am unwell.'

'Do you need me to nurse you again?' she smirked.

'No it is a female matter.'

Her face fell. 'Well tell Wolf to bring up some laudanum. You don't have to sulk in your room.'

I leaned against the doorframe and smiled, taking in this ruffled Witch. Several weeks ago she would have been ordering me out of her study in outrage at being interrupted, refusing even a second of my company. Now she grumbled at being denied it.

'I will be better tomorrow. Let me sleep tonight.'

'Very well,' she said. 'But I will have you know I am most displeased.'

'I am glad to hear it. I hope you pine.' I went back to my room, the memory of her playing bright and warm in my mind.

Then the thought that soured it: she had been taught by a previous companion. Perhaps our fear about the fate of the companions was unfounded. Edgar's unfinished letter nothing more than a distracted boy. I wished for a moment that I had not delivered it to the Hässlers so that I could study it further for any sign of his fate.

Still wrapped in the counterpane, I retrieved the key to Edgar's room and slipped inside. It was the same as it had been before, bare, tidy, unused. The messy desk was only that: empty ink bottles, snapped quills, blank, brittle paper.

There were no answers here.

I had promised not to pry. The Witch had done far more than she was obliged to in keeping her end of the bargain; she had let me visit my father, taken an interest in me. What had I done but broken her trust?

I snapped the lid of the escritoire shut.

The Witch had told Edgar something, that much I

remembered of his letter. Perhaps if I let her trust in me grow, she would share the secrets I searched for in time.

*

For a while, that hope was like a spell I cast over myself.

It was all too easy to lose track of the days, living as we did in a perpetual cycle of breakfasts together, days spent alone walking the castle to stave off boredom or digging through the three different libraries, then evenings holed up in a truce that had become more like friendship. I slept deep and long, in a way I had not for a long time, languid and content. I had attempted to speak to the women in the village again, but they turned their backs on me as one. It was as though, to them, I simply didn't exist.

I instructed Wolf to mark the days with different meals – preserved cherries only to be served on Mondays, or poached eggs on Friday. Christmas passed without remark. I ate ham on Christmas Eve and looked out of my bedroom window to the valley where the village was hidden below; there were no lights, no church bells. I wondered if my family thought of me as they exchanged presents, sang carols. I thought about Edgar and his family. They had wanted him back, unlike mine, and yet I had been the one able to return. Some mornings at breakfast I toyed with mentioning his name to the Witch, but never worked up the courage. I did not want to risk hurting her again; the peace between us was too fragile and precious.

Winter dragged long and slow through January, freezing the birds to the branches in the forest, but we made a warm home inside the castle, the two of us nested in the study with the fire always stoked and bright. I could feel myself begin to relax, held enough by the familiarity to feel safe – to feel *home*. The river, too, froze, a thick crust of ice with fish trapped like insects in amber, twisted and grotesque. I found several battered pairs of old skates in one of the junk rooms and dragged her down to spend an afternoon skittering and skidding between the banks, grabbing at each other and growing red and breathless with laughter. It was outside the bounds of our agreement, but those lines had been sloughing away with each week together.

We passed snowed-in evenings around the fire playing whist and card games the Witch insisted were popular even though I'd never heard of them, eating spiced ginger biscuits Wolf baked in vast batches. I tried again with my mother's drop spindle and a book on spinning; I caught the Witch watching me strangely as I worked, and in embarrassment, I put the spindle away.

At breakfast one morning in mid-January, I came down in a tea dress with three India shawls wrapped around me for warmth. The Witch had already poured me a cup of coffee and buttered me a roll.

Without missing a beat, she said, 'I have decided we will celebrate your birthday. When is it?'

Surprised, I gave the date, a few weeks away.

'Then it is settled. Instruct Wolf however you please.'

I went through the rest of my day lighter, buoyed up by this unexpected kindness. My birthday had never been much of an event at the palace, and I was touched that the Witch had thought of it.

Wolf made simple work of the preparations. There were only two of us, so it hardly required changing her menus and the castle kitchen was packed with food stores. I dug around for anything I could use to decorate our breakfast room. All I owned was rocks. In the end I made do with what I would have used for Christmas: pine cones and fir branches and swags of ivy. I cut up a silk petticoat and sewed the pieces into something approaching flowers.

The day came and I spent too much time going through my things – all my stupid, boring, plain, sensible things – and hated myself for hiding behind tweed and serge and shapeless wool. There was little I could do about it, stuck as I was with my cage crinoline that was too wide to take in my dresses to a proper, fashionable shape. In a moment of desperation and inspiration, I tied the two sides of the cage together, pulling the elliptical shape into a lozenge, with the bulk of it to my back side to create a bustle. Then with a petticoat and dress over it, it looked like I was at least a little fashionable.

The dress I settled on was a rich green silk and taffeta with a scoop neckline that showed off rather more of my bust than I would usually be comfortable with, an underskirt in gold, with gold and black ruffles looping the overskirt and neckline, and great puffs of fabric in the skirt bunched up until I looked like a strange cloud. The maid Wolf had found to 'do' for me wrestled with my hair, brushing it out into a frizzy blonde nest, then braiding it up in a crown.

At last I was ready.

I had never been so nervous about a dinner in my life.

The Witch and I arrived within minutes of each other and

we took our chairs with a few awkward exchanges. She had dressed in something truly spectacular, a black shot silk dress from the previous century cut à la française with a full sack-back and square, low-cut neckline, and panniers so wide she came through the door sideways. We ate well, a whole roast goose accompanied by apple and sausage stuffing, red cabbage and potato dumplings, bottles of hock and claret finished off by a slab of cake Wolf brought on a silver platter.

After, the Witch beckoned for me to follow her; we passed through shadowy ice-cold hallways, her hand hot in mine as she led me on. The study was as over-full as always, so it took me a minute to realise what had changed: the collection of couches, armchairs and footstools normally gathered around the fireplace had been rearranged, and now a new desk was set to the left-hand side, with my books and things stacked upon it. I was speechless, one hand at my throat as I took it in.

'I thought you should have a place of your own,' said the Witch. She showed me the drawers stocked with ink and paper, the oil lamp to better see my samples and the chair tucked neatly underneath.

'Oh.' It was all I could safely say without crying.

'Do you not like it?' Her brows knitted tight in concern.

I put my arms around her and said against her neck, 'I love it.' She went still; I could feel the tension in her muscles so strong, she was trembling. Then she disentangled us, and stepped a good half metre back.

'It is only a desk.'

We both knew it was more than that, but I understood what she needed.

I ran my hand along its surface and took in the view from my new place. 'Thank you.' From my old cupboard, I took out a lumpy parcel wrapped in a shawl. 'Don't think I forgot you,' I said and handed it to the Witch.

She held it like it might explode. 'Why are you giving me something? What is inside?'

'You have to open it to find out. You've given me two gifts now. I wanted to return the gesture.'

She arched an eyebrow, but she complied. The shawl fell away to reveal a pair of woollen socks in dark grey yarn.

'I'm not very good,' I said, 'and I had to estimate the size but they should at least be warm.'

The Witch was silent, looking at the parcel in her lap. I had asked Wolf for any spare yarn and a set of double point needles once the idea had come to my head. When Wolf brought me several skeins of yarn, it was undyed, raw wool carded and spun by the women in the village. I took great pleasure in dying the skeins with Wolf, boiling walnut hulls and iris roots in water and soaking the wool, hoping for black but being satisfied with grey. I had never enjoyed this sort of craft before, but now I understood it. It felt different when it was for someone you cared about.

'You always have bare feet,' I continued. 'And it's so cold now I wanted you to have something a little comforting. I care about that even if you don't.'

I had found her filthy feet repulsive when I had first known her, but now they only inspired pity in me that she cared so little for herself. That there was no one else to care on her behalf.

She smoothed a hand over the wool. 'Thank you.'

I almost asked her to try them on, but I knew not to push too far.

Then she did something that shocked me more than any single thing that had come before. Gently, she placed the socks and shawl and string down on the side table, before rising to put her arms gingerly around me in a return of my own gesture before. It was an embrace – only a brief second of contact, her chest to mine, the swell of her breast and the thrum of her heart pressed close against me, the smoothness of her cheek and the sandalwood scent of her hair.

She drew back and turned to stoke the fire as if it had never happened.

But the memory of her skin against mine was intoxicating.

One night in February, when I looked to the sky to hope for its lightening and still wiped frost from inside my window panes, Wolf summoned the Witch from the study with a curious message about a 'snag' that I couldn't understand. The Witch went ashen, and followed Wolf to the kitchens. I was tempted for a moment to follow her.

During the days, the Witch would still disappear for hours and hours into the Tower to do her 'work', of which I understood nothing. The door was always locked, the key on a string around the Witch's neck. If I lingered nearby, an unbearable pressure built in my skull like a vice clamped around my head like a warning. Now, she breached the careful terms of our agreement to attend to some emergency. I had tried to swallow my curiosity, but curiosity had driven me up mountains and down into the bedrock, and now it sent my thoughts after the Witch, up into the Tower and its mystery.

No. I must not.

Instead I took myself to bed. A storm had blown in and the noise of the thunder was too loud to sleep, so I returned to my room and stayed up until the small hours reading. The volume was one the Witch had lent me: a new English literary magazine with serialised novels. Tonight I was gripped by a story entitled *Carmilla*.

When the floorboards creaked outside my door I startled so badly I knocked the oil lamp from my bedside table. The glass chimney smashed and the light was snuffed at once. Against the hammering rain, all I could hear was the sound of the metal lamp base rolling away across the floor.

Then the footsteps began to pace.

Had it been the Witch I had seen before? Or did nothing move outside my door at all?

I was afraid, and frustrated at my fear. Was the castle not my home now? Was the Witch not gracious to me? Why, then, did I tremble at the footsteps, harbour doubts about her past?

As quickly as the footsteps came, they passed, and after a moment of deliberation, I left my bed to fetch fresh candles and matches.

I yelped in pain as the soles of my feet met the glass strewn across the floor. Foolish, so foolish. In the dark I could not see where the shards had fallen, and tripped forward, feeling my skin slice open with each step. I sank against the wall by the door and inspected my feet in turn with the tips of my fingers, running them along the arch and curve of my sole to locate each glass fragment and tease it out. Perhaps the dark was a blessing: I could not see the damage I had done.

Limping, I went down to the kitchens where I could find candles, but also water and something to clean my wounds. The castle was not kind at night. An alien, stone world unfit for the living. In pain and fearful of hurting myself more, I moved slowly like a small mammal amongst the grasses, easing myself from shelter to shelter, fearful and twitching. I could not run, injured as I was, and as I descended into the bowels of the castle I had some terrible sense that I was making a mistake.

I had never been to the kitchens after dark and I was quickly lost. There was the last of the water brought up from the well yesterday by the sink, but to clean my feet I would need light and I couldn't begin to think where the candles were now I was presented by a series of drawers and cupboards. The banked cooking fire glowed malevolently, smouldering logs radiating a shocking warmth in the winter cold.

For goodness' sake, I was not a child afraid of shadows. I needed candles, matches, to clean my foot and wrap it in something. I could complete this task without fleeing like a coward.

I tried one drawer and then the next and found spoons, reels of twine, table linen, whisks and forks and whetstones. But no candles. No matches. Damn. The kitchen was too vast and my feet hurt with every step. There were a series of rooms set off the kitchen, a silverware store, a larder, a scullery. But tonight there was another open door. I saw my mistake before: I had thought it a cupboard, half buried behind stacks of rusting pans and broken crockery. Now it had all been pushed to one side and the door was open a crack.

I didn't want to go back a failure, so nudged it wider, hoping for a store room. Instead, I found a large but empty space, and I was struck by the scent of jasmine.

Then I noticed the girl.

Petite and wearing a maid's uniform, a figure stood in the corner, facing the wall.

The skin at the back of my neck prickled.

'Hello?' My voice was a whisper.

The girl didn't move. I knew I should go to her but I couldn't make myself move.

The room had a single window showing a stretch of grass and trees painted in navy and black; it was thrown open to the night, letting in a warm breeze and the rich floral scent of night blooms. Somehow, that was the most sinister thing, the warm rush of summer trapped in the room.

'Hello?' I said again. 'Is everything all right?'

The maid stood in the corner, silent. All I saw was the back of her head in the unnatural moonlight, her arms slack by her side.

I took a step forward.

'Do you need help?'

I still got no reply, so I took another step and another. Halfway across the room, I couldn't move any further. The only thing more frightening than the unmoving figure with its back to me was the idea of seeing its face.

Something made a noise behind me, the quiet hush of fabric over stone and I turned.

The Witch stood before me, face hidden by shadow. My breath caught in my throat.

'Oh!'

I had thought the Witch was someone familiar to me now but suddenly she seemed a stranger in the dark and the quiet. All I could see was the flash of her eyes, glittering.

'Go to bed, Mina.' Her voice was cold.

All my confidence fled, and I with it.

My feet left a trail of blood behind me. I did not understand what I had seen, and what the Witch's role in it was. The only thing I knew for sure was that the Witch was hiding something. I had promised not to pry but I could feel my resolve waning.

What secret was so terrible a Witch would fear it coming out?

*

The day after my unnerving encounter with the Witch in the kitchens, I went walking after breakfast. It had been a tense affair, and I had left it with a compulsion to try and understand a little better what I had seen. After bandaging my feet and stuffing them into thick socks, I limped outside.

A grey blanket of cloud hung low over the mountains and the castle seemed so tall its towers scraped their base, the off-white stone another bank of snow between the trees. I could not turn my mind from the image of the maid stood mute in the corner in that strange room. I traced a path around the foundations, trying to map the interior to the walls and windows I could see. I found at last the staved-in windows of the room banked with snow, but that was as far as I could improve my understanding. The harder I tried to understand my new home, the more it evaded me. Strange, unnerving things occurred within its walls, and no power of observation or academic study could elucidate the problem.

I came home damp up to my thighs with grey slush and harbouring a deep need to scrub myself raw. I stripped off, dropping my dress, corset, bustle, petticoats and bloomers across the floor like wrapping torn from a present. A team of maids brought the wooden bath to my room and water from the kitchens; I watched each face closely but I could not tell if any had been the girl from last night. I had never seen her face.

Once the bath was full I sunk into the hot water like a stone, weariness tethering me down.

What secret was so terrible a Witch would fear it coming out?

I could not shake the question from my mind.

In my long walk I had turned the events of the night before over in my mind: the maid in the corner, the Witch at my back. The strange summer room. With the crunch of snow beneath my boots and the bright blue of the winter sky above me, it had felt a little foolish to have been so frightened and I berated myself for it. But now as I tested out explanations, I came up short. It would make enough sense for a maid to be in the kitchens, except when I first arrived Wolf had told me no one else stayed overnight in the castle. Perhaps whatever emergency Wolf had summoned the Witch to yesterday evening had involved the maid and she had stayed?

I frowned, picking at the skin around my nails.

Another memory came back to me: the woman in the

village bakery had said that people went up to work in the castle for a day and lost a whole month.

A knot of dread had settled in the pit of my stomach. I had decided to return to the Witch because I was needed here, and the joy I had found in our growing intimacy had confirmed my choice.

And yet.

There was so much I didn't know, and I found myself unable to ignore it.

Perhaps I had made a terrible mistake, and I might not understand exactly why until too late.

As if summoned by my thoughts, the door opened without a knock and the Witch came into my room.

Flushed with shock, I struggled up, groping for the towel. My fingers touched the edge of the cloth – then my sore foot slipped and I went crashing down, face first into the metal edge.

Before I met its sharp blade, I was caught, a body bracing me.

The Witch had moved impossibly fast, and I clung to her, trembling. I wore my shift to bathe as most women did, and I was acutely aware of only a thin, translucent barrier between us. Her grip was powerful; I could not have freed myself if I wanted to.

I was not sure I wanted to.

'That's the second time I've had to save you,' she said.

I felt it, the fragile weight of my life in her hands.

So much rested on her regard for me. My happiness. My future.

'You startled me,' I breathed.

This close I could see every black lash against her cheek, the full curve of her lip. The impenetrable hollow of her pupils.

I swallowed.

I recalled Frau Hässler grasping my wrist and demanding to know why. Why had the Witch let me go? Was I special?

'Put me down,' I whispered.

'As you wish.'

She released me. My shift clung to my breasts and hips, and water ran down my body, hair sticking to my shoulders and chest in wet coils. Her eyes lingered on the shape of me a moment too long, and a blush crept across my cheeks. We were both women and there was nothing I had that she hadn't seen before; she had nursed me when I was sick and who knew what state of undress she'd seen me in then. And yet I was flush with embarrassment, acutely aware of every inch of me exposed to her gaze.

I found it not entirely objectionable.

Maybe I *was* special.

Maybe I was safe here, whatever secrets my Witch kept. Maybe I could have what I wanted.

'Can I help you?' I asked.

Her eyes flicked up and a pink stain spread across her milk white face. 'No. I did not expect you to be here.'

'Well I *am* here,' I said, mouth dry. 'Might I be allowed to finish my bath?'

The Witch stared at me a moment longer, then with a

flourish of skirts she stalked out and I sank back under the cooling water, this new knowledge large in my mind: the Witch wanted to look at me, and I wanted to be looked at.

✳

After dinner that night I wrapped myself in a quilt and sat by my window looking at the snowy crop of trees that bordered the castle. I felt at a crossroads. I had been drawn back to the Witch for so many reasons: the duty my father lay upon my shoulders, fear of remaining trapped in my old home, curiosity about the truth behind the Witch. But I was not so blind to myself that I could not admit that at the heart of it was this simple truth: it was only with the Witch that I was needed. Today had made it undeniable that what I felt for the Witch was different to anything I had felt for anyone before. The Witch had saved me from my misery.

For better or worse, I belonged here, and I so desperately hoped that could mean something good.

And yet I could not escape the secrets that were woven around me. It was as though every time I let myself think I had made the right choice, I was stung by some lurking creature.

Then another thought: if the Witch had not expected me to be in my room, why had she come?

The footsteps outside my door – I still did not understand what she did at night. But perhaps one thing was clear: I was being watched. This was her castle; there was nowhere that was mine alone. Nowhere I could hide. I thought of my visits to Edgar's room and the key I kept at the bottom of a drawer.

My chest hollowed out. Perhaps she already knew I had broken my promise and pried.

Two paths lay ahead of me. I could dig and dig, and I might not like what I found.

Or I could let it lie. I could keep my promise.

For now.

XII

Winter gave small blessings: with ice in the window panes and heavy curtains drawn over every door against the creeping cold, the Witch left the chill of her desk and joined me by the fireplace, abandoning her ledgers more evenings than not to pick over my geological specimens, demanding to know the difference between igneous, sedimentary and metamorphic, running her fingertips over slate and granite and quartz. I savoured our moments together, the wry smile she gave when I spoke of my passions, the way she chewed her lip in concentration over the next move in a game. I liked how she would watch me when I wasn't looking, and the care she took to have my desk stocked with paper and ink. I felt held in mind.

In turn I fussed at her to wear her cloak against the cold, and insisted she join me for a hand of Schafkopf, fanning the deck of cards between our bowed heads. One morning in late February, brittle with frost, we had brought them to her study after breakfast: a rematch after a particularly heated battle the night before in which I had emerged triumphant. My Witch that day looked sleepless and preoccupied in a moth-eaten black silk robe and her hair in a rats' nest and I peppered her with jabs that perhaps she lost sleep over my victory.

Our peace was fractured by the sound of Wolf's voice, shockingly loud. I had never heard Wolf raise her voice. The Witch and I were of one mind, moving towards the clamour.

When we drew near, I recognised a second voice.

'Let me in! Where is she?'

A wild-haired woman was in the great hall tussling with Wolf; when she saw me, she broke free and came towards the stairs.

For a moment I was dumb with shock. This was impossible. She shouldn't be here. She *couldn't* be here.

I found my voice and cried out, 'Frieda?'

Her hair had come loose from its tight bun and she no longer held herself with control, but I recognised Frieda Hässler immediately.

The Witch's castle was not somewhere that allowed itself to be easily found. I didn't understand how Frieda had done it. She had been all reserve and iron will when I had met her, now she looked to be unravelling at the seams, like a stretch of yarn losing its twist, turning from thread to raw wool.

I started down the worm-eaten stairs, and stopped just above a rotten step. I could not help but want a barrier between myself and Frieda.

She came to the foot of the stairs – Wolf followed but I shook my head at her.

Frieda was my responsibility.

'I knew it, you went back to her. Little fool,' she sneered.

171

I clasped my hands before me. 'What are you doing here? How did you find us?'

'You think your Witch so clever she cannot be found? The forest played its tricks on me but I persisted, and here I am.'

I frowned. It would take a degree of dedication to find the Witch that bordered on fanatic. I had not even known it was possible. How long had she wandered the forest? She had lost a lot of weight, all bone and wild, intense light in her eyes. The hem of her dress was mud-stained and torn, and a half-healed scrape marred the side of her face. I thought of the stories about the families of companions setting out to search for the Witch and her castle. Few ever returned. I always assumed those who went missing met some sad end at the bottom of a ravine or frozen in the night; now a thought struck me with slow horror: just because they had not returned did not mean they had not found what they were looking for.

'I would have walked to the ends of the earth if I had to,' continued Frieda. 'After you came, my mother did not know peace. She did not sleep, she did not eat, all she did was weep for the son who was ripped from her. You made it so much worse, giving her hope that anyone can survive this place. Survive *her*.'

A flare of panic. The Witch couldn't find out that I had taken Edgar's letter to them. 'You came all this way to say that to me?'

'No. I came for answers. I must see the Witch.'

I turned to look behind me, but the Witch had melted away. All I could see was the edge of black skirts by the doors at the top of the stairs.

'Where is she?' demanded Frieda. 'Where is that monster?'

The sympathy I had felt vanished like a candle blown out.

'She's not a monster.'

Frieda sneered and started up the stairs towards me, dodging Wolf. 'Witch! Come and face me.' Her voice echoed off stone. 'I see you hiding!'

The Witch had peeked her moon-pale face around the doorframe and was spotted at once. I hummed with nerves, torn between Frieda and the Witch, and tried to catch Frieda as she passed me on the stairs but her angry steps made the fragile frame shake and I feared any violent action on my part would bring the structure to pieces.

Frieda descended on the Witch like a bird of prey, talons extended and eyes flashing.

'What did you do with my brother?'

My Witch froze like a doe in hunting season.

I thought she would be angry at the intrusion; I had not expected her to be terrified.

Frieda snatched up a handful of the Witch's dress and yanked her so close I thought she might bite her.

'Stop —' At this threat I was moved to act. I launched forward but Wolf had come up the stairs behind me, the sagging steps groaning under the weight of the four of us, to snag my arm and hold me back.

'Tell me the truth,' Frieda cried. 'What happened to my brother? I cannot live a day longer without answers.'

'You do not know what you ask,' whispered the Witch.

'We couldn't even bury him.'

I remembered Wolf's words months ago: *they have no grave.*

Frieda shook her like a doll and the Witch submitted to her anger. 'You ruin lives.' Frieda's voice broke. 'You destroy families and you don't care at all.'

I had never seen my Witch so helpless. I could not understand it.

She said something so soft I could barely make it out, but it sounded like *I care.*

Frieda snapped. With a yell she flung the Witch against the wall, raising a hand to strike her. But this time Wolf intervened before I could. She caught Frieda's hand with a surprisingly strong grip.

'Enough of that. It's time for you to go.'

'No. Make her answer. I need an answer.'

Wolf pulled at Frieda again and they fell against the bannister. To my horror, the spindles gave way. The Witch lunged for Wolf and I for Frieda and together we righted them before they could topple several metres to the floor below.

The shock seemed to quell Frieda's rage for a moment, and the Witch took her opportunity to scramble through the door and away. Now we were three.

'Let me arrange for a carriage to take you back,' said Wolf.

Frieda shook her off. 'No. I want *nothing* from you monsters.'

Frieda stormed down the shaking stairs and out of the great hall.

I hung back, torn between two paths ahead.

I wanted to follow Frieda. Her rage had frightened me, but

I could not deny our questions were the same. The Witch kept a dark secret and I both feared and longed to know it.

Then I thought about the horror on my Witch's face, the fear and sadness and despair like a child abandoned.

I could not let her fear be proved true.

I followed her.

All illusions I had of comforting her vanished as soon as I entered her study. A vase of dried flowers lay smashed across the floor and she had taken a hunting knife to the cushions of the chaise longue, ripping hunks of feathers and fabric in her rage and anguish. She turned to me, tear-streaked face and knife still in hand.

'Did you do this? Did you bring her here?'

I flushed with guilt. 'Of course not.'

'I should never have let you go back to that damn town.' She slammed the knife into her desk so it stood vibrating on its point. 'All you do is bring trouble.'

I felt the words like a blow and my own anger roused. 'This is not my fault. Is it really so unreasonable for someone to want to know what happened to their loved one?'

Was it so unreasonable for me to want to know my own fate?

'Oh, I'm *sorry*,' she sneered, yanking handfuls of books from the shelves in a whirl of paper and ink. 'Am I being *unreasonable*?'

It was strange to feel concern for someone one minute and anger the next. She was infuriating.

'Do you take pleasure in your cruelty?' I snapped. 'What does it cost you to tell her what happened to her brother? She and her mother live trapped in a grief they cannot escape, all for the want of what *you* can give them.'

The Witch fell silent. A dark light flared in her eyes, and then she stared down at the destruction strewn across the room, a curtain of black hair concealing her face. 'Cruelty is my nature. It is who I am. You came to live with a monster all others feared. Why did you expect me to be any different?'

'I know you are no monster.'

'Do you? Do you know that?'

'I believe it.'

She gave a laugh that broke into a sob and turned to the window to hide herself from me. Snowfall had thinned and now a little more sun reached us inside the castle; a cold, milky light that iced the hallways and cast the world into a perpetual blue-grey dawn. 'You have no idea what my life here has cost me,' she said. 'Do not ask I pay more.'

My patience broke. 'Pay nothing and nothing is what you will receive in return. You dragged me here and yet you will not let me near you. You will not tell me why I am here. What was the point? Am I a toy to you?'

She spoke in deadened tones. 'You are nothing to me.'

It should not have wounded me as badly as it did. 'You're lying,' I said, but I wondered whether I truly believed the words.

The Witch didn't reply. She remained with her back to me, face upturned to the pallid winter light. We were two amateurs, leading each other foolishly through the rocky path to – to what? Did I mean friendship? Family?

Love?

She did not know the way and nor did I.

*

I could not bear to be under the same roof as the Witch after our fight so I went to the forest immediately, following the path to the village. I needed to feel the sting of winter air in my lungs and the ache of my thighs. I felt so confused. I had thought myself loyal to the Witch but my reward had been her anger. I did not understand what I had done wrong, and I did not understand the way I lost control around her. I had not meant to say the things I had but I could not deny the truth in them. She could solve Frieda's pain with a few words and yet she would not. Just as she would not ease my uncertainty. She guarded her secrets precious above all else and I resented it.

My feet had brought me to the village as the sun reached the treetops. A path had been cleared in the snow between the houses, and I found myself outside the inn. The shutters were open and inside I could see clusters of drinkers around the broad fireplace.

And Frieda.

She sat at a table, head in her hands and an untouched drink at her elbow.

I hesitated. Had I meant to come to her? Perhaps my feet had known what my mind would not admit: I needed to talk to her. I knew that engaging with Frieda would only make things more complicated, but I could not let her leave without speaking to her once more.

I went inside and sat down opposite, acutely aware of eyes

around the room watching me. It was stuffy and, unlike when I'd first arrived with the Witch, lively with conversation. Still, a ring of empty space opened up around us. Here, as in Blumwald, the taint of the Witch marked me out.

'Why did you have to come to us?' said Frieda, not raising her head. 'We were not happy before, but we survived.'

Now I was here I did not know what I wanted from Frieda. Absolution? Answers? Beneath the table I picked at the skin around my nails.

'Please, just go,' I said eventually. 'There's nothing to find out. Trust me.'

I should know. I had been here for months and failed to learn anything meaningful about this place or my role as the Witch's companion.

'Why should I trust you?' Frieda dismissed me.

I had no answer.

I had not taken off my cloak when I sat down and now I was sweating beneath the heavy wool. 'How can this possibly help, coming here? It cannot bring your brother back.'

'Dead or not, he is my brother. I owe it to him. *Some* of us care about our families.'

She could not know how well her blow landed. I thought of my father putting up no fight when I bound myself to the Witch, urging me away. None of them would come searching for me. None of them would cry over my fate for years. No, they were planning weddings and railways. They had moved on.

When Frieda looked up, her eyes were bloodshot, the creases around sunk deep. 'Help me. You are her next companion. Surely you of all people want the truth out of her?'

I looked at my hands. I did. And I didn't.

'I can't.'

'You are scared of her.'

'No.'

'You cannot truly *want* to stay here.'

Only a few hours ago I had been happily with the Witch, sharing our small, comfortable life together.

Couldn't I want to stay?

I felt the pull of her like a tug at my navel. Just because we had fought didn't mean I would betray her to Frieda.

'I am so sorry,' I said. 'I shouldn't have brought Edgar's letter. I thought I was doing the right thing.'

Anger washed over Frieda's face once more.

'The *right thing* is for the Witch to be done away with. How long will Blumwald sit at her mercy, how long will we feed her our sons – and for what? I know I should bow and scrape to you, the duke's daughter, but what good will his railway and this new German Empire be if we still live at her mercy?'

My own anger met hers. What did she truly know of my Witch?

'Did you ever think she might truly want a companion? It is a lonely life she lives.'

Frieda scoffed. 'Pretty little fool. You deserve what you will get.'

'You think loneliness so easy a thing to live with?' I snapped. I may have hurt Frieda by resurrecting the pain of her brother's death, but that did not mean I would take any jab she dealt.

'I know very well it is not. But it is no excuse for murder.'

My heart raced. 'You have no proof.'

'Why are you so desperate to believe in her?'

'Why are you so quick to doubt?'

'Go on. Tell me then, what do you think happened to my brother? Why did he never finish that letter? Why has no companion ever been heard from again?'

I opened my mouth, then closed it again. There was nothing I could say.

'There. You cannot defend her. She is indefensible,' sneered Frieda.

I could not speak because the truth was not something I was ready to hear. I was ashamed of my own heart. If I had made a mistake choosing to return to the Witch, then my life truly had no future to it, not here and not in Blumwald. Perhaps there was danger in the castle, a secret that may hurt me, but between my old life and this, what choice truly was it?

At least here I mattered. There was something between the Witch and I now that was greater than the vow that had bound me as her companion, something almost tender in its own way. I thought of her gaze raking over me in the bath and a fresh blush rose to my cheeks. Tender, but also fierce and demanding. At first I had wanted answers from her; now I wanted so much more, and some undaunted part of me hoped she might feel the same.

I could not meet Frieda's eye.

'Go. Let Edgar lie in the past.' I set a few coins on the table for her drink. 'I'm sorry for what happened to your family. But leave us alone. For your own good.'

The Witch and I dined apart that evening and I went to bed uneasy. I had done nothing in talking to Frieda, but still I felt somehow as though I'd betrayed the Witch.

I thought of her earlier, frightened and lashing out. She had taken the risk of trusting me, allowing me to share her life – even sending me back to visit my father. She was terrified that trust would be broken. With space between us, I could see that now. The Witch's behaviour was not so hard to understand. I had been here mere months and it had broken me open. How many years had she spent alone?

Too many thoughts warred in my mind as I drifted near sleep. I was moved by her pain and frightened by her secrets. And I wanted what she could give me: a place to belong.

I woke suddenly to a noise – loud, discordant, and entirely human.

I sat up.

It came again, and a voice too.

In nothing but my white nightdress, I took up the candlestick from the mantlepiece. The castle was eerie at this hour, sliding and shifting underfoot, each little sound amplified. The moon was high and bright, and the air frosted with my breath. I followed the snatches of noise that wrapped around the castle, my unease growing. I had encountered many strange things, but this felt different. New.

I heard the voice again.

Something crackled, snapped. An acrid scent. A light ahead.

I realised I could no longer see my breath.

It was warmer.

In a panic I flew forward, nightgown flapping around my thighs, and rounded the corner to find the grand staircase aflame. I stood in the doorway of the second-floor corridor that opened onto the stairs, wreathed in smoke. Frieda stood at the bottom, torch in hand, her face uplit by the fire.

'I have to end this,' she called when she saw me. 'I cannot let her continue to enact her evil upon us all.'

The smoke was thick, the ancient wood burning like tinder. I covered my mouth with the cloth of my sleeve.

'You will kill us!'

'If I must.'

The flame arced higher and I lost sight of her. My throat was raw. The base had been consumed and flames licked their way up the steps. The stone walls of the castle wouldn't burn, but the floors were all wood, held up by vast wooden beams. If the fire took hold, there would be nothing left but a shell.

At the other end of this corridor was the door to the Witch's study. If I meant to go to her, it would have to be now; already the floorboards beneath my feet felt warm. Coughing in the smoke, I hesitated at the doors to her private space – she would be angry at the intrusion – but there was no time for manners. I found her in her bed, a streak of black hair against white sheets and delicate lashes brushing the tender skin beneath her eyes. I shook her awake and she pushed up on her elbows, blinking the sleep away.

'Mina? What is it?' Her voice soft and confused.

'There's a fire. Come quickly.'

Back in the corridor smoke was boiling across the ceiling, pouring round the door to the stairs. Half the steps were alight, flames roaring ever upwards. Sparks jumped and danced. Burn marks already marred the nearby tapestries, only saved by the heavy damp in their fibres.

I pulled up short and the Witch collided with my back.

'What do we do?'

Her fingers dug into my shoulders and I realised she was afraid. Smoke made my eyes water; I pulled us back as the Witch began to cough.

'It's too big to put out,' I said. 'We could never bring enough water.'

I looked to the Witch, waiting for her to bark an order at me, or tell me of the castle's fire defences. But she did nothing, only watched wide-eyed as the fire swallowed the stairs, her hand still clamped around mine in desperation.

The bannisters caught like a ribbon of flame, fire eating along the ancient wood like poison.

A thought struck me.

I had seen fires tear through the forest around Blumwald at the end of long, dry summers, bracken and brush like so much kindling. The woodsmen would carve out wide avenues, felling trees and clearing scrub to halt the inferno before it could reach us.

I disentangled myself and darted along the corridor, checking each door until I came to the room I was looking for: a junk room. And amongst the centuries of detritus: axes.

I took the two sharpest ones and raced back to the Witch, who cowered against the wall, frozen in fear. I pushed one axe into her hand.

'We have to make a firebreak.'

I pulled the neck of my nightdress over my mouth and nose and edged out onto the top of the stairs. The flames had made rapid progress but there was a swathe of unburned wood. Before, the rotten steps riddled with woodworm had been a threat to my safety – now that would be our saviour.

I took an experimental swing at the bannister and it splintered under the bite of the blade, and I yanked it out to raise overhead again.

'Help me.' When the Witch didn't rise I gave her a sharp look, and snapped, 'Get up. Now.'

The shock of my harsh words broke her paralysis and she rose, tied up her nightdress at her hip, exposing her slender, muscled thighs, and shakily holding the axe, joined me at the stairs. Following my lead, we hacked at the steps, fire so close the hair on my arms curled and my lungs felt tight and itchy from the smoke. I felt the blisters forming under the skin of my hands, sweat running from my forehead and the back of my neck and under my arms. Side by side, arms swinging, sweat sticking our nightdresses to our bodies, hair tangled and fire-singed, throats burning. After a while, we no longer spoke, exhaustion threatening to overtake us. The bannisters went easily; the steps took more work, bent forward precariously. We hung between one danger and another: the flames, and the fall.

'Hold on,' I said, extending the handle of my axe to the

Witch. She took it without question, and with her anchoring me, I held the head of the axe and leaned further out to kick at the rotten wood until the whole step had gone. Now, there was only the frame on either side.

The drop below us was vertiginous. My head span.

The Witch coughed beside me. Ash was streaked across her forehead and in her hair, her eyes were glassy and flicked rapidly from the fire, to the frame, to the hall beneath us.

'We can do this.' I clasped her hand tightly but she shook her head.

'Witch.' I softened my tone. 'Do you trust me?'

I expected a snide remark in response but she said nothing.

I said again, 'Do you trust me?'

Slowly, she nodded.

Her arm holding firm around my waist, I bent forward to wield the axe at the frame. I was reaching exhaustion, but with the Witch by my side, I found my last scrap of strength over and over. I was working not only to save myself, but to save her and her home too.

The frame gave, and for a moment the stairs remained standing, a path of fire arcing through the open air of the hall.

And then the remaining strut on the other side snapped under the lopsided weight and the staircase collapsed in a torrent of flames and ash. As it went, it tore the remaining steps at the top loose from their joists. The boards beneath me gave way and fear consumed me in one terrible moment as I saw my death come hurtling closer – then the Witch was hauling me up as the steps disappeared and together we slammed into the corridor, arms and legs tangled; I took the brunt of it, and she landed on top of me as we collapsed to the floor. She was trembling. I held her close for a moment, stroked the curl of hair at the base of her neck.

'See? We did it.'

The words were as much to comfort me as her.

But it was true. The fire burned on below us, but now in the empty stone chamber of the great hall it had nothing to feed on but the staircase it had already destroyed. Smoke rolled across the ceiling in a dense black cloud, and filled the corridor. I half carried the Witch to my room that was well away from the smoke and left her on my bed, all the windows thrown wide open.

I patrolled the castle but there was no other sign of fire. From the kitchens, I fetched a fresh jug of water, and salve and bandages for our burns. But the Witch stilled my hands, took the dressings from me and pulled my arm towards her, where a line of shiny puckered skin showed my closest brush with injury.

'You could have stayed in Blumwald,' she said. 'When you went to see your father, I didn't know if you would come back. You could have left with Frieda or taken her side.' She smoothed a layer of honey salve along my skin, fingers gentle and precise, then looked at me from under her lashes, cautious, unsure. Hopeful. 'But you didn't.'

'No, I didn't.'

The air between us was too thin, I felt every prickle of her gaze on me, I could feel the warmth of her body, the beat of her heart like it was mine.

'You would choose to stay?' she asked, a tremor in her voice. 'For me?'

I wet my lips, dry and cracked from the immense heat of the fire. Her eyes were not the solid black I had thought them, I saw specks of amber and grey, and a delicate filigree of lines around them.

I thought I had never loved anything more.

'Yes,' I said, without hesitation. 'I choose you.'

XIII

When dawn came, I slipped away quietly, thinking of Wolf and breakfast. I wanted to tell her what had happened before she came across the destruction in the great hall, and perhaps discuss Frieda, and whether we should send anyone after her.

I was too late.

Wrapped in my dressing gown, I found Wolf in the hall beside the charred remains of the staircase. She looked at something among the ashes.

Frowning, I joined her.

Then there, amongst the fallen beams, was Frieda.

There was no question that she was dead.

Falling debris had pinned her leg before she could run, and a patina of burned skin and cloth ran up the exposed front of her body. One arm was flung over her face for protection, the skin melted like wax, making a claw of her hand.

Horror rushed through me and before I understood what was happening I was doubled over, emptying the contents of my stomach onto the floor.

This could not be.

I cast my mind through the night before. Frieda at the foot of the stairs, bearing the flaming torch that had set the fire – and then, nothing. I had no memory of her after that. Had she stood there hypnotised by the effect wrought by her own hand? Or had she wanted to witness us in our death throes? I could not understand it. Never for a moment had I considered she could still be within the castle.

Whatever reason she'd had, when we cut down the stairs, she had been caught in the wreckage.

Wolf watched me with no sympathy. I wiped my mouth and straightened up, shaking.

Worse, among my guilt and shame, was a glimmer of relief. I was sorry to see her dead but I was not sorry to see the problem of Frieda over.

What a cold thought. The longer I stayed here, the more like the Witch I became.

'What happened here?' asked Wolf.

Haltingly, I explained.

'Wolf. Would you—'

'I will take care of it.'

I thought of Frieda's mother in Blumwald, waiting again on a child who had gone away and never come back.

'Thank you,' I said to Wolf.

There was open disgust on her face, a simmering anger. 'You brought this trouble to our doors,' she said and left me amongst the ashes.

I did not know what to do about the great hall. The remains

of the grand staircase were spread across the flagstones, vast beams three metres long and melted nails and hunks of burned tapestry. Frieda's body still lay amongst it, dusted grey with ash. I thought I should find something to cover her with, until Wolf brought men from the village to take her. I cleared up the smaller pieces as best I could, but the beams were twice as long as I was tall and so heavy, my strength failed at once. Perhaps they would have to become another feature of the hall, like the jut of limestone from the mountain below.

When the Witch roused and found me in the hall, her eyes slid over the corpse like it was another piece of charred wood. Like death was nothing to her. I did not know what to think of that. My Witch had been so undone by Frieda's arrival, so helpless the night before – yet now she stalked through the world as though none of it had passed, her composure regained at such terrible cost.

I stood mute and alone in the aftermath of my choices.

Denial. That is the only name I can put to what came over me the following weeks. I had seen a horror too great in Frieda's pain and death; it was as if it were too vast a feeling to contain in my body, so I simply didn't feel it. I turned my mind away again as I had meant to before I'd known about Edgar's letter, the footsteps, the maid in the kitchens at night, and stumbled through the routine of my day. I had thrown my lot in with the Witch, and the only way I could believe it to be the right path was to close off any other possibility. I had to make this work.

.I understood now: it was a deal I would make, had been making from the start.

What would I not do, if it meant I could be loved?

✴

As March melted the snow and the days grew brighter, I set about replanting the kitchen gardens. It was a little early but I knew there would be work assessing and clearing the wilderness that had consumed its beds before I could start a regimented sowing plan. The seeds I had asked for arrived, and I arranged the packets on my desk in a miniature map of the garden I planned to build. Salad vegetables at one end, herbs at the other. Medicinal plants kept carefully to the side; the current indiscriminate scatter of deadly blooms made me uneasy.

Planting took time, a surrender to the seasons and the forces of weather that were far beyond my control. Whether I came out one morning to find the rosemary flowering, or my thyme savaged by marauding squirrels, it was all the same thing. A process, a world far beyond my human dominion. I could not hurry it, or control it, only invest my time and care, and carry on with a hope and belief in the future.

I took to going barefoot while gardening, finding pleasure in the feeling of soil between my toes and knowing that this was another thing I would never have been allowed to do back in Blumwald. This was something distinctly part of my new life, the one I had chosen for myself and I relished it. I sang as I worked, digging and sowing and pruning and watering, sang as I brought finds back to the study, examined flints and white-streaked granite, sang even when the Witch laughed, called me sentimental and soft. But I didn't care if she saw my softness. After that moment in the bath I understood: I wanted her to see me. All of me. I wondered now if I finally understood what Klara felt at those balls, brushing fingers with eligible young men as they danced, the lingering of eyes and the shortness of breath. All that I found now here, with the Witch. When her fingers grazed mine as I passed her a piece of fruit it was like being burned by sparks jumping from the fire. When she fixed a stray curl of my hair, or the trailing corner of my shawl, it was a revelation. Her body was something I was always aware of, its proximity to my own, its heat, its curves, the hidden silk of her skin.

Perhaps I was alone in this. But when she blushed as I caught her watching me, or when her breath grew rapid and shallow if I leaned across her to reach for a bottle of ink, I thought: perhaps not.

That kernel of something between the Witch and I grew like a weed, rapid and rampant in the cracks between the stone of our clashing natures, wild and beautiful all the same. I tended to my love like a garden, an unfamiliar seed planted out of curiosity and hope, and all I could do was wait to see what might come of it.

I realised, later, that I had misunderstood her. If I had been a little less consumed by nursing my own pain, I might have seen the loneliness in her for what it was. When I saw her slumped in a chair in the echoing dining room, I thought her angry, not unhappy. When she paced the great hall, looping the limestone spur, one hand always touching its ragged bulk, I thought her scheming, not melancholy. I did exactly as she did, lingered and unravelled in the same ways, but I could not see it. Perhaps that was why I could not understand the blank face she turned to Frieda's death. I feared it signalled some inhuman coldness in her heart, but perhaps it was not so different to my own response: she coped as I did, with denial.

I found myself attending to her in a way I had never done with anyone before. I had never been so aware of another person. When she stabbed her finger with her quill I was there with a cloth to wash and bind the cut, when her hair became tangled I sat behind her as she picked at the knot with a comb. This was natural kindness that anyone would do, I told myself.

Once, I woke there, the clock chiming the small hours and found my glasses had been removed, and a blanket drawn over me. I had fallen asleep on the settle, lulled by the warmth and crackle of the fire, and the scratch of the pen nib as the Witch worked on her ledgers. All those dates and times marching along in some complex calculation I couldn't understand. Now the fire burned low, only glowing embers and all but the oil lamp at her desk had been extinguished. My Witch was still working. I wanted to take the pen from her, to pull her onto the sofa with me to rest. I wanted to take the burden she carried and set it down, though I still didn't know what that burden was.

She was *my* Witch, and I wanted her to know it.

She was mine, and I was hers.

I should have learned the lesson of my garden: what seeds are sown cannot help but grow. Cloth woven of a certain thread cannot become one of another.

Our life together was built on secrets and death, and nothing wholly simple or pure could take form in it. I buried thoughts of Frieda, but they sprang up in my dreams like nettles. When I closed my eyes she came to me, her manic face through the flames, and the twisted ruin of her dead body. And with it came thoughts of Edgar, and Frau Hässler – and worse, the maid standing mute in the corner, and the Witch cold and silent, walking the halls at night. My life here was the stuff of nightmares.

Soon, I grew sluggish and short in my days, making simple mistakes and snapping at minor inconveniences. I was exhausted from sleepless nights, and overwhelmed by a sense of frustration. How many times had I told myself I could live by my promise not to pry, how many times had I tried to close my eyes to the secrets within the castle?

A month passed after Frieda, and I lay awake under a gibbous moon. With the warmth of oncoming spring and the Witch at my side it was easier to believe I had done the right thing; but at night, when the cold came creeping from the stones and I lay all alone in the vast castle, dread took over. I could not sleep for fear of bad dreams, and had caught myself dragging my nails along my thigh before pinching the top. The realisation that I had fallen into old patterns again had sent a pang of hopelessness through me. This aspect of myself that I could not escape.

When the footsteps passed outside my door it was almost too much, and I buried my head beneath my pillow. Why could

I not want something in the Witch and have it? Why did it have to be a torment?

I thought I would pay anything to be needed. To have a place I belonged.

✳

The Witch pulled me up at breakfast the next morning when I sniped at her for eating the last of the marmalade. 'What is wrong with you?'

'Nothing.'

The Witch narrowed her eyes. 'Don't lie to me.'

I was in no mood for it this morning. 'No, I suppose lying is your job.'

The Witch set down her knife with the clink of metal on china. 'This seems quite an escalation from the issue of marmalade. Will you tell me what is wrong or should I leave you alone to sulk?'

I shut my eyes. I was so tired.

'A woman died,' I said slowly, 'because of me.' *Because I chose you.*

It took her a moment to follow my meaning. 'Frieda?'

'Who else?'

The Witch waved a dismissive hand. 'That was not your doing. She set the fire. If she was fool enough to stay then it is on her head.'

I had not thought of it in that way but the Witch was right. Frieda could have left. Frieda could not have come at all. All the same, it sat badly with me that the Witch could dismiss her death so easily.

'I heard you last night. Outside my door.' I don't know what bravery possessed me, but I found myself speaking before I realised what I would say.

'Oh?'

'Yes. I have heard you many nights.'

Silence.

'Do you have some business in my quarters?'

'Remember our bargain. You do not pry, and I give you what you claim to want.'

I confess, I was wounded. 'Is that still all this is to you?'

The Witch did not reply. I rarely saw her blush, but the way she turned her attention to her cup of coffee, busied herself stirring in the sugar, gave me the answer all the same. No, I was not wrong.

The bond between us was more than the bargain we had struck.

I probed the thought like a tongue against a loose tooth.

'I understand why you want to keep your work in the Tower and your ledgers private, that is your right.' My mouth was dry with fear. 'But that night in the kitchens . . . what was wrong with that girl?'

'Why are you so set on making things more complicated than they need to be?'

'Because if you will not tell me then I must assume Frieda was right. You hide something that concerns me. Something dangerous.'

'Is that what you think?'

Her voice was too low and too quiet and I knew we stood on the brink of an argument I was not sure I was ready to face.

I needed her, and I was frightened of what she hid. I did not know how to live with those two warring sides.

I passed another sleepless night, preoccupied with the need to smooth over the cracks between us. If I were in Blumwald, Klara would tell me to take her hyacinths for forgiveness, but here I had only a swathe of hardy nettles to make do. I brought an armful to the kitchen and persuaded Wolf to boil them up into tea sweetened with honey, then I arranged a tray with a teapot, cup, a plate of dried fruit and brought it to our breakfast room. The dried herbs and flowers I had arranged that first morning were bent and crumbled, dusting the cloth beneath them with a fine shower of petals.

The Witch's dress today was not one I had seen before, something from the thirties with a wide, straight neckline that cut from shoulder to shoulder and large balloon-like sleeves gathered at the elbow. Her waist was cinched in painfully small, and her hair had been half pinned up, revealing the pale shell of her ear.

'I made you breakfast.' I placed the tray before her.

She looked up. 'I thought we had Wolf for that?'

'It's an apology for prying.' I poured a cup of tea and placed it before her. 'I am sorry.'

'I am sorry, too. I should not have been short with you.' The Witch took an obliging sip of tea, but she looked as uneasy as I felt.

After a moment, she said, 'Take me on a walk.'

It was not that I misunderstood her request, but the

phrasing of it caused my mouth to quirk in amusement. To *take her for a walk* as though she were a small lap dog that needed airing.

She saw my amusement, and scowled. 'You *like* to walk in the forest, do you not? Or are you an idiot that gets trapped in the snow only because you are too stupid to know to stay at home?'

'Yes, I like to walk.'

'So take me. I want to see why it interests you. Like your rocks, it is baffling to me and I do not like there to be things I do not understand.'

'Very well.'

We picked a bright, cold day with little wind and packed a picnic provided by Wolf into knapsacks; I laced myself carefully into my walking boots. The sun was strong and the sky a vivid lapis lazuli from mountaintop to mountaintop. Nothing like the snow before; we would be safe.

Still, apprehension prickled along my spine as we set off, tracking east along a low path between broad, soft-boughed beech trees that followed the course of the river. Now I understood what I felt for the Witch, I was acutely aware of her body, how far she stood from me, the warmth of her arm brushed too close, the curve of breast or hip beneath the fabric of whatever black dress she wore that day. It was maddening. I wanted something more from her, but I could hardly let myself dare think of it. It wasn't what women wanted from each other, at least as far as I had ever been told, but then again it wasn't something I had been told women wanted at *all*.

I found myself advancing through the forest so quickly the Witch pulled me to slow down.

'You run this walk like a race, determined to leave me in last place,' she growled. 'Is that it?'

'It's not a race.'

I slowed enough for her to stay beside me.

'What's that?' she asked, pointing to a large tree.

'An ash. Don't you know the names of the trees?'

I thought I might have seen a hint of colour in those alabaster cheeks, but she only looked at me haughtily and said, 'I have far more important things to occupy my mind than *plants*.'

'So why ask me?'

She rearranged the wide-hipped dress she wore like a bird settling ruffled feathers. It was entirely inappropriate for a walk in the forest, square cut and boxy as though the skirt hung off a shelf at her hips to trail in the mulch, the bodice a flat-fronted stomacher that pushed up her breasts.

'Because I am an elegant and generous conversationalist when I want to be. You like trees: tell me about them.'

We walked past the stand of ash in silence as I worked myself around the idea that twice now she had insisted she wanted to know about the things I liked. I knew there was something here worth enduring for.

'That's an oak,' I said, pointing to a trunk so tall and straight it was a wonder no one had cut it down for a ship's mast. 'And here, to the right of the path, that must be an abandoned hazel coppice. They make good walking sticks, and fencing, but no one has cut them down in a long time – look how thick and tall that one is? It's rare to see any left alone to grow that long.'

I pointed out boxwood, something she would never have left on her land unmanaged if she'd known its value in carpentry, lithe willows bending towards the water, silver birch with its curling paper bark and sweet chestnut growing too deep in the shade to bear fruit. The Witch listened attentively, asking astute questions about plant use, how to tell wild forest from managed land. I stopped in a hazel grove to find two branches of the right height and thickness and cut them off with my pocketknife to make us two walking sticks. They would have to be properly dried and treated to last – perhaps I would try to learn how if I could find a book on it – and we turned uphill, working towards the crest of a foothill.

We stopped at a rocky outcrop where the topsoil had washed away and nothing but scrubby heather and thistle could take root. The valley rolled out on either side, before and behind us the tree-clad mountains rising like cupped hands trapping sunlight and warmth between them. We spread the blanket and set out the picnic of roast chicken, soft cheese and rye bread, a tied cloth of apples, and a glass bottle of elderflower cordial. There was still winter in the air once we stopped moving, a note of ice on the wind blowing off the snow-capped mountaintops.

'Do you have a question for me?' she asked so suddenly I only blinked in surprise.

'A question?'

'You were full of them before.'

I blushed and took an apple and began to quarter it with my pocketknife for something to busy my trembling hands. 'I apologised for prying. My curiosity got the better of me.'

'You will learn curiosity is not always a virtue,' she said coldly, and I thought of the way I had spied on her at the start. From *curiosity*. Perhaps she was right. 'I have thought on it, and I have decided I will answer one question.'

I looked up sharply.

'One question,' she repeated. 'Ask wisely.'

My mind was full at once of all the things I would know. The maid – oh God, the maid, what happened to her? What was that? Why did the Witch pace the castle at night? Was she monitoring me? Why did Edgar never finish his letter? What was in the Tower and the ledgers?

Laying it all out, it was overwhelming.

The Witch tore a strand of chicken off the bone with her teeth and I felt queasy. Our picnic was strewn with scraps of gristle and cartilage, the beaky ribcage of the bird we had eaten and fingers of wing bone.

My voice was barely a whisper when I spoke.

'What happened to the men before me?'

The Witch held my gaze with a steady eye, her expression perfectly blank and unreadable. 'They remained at the castle until their lives ran out.'

She had answered and said nothing. I should have known it.

'Let me ask one more.'

'Mina,' she warned.

'Just one.' My breath felt tight in my chest. 'Have you ever taken a woman before?'

She studied me, and for a moment I thought she would dismiss me.

Then she spoke.

'No.'

A small word that lit a wild-burning fire.

We packed the remains of the picnic and returned along the same path, this time the Witch walking ahead. I watched the sway of her hips, the flash of ankle, Achilles' heel, the sole of her foot. I thought of the men who had come before me, watched her like I did. *They remained at the castle until their lives ran out.*

I thought then what a strange way to say they had died of old age without returning home.

But later I understood that wasn't what she had meant at all.

SPRING

XIV

With April came another letter for the Witch. I was present for the arrival of this one, sitting in the study, legs slung over the arm of my chair and eating an apple while reading an English novel she had lent me about wide skies and empty moorland and ghosts of the past haunting the present. Wolf delivered the letter on a silver platter before returning to the kitchens, and the Witch read it frowning. I had come to know the different qualities of her expressions and this one carried with it a grave sorrow. She folded the letter and slipped it into her pocket. A ledger lay open before her and she studied its pages thoughtfully, before shutting it with a decisive movement.

'I am going away for a while.' She rose from the desk, today in a heavy stomacher and gauzy ruff, black hair fanning loose across her breasts. 'You will remain here, Wolf will take good care of you. I should only be a week or two.' She cut me off before I could speak. 'No, you cannot come with me.'

I was growing predictable.

'Will you really be gone so long?'

'I am sure you will hardly notice my absence.'

We both knew that was not true at all.

'I'll miss you,' I said.

She paused in the doorway, looking back with a complicated sadness and I felt bereft already. 'Will you?'

I watched her carriage cross the bridge and loop down to the village, and felt my heart going with her. For the first time since I arrived, the iron gates at the bridge were shut.

She really was gone.

At one time, I would have relished it. Now I felt entirely at sea.

I went to the kitchens to find Wolf. She was butchering a chicken, slicing a paring knife around joints and sinew.

'Do you require something?' she asked when she noticed me.

I hovered at the doorframe. I was not so confident in the Witch's regard for me that I would risk her wrath; the questions I had asked on our mountain walk had been dangerous enough.

But surely it wouldn't hurt to loose my curiosity on Wolf.

'Does the Witch go away often?'

I thought of the black-rimmed letter. She had not left then, what could it be that drew her now?

'That is my mistress's business.'

'She received a letter. I thought the postmark from Vienna perhaps?'

'I would not know.'

This, at least, was a lie. Wolf had delivered the letter to our study, Wolf would have seen exactly where it had been sent from.

'Only, I wondered how long the Witch would be absent. Vienna is no short journey.'

Wolf ignored me as she took a cleaver to the bird's spine, severing the ribs on either side and pulling it out in a fleshy line. The spine and feet and neck went into a stockpot, the bird itself she splayed open like a butterfly, pinned in place for the roasting.

'Will you take supper in the dining room?'

I thought of that cavernous space and myself, stranded at one end of a table meant for so many more. 'No. Send a tray to my room.'

As I left, the back of my neck prickled. Wolf was watching me with narrowed eyes, knife in one hand and bones in the other.

The castle was too large and too silent without my Witch. Our study cold and lifeless. I spent the first evening there, trying to work as normal at my desk but the harder I tried the deeper the loneliness dug in.

I wondered how the Witch had managed like this for so long.

I moved to her armchair, feeling the dip in the seat from the weight of her body, the coarse patches on the arms worn away by her hands, and then to her desk, sitting behind it as though I could summon some ghost of her spirit back by occupying her place. Something sharp and painful expanded in my chest and I cast around for anything to distract myself. She had not tidied before she left, and her ledgers filled with rows of unintelligible numbers were scattered around between sheets of blotting paper and almanacs and books in Greek I could not read. My fingers hovered over the pages: here was my chance. An uninterrupted stretch of time to investigate as I had done before.

But I had made a promise.

I rose from the desk sharply, knocking over the chair. My will was weak and I did not trust myself.

I spent the next night in my room away from temptation. For a while it was easier in this place that held so few memories of the Witch, but then I found my thoughts straying back to those nights when I had lain feverish and she had stayed by my side and nursed me; and the night we had spent dozing fitfully side by side after the fire. I could conjure up the feeling of her cool, slim hands on my forehead, the brush of her hair against my cheek, and it set me so sore with longing I could not stand it.

The door to last Tuesday stood quiet and undisturbed since my visit many months ago. I opened the door and looked in. Today was Friday, but through the door I saw the Tuesday just gone.

The Witch was alone, leaning against her desk and staring into the fire. Minutes passed and she did not stir, hypnotised by the flame, until finally she roused herself, took out the viola I saw her so rarely play. She did not raise it to her chin, but instead plucked it like a fiddle, picking out an unfamiliar tune. Lilting and sorrowful and discordant in places; it sounded old, the music of wild boar hunts, ancient forest, sword and shield.

I came back the next night, and the next, watching her silently from the shadows. Every night she moved the same, staring deeply into the fire before picking out that tune on the viola. I realised she was mouthing something along to it – a song. The tune became familiar to me, hooked in my mind as I went about my solitary days.

Until one night I came to the door and she was gone. The room was cold and empty, the grate raked clean of coals, and I realised my mistake: a week had passed.

I was looking at a new Tuesday. A Tuesday without her.

My heart lay heavy in my chest. That was that then. She was gone, fully, until whenever it was she chose to come back.

*

Loneliness had a bite to it.

The Witch and I had twined together like vines, needing only each other. Now I withered alone, and the grief was staggering. I am not sure what madness came over me in those days after she left, but it was something altogether dark and different.

For days at a time I spoke to no one. Wolf had made it clear she disliked me, and so we avoided each other, and the maids who dressed me were mute and scurried about their business as though I was as frightening as the Witch. I would sit at my window and twist my mother's drop spindle between my fingers in echo of a motion I did not understand how to make. Sometimes I would pass the Witch's study, and test the door to her Tower: still locked. For a moment, I could imagine she was still behind it, consumed by her work, and I would see her in a matter of hours. But evening would come and I remained alone.

I had been left, again. I had done what the Witch had asked

and cut off my curiosity, closed my eyes to the secret of the previous companions, but even that bargain had not brought me what I craved. I was alone, abandoned, a fate that no matter what I did I seemed unable to escape.

I took to lying in what I thought of as the summer room, the empty chamber near the kitchens where I'd seen the silent maid. The windows looked over a lush green forest, the scent of wildflowers and sap on the warm air, and light streamed crystalline through the glass. It was the scene of such terrible horror, but also a keen memory of my Witch. In the past, I would have brought heaping armfuls of wildflowers inside as comfort, but now I could not bear to. They were beautiful for a moment, then I was forced to watch them wither and die, abandoning leaves and petals, drooping as they lost their battle to live.

As April wore on the weather outside grew closer to the idyll in the summer room, and I took myself out more often to my kitchen garden. Seasonal streams had appeared around the schloss almost overnight, a whole mountain-head of snowpack rushing to the valley floor, stripping earth and grass and saplings from its path. My herbs were coming in strong, wild little bushes of basil and coriander and thyme. Spring had even released some dormant plants I had not known lingered, wild garlic and sour sorrel filled the gaps between my planting, and bilberries sprinkled across the heath-like scrubland of the abandoned beds. I saw a glimpse of that happy future then, in the soft growing things and the breeze and the yellow stone walls.

I set to. Trowel and shears and apron equipped, I passed the hours turning over fresh earth, weeding and planting, digging irrigation channels and scratching names on wood markers, picking aphids off stems and mending nets to protect the small thicket of strawberries and green beans, tending courgettes into flower, the long hair of carrot tops and fat pea pods ripening in the sun. The herbs thriving and vegetables bedded in, I turned to the final, unused corner of the walled garden. It butted up against the castle, the round sheer stones of the Tower marking the boundary, and all of it overgrown with nettles, bracken, bramble vines and dandelions. I was ready to start the apothecary garden anew, carefully sectioned off from the edible plants, unlike before.

The brambles I cut back, relegating them to a hedge-like shape at the rear of the bed because I hoped to harvest blackberries come autumn. The nettles I yanked up wearing thick gloves and set aside for Wolf to make tea and soup and salve. The bracken was the saddest to dispose of – I knew no other use for it and it grew like a weed in any open clearing. Still, I piled up the fronds to use for mulch. The dandelions I set about last. These at least could be well used in the kitchen, but I also knew they grew vast taproots far below the surface soil, spreading their kingdom like veins and arteries.

I was sweating, kneeling on a bed of bracken, bare hands and trowel digging deep into the earth, following the line of stem and root, hair stuck to my temples and the back of my neck as I worked down, down, down.

My fingers brushed against something hard – the root? It was long and slender enough to be, but hard like iron, like a tree root. It was too far down to see clearly, and I worked the soil out of the way with the tip of the trowel until it came loose. Not a root then – the length of my arm but a smooth knobble at either end, no fibrous snap as it separated from the plant.

I drew it up, and sat back on my heels to look at what I had found.

It was a bone.

White and scored with dirt, a complete bone buried at the base of the castle.

It was so strange I only stared at it in blinking confusion. What was a bone like this doing in my garden? I turned it over, too numbed by shock to be horrified. Was it human? Some unfortunate animal?

I looked at its size, measured it against my arm as the slow, creeping knowledge settled in me. This *was* a human bone. There was a person buried here.

I looked around, half expecting the Witch to be stalking across the grass, black dress flared out behind her and face twisted with rage. I had found something I knew I shouldn't have. But there was no one there, only birdsong and the drift of shadows across the ground as the clouds scudded overhead.

As if in a trance, I leaned forward again and began to dig. At first I turned up little fragments of finger bones, then the curve of a rib, somewhere, the hummock of a hip. The trowel hit something large and solid. I worked around it, easing the soil apart, and then there it was, staring up through the loamy earth: a skull.

I fell back in shock, scrubbing the grave dirt from my hands, and tumbled straight into the thorny thatch of brambles. They tangled in my clothes, my hair, pulling up pinpricks of blood like constellations across my skin. The more I struggled the more entwined I became, heels digging into the soil, wrenching, scraping, until I struck the castle wall with the crack of an elbow and the back of my head.

But not the rattling, metal pain of stone. A dull thud of bone on wood. I twisted as best I could to see what lay behind me: a door. Ivy hung in curtains over it, the brambles twisting around the hinges, hiding it from sight. Still, there it was, swollen with snowmelt and rusted shut, but a door all the same.

A door at the bottom of the Witch's Tower.

Silently, slowly, I unpicked myself from the thorns until I stood free. Only a pace or two back and the door disappeared from view, but I planted its location in my mind, fetched the shears and set to careful work uncovering it.

It was small, unassuming. Enough for one person to slip in or out unnoticed. I'd seen something like it before in books. It was a traitor's door, meant for the lord of the castle to flee during an attack, but notoriously used by traitors escaping to join the enemy. I ran my hand over the soft, damp wood feeling it flake away, tracing the crude iron hinges, the fat, blunt keyhole. Built into the base of the castle, it must have been here since the first stone was laid. And this rust, the brambles, how many years had it lain unused? It might take a little work but with some oil and brute force, it could still be opened.

Above, the turret of the Witch's Tower was a blot on the April sky. I knew I was tugging at things that should not come loose. The Witch was like a flower bud, with each petal I pulled off, another lay curled below; if I kept pulling and pulling, soon I would end up with nothing but a barren stem. The bloom would be dead.

Want and fear warred in me. I could have this happiness here, with the Witch, but it came at a cost. I must turn my eye from horror. See beauty in rot. Home in a charnel house.

But I had seen the door now and it was not knowledge I could forget.

I knew, for better or worse, I would go through it.

*

It took one night's restless sleep for my will to break. I packed up all I needed and descended to the apothecary garden. I buried the bones at sunrise. They were grainy white and perfectly whole, as though someone had lain down at the foot of the Tower and slept until overtaken by death. I placed each gently back into the hole with the dandelion roots, and covered it over with dirt. I did not want the Witch to know what I had discovered.

Oil wicked along the door's rusted hinges like snowmelt coursing through runnels in the mountainside. Between the oil and a crowbar I found in one of the endless rooms of junk, I prised the door open enough for a body to squeeze through. Before I did, I tied the end of a ball of yarn to the hinge and tucked the other into my belt. I had spent enough time in the schloss to understand it could not be trusted, and I had read enough books to know to leave myself a breadcrumb trail back out. Oil lamp lit, I slipped inside and began to climb.

Almost at once the spiral staircase was pitch black. So dark, my eyes strained wide, the world shrunk down to the haze of light from the lamp picking out the steps ahead, the curve of the wall under my hand. From outside I had seen that the Tower was windowless all the way to the top, not even an arrow slit puncturing the smooth stone façade from the base to where a small square window nestled under the eaves. The way ahead of me was long and dark.

And *cold*. That I had not expected, though it made sense that the ancient cold of the mountain would seep into a place so cut off from life. A pervasive smell of dank and mildew filled the air, the steps were slick with moss and algae growing in the ground water; the wall was wet under my bare hand, and so close I felt shut up in a tomb. The going was slow and terrifying. Occasionally my foot slipped, though I was wearing my sturdy mountain-climbing boots, and my thoughts were filled with the image of my body tumbling down and down, neck cracking on stone to lie lifeless, hidden, where no one would look for me until I had rotted away to join the bones buried under the stifling earth.

The yarn ran out at some featureless point in my climb and I abandoned the thread reluctantly. I was determined not to regret my choice, but I could not deny the strong desire I had to turn around. Still, I climbed. I did not know what would be worse, continuing my ascent, or turning back and plunging into that black well of nothingness. It had been long enough since I last climbed a mountain that my thighs were protesting, but this was a discomfort I knew. In the cold and dark it made my body mine again, carved out something like a place that I belonged.

Finally, with a curse on my breath, the stairs evened out into a landing, where a door-shaped line of light was picked out in the wall. I knelt, grateful for the rest, and peered through the locked keyhole. As I'd hoped, beyond was the corridor by the Witch's rooms, dust motes dancing in a shaft of light and everywhere utter stillness and silence. Either I'd been climbing far longer than I'd thought, or the castle was up to its old tricks, because there was a strong midday sun shining through the windows.

The Tower still rose a good way further, but now at least the stairs and walls were dry, a well-worn divot in the centre of each step from years of passing feet. I thought of the Witch climbing the Tower every day, her feet where I now trod, her hand brushing the wall as mine did. I rested again soon, the lamp cradled on my lap. What was I really hoping to achieve doing this? What did I think I was going to find at the top? What did I *want* to find? If I was looking for the Witch, I was chasing her ghost.

Climbing was outside of conscious thought now. I found myself mounting the stairs again without realising, lost in the rhythm of my body, the burn in my thighs and my throat. When the top came it was without fanfare. Only the plateauing of the steps, an unlocked door, the narrow walls opening out to a small circular room with clean, polished boards, a vast fireplace banked with ash and on the far side, the square window I had seen from below. Rafters in the conical roof rose above, painted in royal blue and sprinkled with stars, all faded like the walls of my bedroom. Outside – another trick of the schloss – dusk, or was it dawn, broke milky pink over the crest of the mountains. An in-between time, soft, pregnant with potential. Despite the stone, the open window, the hollow roof, the void beneath the floor, it was so warm, I pushed my sleeves back and unbuttoned my shirt collar.

The heat was coming from the only thing in the room: a spinning wheel taller than I was, its wheel as broad as the span of my arms. It was cruder than the one Frieda had used, an old-fashioned great wheel, the spinner turned by hand. Around the spindle was wound something golden and shimmering, like a candle flame, like fool's gold, like sunlight in water. I had seen this before; when the Witch had bound me to her, something golden had risen from my skin, wrapped around our entwined fingers. I drew closer, pulled to its warmth like a magnet to true north. A great deal of thread had been spun, and now only a little carded fibre was left on the distaff – the spike set at the side of the wheel where raw fleece was skewered. If it could be called fleece; like a dusk cloud limned gold by the sunset, it mounded and blurred so that I could never look at it directly.

Drugged by the warmth, the fuzzing gold halo, I reached out one bare hand and touched the spindle.

XV

The world blinked out.

Like slipping beneath the water, I was dragged down yet buoyed up by something thicker than air, both weightless and like a stone, sinking slowly.

No, *time* blinked out. The walls warped, sun boiling beyond the window, fire flared and died and the wheel turned. Time ran through the wheel like yarn being spun, owing its steady flow to the turn of the wheel.

I had stumbled upon the secret of the castle: the Witch's work.

The light around the spindle and on the distaff was snuffed and I plunged into the cold and dark. I felt it not with my body – that was a lost, ephemeral thing, cobwebs and dandelion heads and milk foam – but with my soul. My body lay rooted in *now* and my soul flew through time untethered.

If I could have screamed I would have brought the stones crashing down.

At last the wheel's spin slowed, and the Tower walls came juddering into focus. It was early morning, cool blue light outside the window, the sense of things waking in the air. My head span, lapping waves of nausea rising and receding; I reached to touch the wheel again but nothing happened. I had a hand and I had nothing. I could feel the shape of it, fingertips and palm but when I moved it there was only a shadow. I was here, and I was not.

Slowly, it dawned on me just how terrible a mistake I had made. I had touched the white heart of the fire and disrupted the Witch's careful work; now I meddled in time. I was lost.

Voices came up the stairs, and three people entered the room. A man, a woman, and a girl of perhaps sixteen, dressed finely but in garments more antiquated than anything I'd ever seen the Witch wear. Artichoke-patterned silk in black and gold, slashed all over to reveal ivory fabric beneath, sharply angled necklines plunging to a high, belted waist to reveal the kirtle underneath, voluminous bag sleeves and all richly adorned. They looked like something from a Renaissance painting. The man and woman circled the room, talking softly and the girl stepped forward to examine the wheel.

Now I understood exactly why the Witch didn't want me here.

This girl was the Witch.

I was sure of it. The arch of her brow, the curve of her jaw, the fine cheekbones and hazel-flecked eyes. I would know that face anywhere.

The man looked like her, he had the same brow and chin, but the woman was different. Tall, graceful, with chestnut hair and a fierce grey streak at her parting, she was nothing like the other two – and yet I saw the Witch in her too. In the way she held herself; alertness and caution dressed in nonchalance, expression guarded, eyes sharp and cunning, and afraid. And over it all, some deep, deep weariness.

I felt suddenly frightened for my Witch. Whatever sympathy the woman's similarity roused in me was quashed immediately by the way she looked at the young girl.

A snake waiting to strike.

Desperate.

'Holda, dear,' said the man holding out an arm to tuck the girl, my Witch, to his side as they looked out of the window. 'Is this not fine? Are you not pleased?'

'Yes, Father,' she mumbled.

'I have kept you too long in the city; to see such beautiful land is a balm for the soul. Your stepmother's residence will suit us both, don't you think?'

My eyes snapped to the woman; stepmother. I understood this all too well.

Holda pulled out of his arms, avoiding his smile. 'Yes, Father.' Between the two adults, Holda seemed as small and ephemeral as a paper toy; something easily batted about. Easily crushed.

The man said, 'Berchta, my love, will you give us a moment alone?'

The girl's stepmother – Berchta – smiled tightly and stepped back onto the landing, a pair of bright eyes in the shadows.

The man took Holda's hands and drew her to sit with him. 'I know this must all feel quite sudden. We are a long way from Vienna, and this land is unfamiliar to you still, but I hope you will try to learn to like it, for my sake.'

She looked resolutely at her knees. 'I want you to be happy, Father, but you are correct, this does seem sudden.'

'Since we lost your mother, I have found myself lonely. I must admit what pleasure it brings me to have companionship once more.'

'I worry what she wants from you.'

'That is not something you need to think about, my dear. Look around you, she is hardly marrying *me* for my wealth. If anything it is the reverse,' he said with a bark of laughter. 'She brings me a fine title.'

Then what does *she want?* I could see the question on Holda's lips as it was on mine, but she held it back.

'She wants what any woman wants,' continued her father, 'the protection of a man, a household to run, the safety of marriage. Something you will have for yourself soon enough, and then you will hardly need me.'

Holda said nothing but looked at her knees sourly.

'Life puts things in our path, good and bad, and it is for us to make the measure of which it shall be.'

He patted her hand. I thought of my own father, and his rejection. Anger flared. Was he so blind to the sadness in her expression? To the loneliness?

Holda only nodded and let herself be kissed on the head. Leaning on the window edge, a stray lock of hair danced in the breeze while her father rejoined his new wife. Berchta considered Holda for a moment, assessing. Then she drew him close, speaking in soft, mellifluous tones and he stilled, eyes glazing over. They moved in sync for a moment, gently swaying on the spot, then he turned, walking slowly to the door.

'I have business.'

Holda turned, frowning. 'Father – I—'

'Stay here,' he said. His voice was flat and dull. 'I have business.'

He didn't look back once as he walked out.

Now Holda and Berchta were alone. A change washed over her, the mask of nonchalance slipping away as the predator emerged.

'What did you say to my father?' demanded Holda.

She folded her arms, jaw tight, in an expression that was achingly familiar.

Berchta positioned herself between Holda and the door, then asked, 'Do you know how to spin?'

Holda blinked. 'A little.'

'Come, I will teach you.' Berchta gestured to the great wheel. 'A girl should learn useful skills.'

Holda hesitated for a beat, but allowed herself to be positioned at the spindle to work the thread and Berchta slowly began to turn the wheel. The spindle rotated, drawing fleece from the distaff and twisting it into thread.

'Normally the spinner works both the wheel and the thread, but I will help you.'

Holda's hesitation faded as the task of feeding fibre into thread at an even thickness absorbed her attention, and the glassy expression her father had worn crept over her face. Once she had it steady, Berchta transferred Holda's other hand to the wheel so she was managing both at once. A slow golden glow began to build around the thread and the wheel, like warmth spreading out from a flame.

'I'm going to share a secret with you: this wheel spins more than thread. Can you tell?'

Holda looked up. 'Yes . . . it's . . . heavy.' A ball of thread was building on the spindle, the steady clack and whir of the wheel hypnotic.

'You hold in your hands the heaviest thing there is: time. It weighs on us, doesn't it? All the things we've seen. All the things we've done.'

Berchta joined her hand to the wheel, and drew out some gold, shimmering thing. Holda shuddered. 'All our memories crowding us, like weights around our ankles.'

The gold mist swirled and formed into a scene, a woman reclined in bed, a young girl crying at her side, like statues of moulded sand. Berchta dragged her fingers through the golden dust, scattering the image and reshaping it. Now, an adult Holda stood beside a grave, a coffin lowering into it. Holda let out a sob.

'And the knowledge of what inevitably must come. It is a slow acting poison, time. Your mother has died, your father will follow. You will be alone. This is the nature of time. It strips everything from us, and we are mercy to its flow.'

Holda sank to the floor, skirts pooling around her, tears flowing steadily down her face. I wanted to go to her, hold her. Her hands shook, a look of naked panic on her upturned moon of a face. 'Stop – please – I don't want to see this.'

A darkness gathered around Berchta that overshadowed the golden figures of the vision. Beyond the window, the sun died, swallowing the Tower in an oppressive darkness.

'Oh, but there are worse things than time flowing forward.

Worse things than the future coming to meet us.' She braced her hand around the wheel and stopped it.

A pressure closed around my head instantly, so splitting I thought I might vomit. The darkness encroached from all sides, and I was consumed by despair. Berchta moulded the air, drawing the golden sand into new shapes. The little girl by her mother's deathbed once again but now her mother squirmed and writhed, trapped forever in the agony of death.

'If time is not spun in steady measure all manner of torment will wreck the world. We could be prisoners of one moment forever, crushed under time's weight. Or we can be unmade entirely.'

Berchta fed the wheel backwards. The thread snagged, tangled, unspooled in knots from the spindle. The graveyard split open and corpses were lifted out, the dead reborn. Crops curled into themselves and disappeared into the ground, rain sucked up from the earth fleeing to the sky. Rivers ran backwards, walls unbuilt themselves.

The world came undone.

She released the wheel from its tortured backwards turn, and the vision disappeared.

Berchta put Holda's hand on the wheel and set it turning forward again. 'Do you see, Holda? Time is a precious and tyrannical ruler. It makes hags of old maids, it will steal your youth and your beauty. It will steal your loved ones, carving away at you until you are alone and desperate enough to do *anything* to change your fate. But it is our master, and we must serve it. The wheel must turn. The thread of time must be spun out in careful measures or the world will be nothing but ash and dust. What you hold in your hands is the fate of the whole world. Do you *understand*?'

Holda shook her head. 'No – please, make this stop.'

'It cannot stop!' ordered Berchta. 'It must never stop! Time must be spun: that is the duty of the wheel. It is a responsibility a woman must bear. And I will bear it no longer.' Weariness consumed her, and I saw a great age settle across her shoulders. Then she wound the golden haze around her fingers and touched them to the kneeling Witch's forehead. 'I pass this curse to you, Holda von Hohenfeld: you will spin alone, until the end of time.'

Tears wet Holda's cheeks. 'What did you do?' she whispered.

'You will see.' Berchta went to the door. 'Be a good girl. Do your duty. We are in your hands now.'

And with that, she left. The click of the lock was loud in the silence.

Holda stumbled to the door and tried it though she and I both knew it was futile. The wheel was losing momentum. The spindle was bare, the thread hung snagged and tangled. Holda was slowed too as time thickened like honey. It was as Berchta said: the wheel spun time and if the thread was not kept even and smooth, time itself bucked. She fought for too long, nails scrabbling at wood.

Then Holda turned to the wheel, staring it down like a soldier in the vanguard; terrified, but with growing resignation. She was face to face with a monstrous task, and there was no one else to take her place in the line.

My heart broke a final time, seeing my Witch make her choice.

She moved like a swimmer battling a fierce current, carving her way back to gather the thread from the floor, set her hand to the wheel and encourage it forward. It juddered, stiff and uncompliant under her inexperienced hand, but it began to turn and after a few minutes' work, the tangled, dropped thread was rewound on the spindle and the crushing pressure lifted from my temples. The sun dawned again, a balmy, cool light spilling across the floor. Somewhere beyond was the sound of a carriage and horses clattering down the switchback road to the village. Still, Holda stood at her work, feeding the fibre into the twist of the thread, measuring out the turn of the wheel with her back as stiff as a tree, rooted and unbent. Her face was wet with tears, but I saw dawning in her what I knew of her now: she would not break. She would not surrender. If this was the challenge before her, she would rise to it, and master it.

I only wonder that in four hundred years she never found a way out.

I could bear to watch this no longer. With my formless body, I reached for the wheel again. For a moment, something like a hand took shape, ethereal enough Holda did not notice, and I thrust my finger into the thread. Into the flow of time.

The world blinked out again and I was dragged into the current. I was drowning, struggling in a riptide that pulled me under.

I fought for the surface, broke into the light for a fraction of a minute – there, Holda again, eyes smudged dark from lack of sleep, and a servant ushering her away from a spindle wound round thick with golden thread. For now, time was well spun. She had done her job.

Something caught my ankle and I plunged under again. I fought the inexorable force of time. Each time I reached the surface, I saw a glimpse of Holda in shorter and shorter snatches, saw her spinning, her life moving at glacial speeds of hours and hours alone in silence, spinning the golden fibre. Saw her shatter the coat of arms above the fireplace in my room, slash the painting of her stepmother. Saw her face harden, the angles grow sharper.

The girl died and the woman I knew survived, beautiful and cold, cursed to spin and shackled to her Tower.

Time had me in its maw and all I could do was pray it would release me in the place I belonged.

Something brushed my wrist.

I turned, slow and dazed, and saw my Witch – *my* Witch.

I had been found.

Her hand closed around my arm so tight I felt her nails puncture skin, her face a terrifying, cold blank mask only inches from mine.

The world winked out.

*

My vomit splattered the boards with acid and bile.

I threw up again, then sat back on my heels, wiping my mouth on my sleeve, eyes shut against the brightness. It had been drawing close to evening when I had reached the Tower's summit, but now the room was flooded with morning light. How long had I been gone?

The Witch was silent.

I knew she was there. I had seen her drop me back in our

time and turn to mend whatever damage I had done to the wheel.

'What was that?' I asked.

'The past,' she said blankly. 'My past.'

'And the wheel?'

'Time runs through the wheel like yarn being spun. It is my responsibility to keep spinning it, and to spin it smoothly. You saw what could happen if I do not.'

I was waiting for the axe to fall. I had betrayed her in the most awful way I knew how. If I loved her, I had to face the consequences. I saw no other way of salvaging what had grown between us.

I opened my eyes, and I understood why she hadn't launched into an attack.

She had finished with the wheel, and was now curled under the window, arms wrapped around her legs and face buried in her knees as she cried. I crawled over to her on my hands and knees.

'I'm sorry.' I touched her shoulder, but she didn't react, so I left my hand there, unsure what she needed from me. 'I know I made a mistake.'

That got her attention.

Her head snapped up and she trained those crystalline eyes on me.

'That was not a *mistake*. A *mistake* is using salt instead of sugar in a cake or arriving for dinner at the wrong hour. Did you trip and fall through a locked door into the one place I *forbade* you from entering?' she scoffed. 'That wasn't a mistake. What you did was *betrayal*. I trusted you, but you don't trust me.'

'Perhaps I don't know how to trust you. I want to but I'm terrified.'

I had never wanted anything as much as I wanted to be with the Witch, and that want was too much to face. I saw myself so clearly: it was easier not to trust her, to do what I knew would pull us apart, than take the risk of loving her with no assurance of love in return.

'I terrify you?' she asked. A moment of hurt, then her expression soured. 'You are correct, you should not trust me. Perhaps you are not as stupid as you look.'

'I didn't want to hurt you. I was scared about my future and there are so many things you won't tell me.'

'So you would steal what I would not willingly give?'

'If we are to trust each other, there can be no more secrets. Your stepmother cursed you to spin alone, that much I understood. I'm so sorry that happened to you.'

'I don't need your comfort.'

'But I want to give it to you. I love you and it hurts me to see you be treated like that and it hurts me to think of you alone here for so long.'

The Witch looked at me blankly, her voice flat. 'You don't love me. You love an idea of me, Mina. You love the person you've built in your head. You can't love *me*. You don't *know* me.'

I went hot and said without thinking, 'If *you* loved *me* you wouldn't have kept me in the dark!'

Her lip curled in a sneer. 'Who said I love you?' But there was no venom in her voice.

I closed my eyes, gathering myself, then I said, 'Let me know you.'

My voice was barely above a whisper. I felt on the cusp of something I had denied for so long, and yet here it was all the same, insistent to be seen. The two of us were a hair's breadth apart, and it would only take the smallest gesture for me to cross it. To kiss her.

'You don't understand what you're asking.'

'I do. Let me in, Holda.' The name was strange and sweet on my tongue. Holda, the tricked girl in the tower, my Witch.

Her calm vanished in the space of one word to the next. She wrenched her arm away from me like I was poison, that fragile cord between us disappearing into smoke.

She looked at me with eyes like ice. 'I'm your monster, don't forget. I remember what you've called me. Witch. Monster. *Cruel*. Get out while you still can.'

'That's not –' A darkness built around us and I felt the hum of tension in my head, an instinctive prickle of adrenaline.

'I mean it,' she hissed. 'Get *out*.' Her voice rose to a shriek. 'Get it through your thick skull. I do not love you. I will *never* love you. Leave and never come back. I don't *ever* want to see you again.'

To my shame, I turned away from the woman I loved, and fled.

XVI

I stormed down to the kitchens to corner a maid and demand a horse be readied so I could ride out and take the air. I could not stand to be confined to this miserable wreck of a home any longer. My father had told me I could not stay in Blumwald, the Witch had told me I wasn't welcome with her. I was sick of not being wanted, of being a problem wherever I went.

In my room I dressed warmly, riding habit and stiff boots, then marched through the castle, the hall with its rotting tapestries and burned-out staircase, past the empty stables to the horse that had been brought up from the village; mounted, I carried on through the misty gatehouse and across the narrow bridge to the forest.

I hated the Witch. I hated her with a fury that frightened me. I wanted to melt the flesh off her bones, I wanted to train birds to peck her eyes out, I wanted to crush her slowly under a huge boulder.

In sharp odds with my sour mood, it was a fresh morning, the midday sun winking between the crowns of the treetops. My horse was a gentle dappled mare quite different from the steeds that had drawn the Witch's carriage. The trees rolled out on either side of me, unending. Ash trees followed me as I rose, marking a swathe of limestone, a few lonely oaks arcing up, and everywhere beech, all garlanded with ivy vines thick as my forearm. The dirt was crisp with dew and a tangle of blackthorn guarded the forest on either side of the path, its wicked spikes dancing dangerously at eye level.

I thought of when I had first come to the schloss, that great thicket of blackthorn encroaching the walls, as effective a defence as any moat. Bitterthorn, my mother had called it, named after its pebbly sloe berries that we picked every autumn after the first frost. A fruit so sour and bitter I had cried the first time I ate them raw as a child. As bitter as the woman now trapped inside.

My mother had been the one to feed me the berries, plucked fresh from a tangled thatch of thorns in the woods behind the palace. Boiled up with sugar they made a tart jam, she had said, or soaked in gin a warming drink. Thinking of the sweet summer fruit of the palace gardens, I had pressed a handful between my lips, broke their skin with my teeth and then the sharp flavour had washed across my tongue, a shock so severe it was like a blow. I had spat out the pulpy mess onto the grass.

My mother had laughed, entertained by her own trick as I cried and scrubbed my mouth out with my sleeve. Not bittersweet, she had said. Only bitter.

Finally, I broke through the canopy. Ahead, the valley broadened and I could see a thin line of fields amongst the woods. Behind, the forest tangled thicker. And among it, the Witch's castle on its barren outcrop.

The idea slunk into my mind. I could simply keep riding and never return. In Blumwald there was nothing left for me, but I could go to Munich, get a job as a governess or some other spinster role.

And be alone again.

Like a magnet that only repels, I was a solitary creature. The Witch had her curse and I had mine.

But now I knew the Witch's loneliness was one of duty, of sacrifice.

What was mine?

I stopped the horse dead. Looked at the narrow path curving along the river, unmarked by any hoofprint or cartwheel. Looked back where the road inclined, climbing towards the schloss and its spur of limestone.

The Witch had railed and cursed at me, but I knew her better now. I understood the terrible secret she kept in the Tower, the lonely curse that had trapped her for so long. The mysteries of the castle seemed benign now, pieces of a puzzle I could begin to fit together with time. The ledgers, why she paced the hallways at night, those answers were surely connected.

I thought for a moment of the body buried in my garden. Why did I see horror so easily? The castle was old, it must have gathered bones from long before the Witch's time.

I had betrayed her trust by going into the Tower – but it was more than that that had upset her. She had been exposed, all her vulnerability and weakness. She had been laid open to me and found it too much to bear.

I turned my mare around and moved up to a brisk trot, hooves eating up the ground, moving faster and faster as I leaned into the decline.

Love was complex, conditional. Not all sweet, but not all bitter.

How many times was I going to be a coward? How would anything ever change for me if I gave up on myself whenever things became hard? If I turned this anger and hurt in on myself?

I had stayed with the Witch before out of fear of my old life, and that there would be no other place I was needed as the Witch needed her companion.

What I did now must be more than that.

The Witch was the closest thing I had ever known to love. To a true home. True family. If I walked away I would be the one cursing myself to loneliness. She was as frightened as I was, and unless one of us did something to break the spell we would let our own fear keep us apart. Alone.

The journey home took too long and yet was over too soon. I hadn't thought what to say, how to explain myself to her. How to make her *understand*. I reached the top of the switchback road, and slipped from my side saddle.

I collared Wolf by the sink.

'Where is she?'

Wolf regarded me with a coolly arched brow. 'I thought perhaps you had fled, my lady.'

'Tell me.'

'Her study, I believe.'

I went to the second floor, acutely aware of how sweaty and bedraggled I must be; the door to her study cracked against the wall as I flung it open. The Witch startled, dropped an ink pot, black liquid seeping over the newspapers. I rounded the back of the desk so we were face to face, half a metre apart. Me: panting, mud-stained, leaves in my hair and my boots tracking dirt across the rugs. Her: tense, white-knuckle grip on the back of her chair, in a loose, Aesthetic dress poorly dyed so the greens of the original silk showed through.

'Why are you—'

I tangled my hand in the fabric of her dress, pulled her to me and pressed our mouths together to swallow the end of her sentence in a kiss.

Oh.

This was how I would make her understand.

It lasted a confused, painful second, my chapped lips against her soft ones, the small parting of her mouth and the hint of something more – then I let go, giddy and afraid.

The Witch stared in shock, hand to her mouth. 'Why did you do that?'

'Because I wanted to.'

'You want to kiss me?'

For a moment, the horrified thought crossed my mind that I had misread her feelings towards me. 'Yes. Don't you want to kiss me?'

The Witch, breathless, her voice almost a whisper, said, '*Yes.*'

So I kissed her again. Softly this time, one hand cupping

her face, the other cradling her waist to draw her close. I was suddenly too aware of both our bodies: our lips, our noses brushing, the shape of her chin, her arms at her side, hands hesitantly coming to rest on my shoulders, the shape of her under the sack of a dress she wore.

In that moment it was as simple as kissing her, and my Witch kissing me back.

When we finally broke apart, pink-cheeked and tangled hair, I didn't know what to do with myself. I had never kissed anyone before, and I hoped I had done it right.

Then she looked down at my muddy, sweaty clothes, wrinkled her nose and said, 'You smell like badger piss. Take a bath.'

Servants were summoned and the huge wooden bathtub was set before the fire, and pails of water heated. I had just enough nerve to ask the Witch whether she wanted to watch me bathe this time too; she smirked at me in a way that made me shiver in anticipation for something I didn't fully understand, then went into her bedroom and shut the door.

I let the maid brush the burrs and thorns from my hair and wash it with rosewater. The shock of the wheel, the fight, my almost-escape, and this revelation of what truly lay between us. It was too much to think of all at once, so I thought of none of it; only yawned and sunk back into the steaming water.

Wolf brought up a meal – I lost track of which one we were eating – and we devoured it sat on the rug in front of the fire, the Witch in black and me in a nightdress and damp hair braided back and tied with a ribbon. There was honey and comb, thick slices of white bread, preserved beetroot, pickled walnuts, tranches of headcheese and tiny salty pickles, a salad of new potatoes and onion and capers, salted cabbage, sorrel leaves dressing wilted spinach, and a rhubarb crumble set to keep warm by the grate. A vast pot of nettle tea enough for four people was hung over the fire, and the Witch got up and down to pour me endless servings in a tiny porcelain cup painted gold and pink with tiny flowers blossoming around the rim.

We didn't speak of what had happened in the Tower. Nor did I raise the skeleton buried in my garden. I had climbed the Tower wanting answers about the past companions, my own future with the Witch, but I had found out far more than I had been ready for. So I held my tongue for now; I was in no rush to spoil this moment. There would be hardship in my future, and loss, and difficult decisions, that I was sure of, but right now I wanted to enjoy the fantasy of what could be.

The fire grew low, and the Witch ended sprawled out in front of it like a cat, her head in my lap. Tentatively, I stroked her hair, feeling the glossy, cool strands slip between my fingers. Her face looked different from this angle, her mouth a little softer, nose a little sharper; I could see a freckle behind her ear, and the corner of her eye where her lashes were stuck together by a little crust of sleep. She was so beautiful in the firelight, full red lips and pebble black eyes, like a siren, like a succubus. A tamed beast resting in my lap, claws sheathed.

For now.

She stared deeply into the fire, silent for a long time.

I was happy, but it came to me with unease that perhaps she was not.

We had both been alone for such a long time, the Witch for far longer than I. It could not be an easy transition to make, an unfamiliar new reality to acquaint herself with. I confess I did not feel quite at home in this yet either.

I carried a dark, lurking knowledge: what I would do, so as never to be alone again.

XVII

The Witch came to me at breakfast the next morning, wearing a fashionable tea gown; sleeves and collar of delicate lace, a long line of buttons from throat to hem, the generous bustle where the fabric split in a precise pleat, all had been made up in shining black.

'Come.'

It wasn't a request.

At the Tower, she pulled the key on its length of cord from beneath her bodice. 'I suppose there's not that much point locking it any more,' she said, hand resting on the knob. Then the two of us began the ascent.

It was a much faster climb this time, only a few loops around until we opened onto the circular room at the top. The wheel stood alone, and around it wound the softly glowing golden thread. Only now there was even less fleece left on the distaff than before.

'You wanted to look so badly. Well, go on then.'

At her invitation, I walked around the wheel, being careful not to touch anything. 'It spins time.'

'Yes.'

I hesitated. She had made the overture so she must be expecting questions, but it felt as though I was walking across the glacial mountaintops, groaning ice and hidden crevasses. 'What happens to the thread once it has been spun?'

The Witch hovered a hand above the golden bobbin. There was no end to the thread wound around, only a point where it faded, its substance dissolving into the shimmer in the air. 'It is used up. I do not fully comprehend how. I do not believe that is for us to know.'

'Did your stepmother know?'

'I have no idea. You saw for yourself all she told me. I made a study of the books she left behind, obtained any tract on magic I could trace, but there is nothing written about the wheel. I taught myself a little of her magic, but I am not the Witch she was.'

'She cursed you to stay here and spin.'

The Witch's face was a study in blankness. 'She was done with it, so someone had to.'

'You didn't try to get anyone else?'

Her eyes narrowed. 'You're asking if I would do to someone else what she did to me? If it were an easy curse to break, don't you think I would have broken it?'

My eyes went back to the golden stuff wound around the spindle. I thought of what Berchta had done, the magic she had worked with it to show the Witch her past and future loss. I thought of the misery I had seen in my time, and felt a shudder of gratitude that it was not my life on show.

'Are there other spinners? How far does your responsibility lie?'

It had sounded from Berchta as though the fate of the whole world rested on the wheel – but could that really be true?

'I don't know,' she said simply. 'I have never travelled too long from this castle. There is only so much thread the spindle can hold at once. I must return to tend it before the thread runs out.' The Witch looked sick. She indicated a notebook and pencil, and a series of measuring instruments that lay in a basket by the wheel. 'I try to understand it as best I can, measure the rate the thread is used up, the rate at which the fleece is spun, but after four hundred years I still know so little . . .'

'Your ledgers,' I said.

The Witch nodded.

She went to the window, looking out over the mountainside tumbling into a verdant spring green. 'No one taught me how to do this. They left me, and I had to work it out for myself. My stepmother was a true witch, I am only a pale imitation. I know how to spin the thread of time, and I know how to untangle it when it becomes snagged. That is all.'

'Is that not enough?'

She didn't answer me, and I wondered what tender wound I had pressed against.

I tried again. 'What happens if you do not spin? Will time stop?'

'Yes. We think of time as something immutable, inevitable . . .'

I thought of my rock samples, the vast eons of time measured out in mica and feldspar.

'But it is not. Summer follows spring because I spin it. Tomorrow follows today because I have kept its thread steady and even. Like any thread, if it is spun too thin it can fray and snap, become knotted or coarse. I untangle the snarls.' She went to the wheel and began to turn it, taking up the thread in her other hand. 'Here, I will show you.'

The wheel rotated at a steady pace, the spokes blurring into softness and the cloud of gold spreading out from the spindle over all of it, even the Witch, who was picked out in lines of yellow and orange like a sunset, like a field of marigolds, like honey or wine or sunlight on water.

I remembered my mother working delicate tufts of fleece into smooth locks of wool between two paddles as big as her hands and covered all over with metal pins. Then from this carded wool, she would do some magic I never fully understood, and connect the fibre to the old-fashioned drop spindle I carried with me still. A neat twist in the thread and soon she was spinning, the wooden bulb bobbing up and down as she teased her way from sheep to yarn.

It was all magic, I thought, in its own way. The mundane alchemy of craft work, turning one thing into another as much a miracle as the strange magic the Witch wove with her wheel. I looked at the Witch and the power in her hands. The power I had seen Berchta work, frightening and terrible and impossible.

'That is how time flows,' said the Witch. 'And I am its keeper.'

The wheel slowed, and she tucked up the slack of the thread. The fleece on the distaff was a little more depleted.

'What is that material?' I asked.

Her eyes went to the thin tuft of golden light then to me. 'The raw stuff time is made of.'

Before I could ask what that meant, she said, 'Get a stool, I have a long piece of work ahead.'

She gestured and there was a stool set against the wall that I had not seen before. I brought it to what seemed like a respectful distance.

'What do you want me to do?'

She gave me that wry smile again, full lip curling. I thought about kissing it, grazing it with my teeth, and quickly looked down, crossing my legs and squeezing them against the feeling that had flared.

'Why, are you not my companion? I want you to keep me company.'

Had it truly been that simple all along? Her companions were exactly what she called them: fellowship across the long, dark years of her work. I had lived in a place of ignorance and fear, and there were still things I did not understand but today felt like a peace offering. The companions were companions, and the bones in my garden were the inheritance of an ancient castle. And the Witch was my Witch.

As the wheel started turning again, a warmth spread through the room like sunlight breaking through the clouds, like a fire in winter, hazy and hypnotic.

'Go on,' she said. 'Tell me about your rocks.'

I roused from the strange trance the warmth had snagged me in.

'You've seen all my collection.'

'No, tell me about the *big* ones. Like in the hall.'

'You mean the mountain?'

She smiled again and my stomach rolled over. I wanted something that was too big to put words to. Something perhaps no one had ever taught me the words for.

I talked to her about everything I knew as she worked, speaking until my mouth was dry and still the stretch of thread didn't seem to have lengthened in her hand. I talked about anything and everything until finally she stopped the wheel, and we went down for a dinner eaten in blissful silence. I drank enough wine to give me the confidence to put my hand on her leg that evening as we read by the fire. The soft-and-hard feeling of skin and muscle under her skirts, the tickle of her hair in my nose, the light, breathless feeling of something teetering on the edge of happening. I *wanted* her.

When I touched myself in bed that night, I came almost immediately then lay there, hot and flushed and a little ashamed. Perhaps she did not lust after me in the same way. Perhaps I would seem so mortal and beastlike to her, my golden Witch. She never initiated anything, but hardly turned away when I did kiss her. I could not understand what it was she did want.

I took a supply of books to the Tower the next day, and a jug of water so I could read to her. When I ran out of pages, I told her stories: of my father's travels to Berlin, of the war with France, of Klara's engagement, of the time I had visited Nuremberg and eaten so much cherry ice cream I had thrown up red vomit and they'd rushed me to the doctor, convinced my stomach was bleeding. The Witch laughed so much at that story, she lost control of the tension in the thread and had to unwind a small section from the spindle, grumbling.

I asked her once if she would teach me a little magic but her expression went cold, and all she said was, 'I would never burden you with that, Mina.'

On the third day, I thought it was time.

'How old are you?' I asked, pausing in the middle of a fat translated English novel about a plain girl who marries a wealthy man but finds out his previous wife is still alive and locked in the attic.

The Witch spluttered. 'I thought the one thing a princess might have is manners.'

'Sadly I have been raised most shockingly.' I tried again. 'Your legend goes back quite a way.'

She shifted her weight, thinking. 'I am not quite sure how to count time here.'

I frowned. 'In what way?'

She was quiet for a while, and I thought I'd exhausted my opportunity for the day, but then she spoke.

'Imagine a spinning disc. The edge and the centre revolve as one, do they not? And yet the edge seems to move so much faster, to cover so much more ground in the same time. That is like me, here. I am at the centre of time, and you are out there, moving as I do, yet hurtling across so much more ground.'

I thought of the schloss with its anomalies, the door to last Tuesday and the room perpetually in summer in the kitchen.

'Is that why time works strangely in the castle? Are we too close to the source?' There was more I wanted to know – what of the maid in the kitchen? Why did she walk the castle at night? – but she had told me so much already, I would not tax her patience.

'That is how I understand it. The castle has been steeped in time and magic for too long, it takes on a life of its own here. The world bends around the wheel like a heavy weight. You will have seen it in the fabric of the castle, the way rooms shift and space does not obey the natural laws of the earth. Time affects everything, the earth, the seasons. What is it but a way to measure the world around us? And can we not measure time by the world? Time, space, they are two sides of the same coin.'

I thought of the way time was visible in the strata of a cliff face.

'I can keep the flow of time smooth beyond these walls, but here it is like how from a distance the sound of a bell comes from one clear direction, but stand directly inside it and the sound is all around you, no clear direction, only an overwhelming excess of noise.'

A sick feeling spread over me.

'Does that mean you will live forever?'

Her lip curled in disgust. 'I certainly hope not. I age.'

I furrowed my brow. 'But you age far slower than me.'

'I must have faith that this will come to an end one way or another.'

I let the unfinished thought lie between us. I knew she understood me.

I might give her my whole life, and yet for her it might be no more than a year taken off her sentence of solitude.

*

I came up with a new scheme for my life at the schloss: turning it into something resembling a home. I started with the great hall. The collapsed remains of the grand staircase still lay where they had fallen; we would need a team of people with ropes and chains to haul the great trunk beams away. I wrote letters to Munich and Nuremberg enquiring about tapestry cleaning and repairs, walked the perimeter with Wolf, dictating an ever-growing list of tasks: cracked flagstones, crumbling mortar, a smashed window, kingdoms of spiders and woodlice in the soft, rotting corners.

The vast crag of limestone that thrust up through the floor was quite another matter. It bisected the room like a wave rising to curl at the crest, brutal and unforgiving and inhuman. I circled its length three times, taking in the chiaroscuro flecks, the divots and runnels worn into its face when it had still been the exposed top of the spur, beaten and lashed by rain and wind and snow. It was a wild thing brought into the heart of the castle.

I loved it.

It would be a crime to break it up to flatten the floor, as would it be to grind down its harsh edges and polish it to an animal softness. No, it must be left as it was. All I would do was clean it.

So I did, the Witch coming to sit a little distance away with her ledgers monitoring the flow of thread and time, to watch me in amusement as I painstakingly worked my way along the rock with a soft cloth and bucket of warm soapy water, dabbing away centuries of smoke and oil and dust and mud to reveal the pale stone beneath. I could hardly say it glowed in its raw, matte form, but it was beautiful to me, a wide white line like the dash of a paintbrush through a gloomy landscape.

The Witch ran her hand over the stone, a complicated expression fracturing the porcelain of her face, then she came to me, ran the same hand along the shape of my jaw, my cheekbone, my brow, and she kissed me so lightly I could have imagined it.

*

A few weeks later and new flagstones had been set, walls repointed, the detritus from the fire cleared and the vast, crumbling tapestries carefully rolled up between crepe paper and taken away to be restored. The Witch and I sat in the walled garden, bare feet stretched out in the sun. The herbs were coming in well, and my little bed of peas and peppers and round fat cabbage heads. We were sorting through a box of flints I had found in one of the rooms on my survey, when Wolf came from the kitchen. Drying her hands on the cloth tucked into the waist of her apron, a stony expression was on her face.

The Witch stilled at once. 'Again?'

Wolf nodded.

The Witch got up, dusting the back of her skirts where she'd been sat on a rock. The urgency in her voice and the slowness of her movements were an unsettling mismatch.

'What do you mean, "again"?' I asked, but they both said nothing and went to the kitchen. I hastily repacked the flints, covering them with a piece of hessian, and followed.

I found them in the scullery, watching a maid washing dishes. My frown deepened.

The Witch was frowning. 'How long?'

Wolf considered the girl. 'Can't say for sure. Didn't see her go home last night or arrive this morning, then found her here. It's getting worse.'

'I know that,' snapped the Witch.

The girl was a narrow thing with flaxen hair and no chin to speak of; she wore the plain dress, apron and wooden clogs of any scullery girl, and her sleeves had been pushed up to the elbow to keep them out of the soapy water. Only, it was no longer soapy but brackish and greasy like sink water left to sit too long, and her arms were red; fingers, when they emerged with each dish, wrinkled like raisins.

Something grew tense in my stomach. I remembered the disturbing image of the maid stood silently in the corner of the kitchen room at night.

'What's her name?'

'Hanna.'

The Witch padded softly over the well-worn flags of the scullery to the girl. 'Hanna. Tell me: what you are doing?'

The girl turned, brows furrowed, then her face brightened at once. 'Oh! Yes, Frau Wolf, I have the loaves rising here.' She turned and walked past the Witch, Wolf and I to the other side where she indicated an empty alcove next to the fire used to boil water for the cleaning. She stood glassy-eyed for a moment, not registering the missing loaves, then turned again, going back to the sink. 'I'll clear these last dishes and go home, if it pleases you.' She put the clean dishes into the water and began to scrub again. I could see she had scrubbed them so many times the pattern had started to wear away.

'What's wrong with her?' I wanted to ask if it was the

same as what had happened to the maid that night, and why the Witch had been down there with her, but I did not want to interrupt further.

The Witch began to speak softly to Hanna, touching her temples, moving her hand back and forth as though pulling thread from fibre at the spinning wheel, working in the twist. Gradually, the fog seemed to lift from her face, the slackness of her expression shifting to a dazed blinking, like someone roused from a daydream. Hanna came back into the world, and drew her hands from the water, looking at them in confusion.

'I was washing the dishes.'

'And what a good job you did,' said Wolf, sweeping past and pulling Hanna's shawl and hat from the peg. 'We expect a quiet day today, so why don't you take the rest of it off?'

She helped a befuddled Hanna out the door and the Witch and I were alone.

'What was that?'

She looked at her own hands that had drawn whatever thread of time back into place, and the dishes on the draining board, pattern scrubbed clean. 'People get tangled sometimes, if they spend too long in the castle.'

Like the anomalies, too much raw time spilling out from the wheel.

'Does it happen to all the servants?'

'No. But many. I work through the night to fix any snags I can find before anyone is affected. But I cannot find them all.'

'Like that night in the kitchens? The previous maid?'

She nodded.

Horror flooded through me. I had thought myself jumping at shadows but a nightmare had truly been unravelling around me. That poor girl.

Another unpleasant thought struck me. 'Have I ever been . . . tangled?'

'No. When I bound you that first night the magic I worked conferred a little protection upon you, just as I have been able to protect Wolf. You sail through it like the storm can't touch you.'

She didn't say it as though it were a good thing.

The past months raced through my mind: the Witch pacing outside my door, the fear I had felt, never knowing she was not the source of it but my saviour. I thought of the day she found me in the bath – had she come to my room to work her magic and keep me safe?

She carried such a burden and I wished desperately there was some way I could share the weight.

I reached for her but she stepped away. 'Go back to your plants, Mina.'

I was dismissed. She went to her Tower and I went back to my garden and the abandoned box of flints. I didn't understand what had happened. She had told me how the wheel worked, but I could see there was more she held back. Something that made her unhappy.

I sat down heavily, deflated by her thorns that had punctured me. I had hoped we could hide in our fledgling happiness a little longer, but I knew it would fail at some point.

I thought of the bones buried beneath me, and all the questions I was still too frightened to ask. If the companions truly were just that, why had she kept it from me for so long?

I had sown the seeds of love in grave dirt; who could say what monstrous bloom would grow?

XVIII

I tired of the spinning after a few weeks; the Witch saw it, and ordered me out. She talked less and less as the fleece on the distaff depleted, her work to keep the thread steady becoming more delicate and demanding. I felt guilty slinking back down the spiral stairs, but I also knew that fighting with her about it would come to no good so I left her to her choice. If I had grown weary of it after only a matter of weeks, I could only imagine how she must feel after centuries.

I made it my business instead to make regular visits, bringing her newly plucked mint and sorrel from the garden, pears sliced so thin you could see a foggy window of the other side, tiny freshly baked buns studded with cardamon and cloves, cups of spiced wine on the final cold days before summer took root.

Some nights the Witch would follow me to my room and curl up upon my bed like a cat, twitching occasionally with a dream. She looked beautiful in sleep. The harsh lines of her old expression softened, and the curve of her ear peeking through her hair, the fan of her lashes against her cheeks, were fragile details that seemed so human for someone as impossible and wild as the Witch. I would draw a blanket across her and edge the bed warmer towards her feet.

That was the unexpected thing the Witch had taught me: the value of offering an act of care to another. I never pictured myself as the kind of person to take pleasure from cooking a meal or folding laundry, but then here with the Witch, someone who seemed to give those things even less regard than I did, I saw it differently. She had slipped so far from love that she didn't think to take care of herself; she walked barefoot through icy flagstoned rooms, ate sparingly, wore the same ink-stained gowns for days on end. She outright refused to take a moment of kindness for herself. It made me realise that I had been living like that too, in my own way. I had always known myself as a problem to be dealt with. 'Care' was not a word that meant something to me – if I ate, kept clean, it was to not be a burden. Seeing it in the Witch, the sadness of it struck me like a blow. I would care for her because I loved her, not because she was a burden or a problem. I would do the same for myself.

So I elbowed my way into the kitchen alongside Wolf, rolled up my sleeves and started to learn. I began with bread. Stodgy loaves I forgot to salt, with crusts like leather that were good for nothing but feeding the birds. I practised: I baked pies with flaky, buttery crusts, plucked armfuls of ripe cherries that hung heavy from the tree branches. I boiled up vats of jam in heavy pots, an easy, spiced mixture of fruit so ripe they split their skins.

'How did you come to work for the Witch?' I asked Wolf, as we stood side by side kneading dough.

I wondered what sort of half-answer I would get today.

'I came from the village to work in the kitchen,' she said, then surprised me when she continued. 'My husband died when I was still very young, so I needed work. Most who work here don't stay long. Most can't cope. But when I saw my mistress, I thought she needed someone to look out for her.' Wolf had stopped kneading, lost in memory. It was as though she'd forgotten I was there. 'Everyone else was too scared to notice, but I did.'

'How long ago was that?' I spoke softly, hoping not to break her from her reverie.

'A long time, I should think. In a place like this, you learn to stop counting in years.'

The kettle boiled, filling the kitchen with a piercing whistle and Wolf snapped back to herself. 'Get that off the fire now, you daft girl, or do you like listening to this racket?'

I did as I was told, pouring the water over a mixture of tea leaves and ginger to steep for a cake, holding close the small piece of the Witch's past I had been gifted.

At first I'm not sure she noticed the difference between the food Wolf had always delivered, and that which bore the mark of my hand – but she didn't remark on the poor quality of my work and that was praise enough. One evening she asked for a second serving of jugged hare and I flushed with elation.

I could not be with her every moment in the Tower – that would not do either of us good – but I could make my love known in other ways.

The rest of the time I was free to pursue my own interests. My garden was growing fierce and strong, an Eden of plants thriving in the rich soil and bright sun. I still turned up bones when I dug, found vines of pea shoots winding around ribs or knucklebones strung along a tomato plant. Everything grew so well, I couldn't help but think about what had fertilised this land. But it was like a madness had taken control of me, an infernal bargain I had struck to be loved. The more I found, the less I let myself see. If I truly thought about what was buried below, a door would be opened that could never be shut. The bite of an apple I could not spit out.

I knelt in a graveyard and told myself it was paradise.

The strangeness of time at the schloss made its presence felt even here. One morning I came to inspect my beds to find a row of kale greens shrunk down to their tiny, budding forms, as though they were growing backwards. On another day, a whole head of cauliflower so big I could hardly take it in my arms had sprung up in an afternoon. Perhaps the messy sprawl of time in the castle had spread. I saw these as benign mistakes, but Hanna the scullery maid never returned and when I asked Wolf why, she gave me a pinched look and said, 'For the girl's own good.'

I decided to use the castle's chaotic time to my own benefit. The summer room by the kitchens I used as a greenhouse to grow fat tomatoes and juicy strawberries. I found the room with the smashed windows was still banked with snow, and I wedged produce into the drifts, ready for whenever Wolf needed it. She seemed a little confused by this influx of supplies, accustomed as she was to carrying everything we needed up from the village and its market. I had found the room frightening before, but now I saw it as another oddity of the wheel's influence, part of this strange home I had come to love.

If I were to spend my life here, I realised I needed to rehabilitate the schloss's reputation with the villagers. I decided to start by selling my fruit and vegetables in the market. I harvested and dried the herbs from the apothecary garden, closely following along the book of herb lore I'd found in the Witch's library. Willow bark for pain and ginger for nausea were straightforward enough that anyone would buy or sell them, but some of the other things growing – foxglove for heart problems, saint john's wort for melancholy – might be less palatable. It occurred to me as I hung up bundles of herbs by the fire to dry, grinding some into powders or steeping in honey or sugar syrup, that turning up to a market peddling spells and potions, people might call me witch myself. I broke into a smile as I portioned up mint leaves to sell as tea for digestion.

I found out the next market day from Wolf, and packed baskets of goods to take down, along with a list of errands: find someone to limewash the disused rooms, a stonemason to look at a crumbling wall and a carpenter to consult about the woodworm and rotting beams. I rounded up the scant servants and gave them orders.

A couple of days before the market, I made a sweep of the castle to check there were no further errands I should add to my list. I left the Witch spinning with a wind chime I'd fashioned out of pieces of wood hung in the window for something like music to keep her company, and stared from the great hall that was now looking bright and clean, if a little empty while we waited for the tapestries to be rehung, and worked up past the summer room, our dining room, my bedroom, the winter room and the Witch's study, until I was drifting past rooms I hadn't bothered with since my arrival at the schloss. Here were the rooms of junk, the broken chairs and staved-in trunks, broken tennis rackets, spotted mirrors, moth-eaten curtains heaped up by cracked chamber pots. Perhaps I could get some of it mended and sold, or put to use in the many empty chambers.

In the room of travelling cases, I stopped. Like a stone in my shoe they had been a disquieting thought in the corner of my mind since I had found them. There they still were, the seven cases that could only belong to my predecessors, discarded like refuse. I dragged them into a line, and organised them from least decayed to most. Here was the history of the people who had come before me. The *men* who had come before me. Jealousy flared in my belly; the Witch hadn't *really* been alone, she'd had these men to keep her company for centuries. Perhaps she'd loved some of them, too. Maybe they'd known how to mind their own business and the Witch had liked them from the start.

I knew nothing good could come of opening the trunks, but I also knew I was going to do it anyway. Like picking a scab or drinking to excess, the allure was stronger than the fear of the consequences.

I knelt by the newest. It was only a little faded, battered at the corners and sporting a fine lock, engraved with the initials *E.H.* The date 1818 had been added next to the maker's mark. Edgar Hässler's case.

Naturally, it was locked. I looked warily at the other trunks, each with a lock or fastening of some variety. The second in line was smaller, more modest. Leather and camphor wood, with straps holding it closed which had grown brittle with time. I tugged at one, and felt guilt like mould growing inside of me as it snapped. Someone had locked it for a reason, shutting away the last of their life spent alone in this place, old age claiming them before they could ever leave. Or perhaps the Witch had been the one to lock their possessions away after they died. Packing away another life that had been over before hers.

I eased the strap off, and lifted the lid. Inside were stacks of neatly folded shirts and embroidered silk breeches and waistcoats of a style I recognised from portraits of my great-grandparents. They must be at least a hundred years old, handsome things well packed with mothballs between delicate linens and sheets of tissue that crumbled when I touched them. Men's clothes, as I'd thought. The only personal effects were a gold cross on a chain, and a small pair of wire-rimmed spectacles. I wondered who he'd been, how he had spent his solitude in the castle.

I opened the next trunk using my pocketknife to lever the crumbling wood apart, and found similar contents, linen underthings, breeches and this time sumptuous knee-length overcoats in velvet and brocade. There was a leather-bound Bible in English and dried-up pots of ink nestled amongst the clothing, and one threadbare quill. A writer, then.

The next three had been badly affected by moths, but I could see sets of clothes, smelled the sweat still soaked into the armpits and crotches.

The final chest was the hardest to open, its formidable lock waiting for some key centuries lost. I used the point of my knife to wiggle around inside the mechanism more in curiosity than hope, and was rewarded with a crunching and the lid separating. The chest walls had been lined in camphor wood, each item carefully folded and separated by cloth, astonishingly well preserved. Clothes I barely knew the name for, slashed doublets, wool hose and silk garters, all splattered in a dark, flaking stain like rust.

With trembling fingers I touched the stain; red, almost black with age. Blood.

I slammed the trunk shut and sat at a distance from where they were all lined up like a series of gravestones, each one a life run out.

*

Raised voices came from the study when I returned from looking through the trunks. I opened the door and found the Witch and Wolf at each other's throat before the fireplace. Wolf was red-faced and the Witch was dangerously still, a cold look I had come to fear.

'Mina. Go away.' The Witch dismissed me without looking.

'No. Stay.' Wolf rounded on me, all her stiff politeness stripped away. 'This started with you.'

I frowned. 'What started with me?' I looked to the Witch but she provided no answer.

'Wolf, enough. You have said your piece, now leave.'

'And how many more times will I have to say it?' She grasped the Witch's elbow, drew her close in a gesture of intimacy that surprised me, though it shouldn't have. Wolf had been the Witch's only confidante for more years than I knew. 'You are pushing yourself to the brink, spinning like this. There is only so much longer that this charade can continue. You must do it now. Please.'

The Witch's eyes flicked to me, then away. My presence was making her deeply uncomfortable. 'No. This is my responsibility. I'll manage it as I please.'

'This isn't about you *managing* things,' spat Wolf. 'This girl has addled your mind and I do not understand it.'

'Then perhaps it is not for you to understand!' The Witch's voice rose to a crescendo. 'You overstep.'

'I am *frightened* for you. I cannot sit silently and watch you hurt yourself like this. I care too much to allow it.'

I stepped forward, one hand raised in supplication. 'Will someone tell me what's wrong? If this is my fault—'

'It is not,' snapped the Witch. 'Keep out of this.'

Before I could say anything else, Wolf spoke again.

'I'm finished.'

'Good, then leave us and stop throwing a tantrum in my study.'

'No. I am finished with *this*.' She shot me a furious look. 'Either you do it, or I leave.'

The Witch paled, but held her ground, tilted her chin in a sneer. 'Don't bluff. You're not clever enough for that.'

'It's her or me.' Wolf was too calm.

'I won't be forced by some facile ultimatum.'

Wolf looked truly pained as she waited for the Witch to bend. But it did not come, as we all knew it wouldn't, and Wolf left the Witch triumphant and alone by the cold grate.

Once the door was closed, the Witch shook herself off like a bird smoothing its feathers, and took her place behind her desk. I followed her.

'What happened? What have I done?'

'Nothing.'

I took the Witch's chin in my hand, tilted her face to look at me. 'That argument was about me. Wolf is threatening to leave because of *me*. I know what she means to you. Tell me what I can do to make it right.'

A look of fear crossed her eyes and I faltered, fingers lifting from her skin. Then her mask snapped back in place and she sneered and said, 'She won't leave.'

I tried to shake off my disquiet. 'She seemed quite serious.'

The Witch pulled a ledger open and dipped her quill into the ink. 'She's not a prisoner. If she wants to leave, she can leave.'

I fell quiet. The Witch didn't look up from her figures, so I went to my chair by the fire, looked unseeingly at a paper on mineral deposits in the Rhine valley. My mind was filled with the image of the trunks all in a line. Wolf was no prisoner, she could leave.

But I could not.

I was the prisoner here.

And so was the Witch.

*

That evening the Witch insisted she needed time alone, so instead I went back via the door to last Tuesday, looking for a book that I had misplaced. It was quiet in the study, no fire in the grate and the day outside pallid and lifeless. The book was nowhere around my desk, so I looked over at the Witch's – I had spent enough time with her now that I was familiar with its chaos. It felt like a lifetime ago that I had been hidden behind the settle, spying on her reading a letter rimmed with black. I wondered again who it had been from.

I moved the papers aside with the tip of my finger in idle curiosity. Half the surface was taken up by her ledgers, the pages covered in spidery figures tracking her work on the wheel. There were a few pieces of correspondence with the names of politicians in Bavaria and Austria, even as far as Prussia and Luxembourg, all discussing her work in the most abstract terms. The newspaper headlines were full of Bismarck and unification and the expansion of the railway, something that felt a world away now. Perhaps it would come to affect us someday. Time spun on and we could not hold it back.

There, tucked towards the bottom, was the letter with black edges.

I shouldn't. I had promised.

Though I knew about the wheel now. Surely that promise had outlived its necessity.

I thought of that day I had seen her receive the letter and how distraught she had been. My Witch, bent and broken with grief. And I thought of Wolf's accusations that the Witch was making herself miserable on my account. If I knew what had hurt her, perhaps I could know how to comfort her better.

I eased the paper out. At its head was a coat of arms that

seemed familiar; it took me a moment to recognise it as similar to the crest that had been hacked from the wall above my fireplace.

Frowning, I read on.

It was a short message, in the firm hand of a clerk.

. . . I write to inform you of the death of Konrad von Hohenfeld, last of the Hohenfeld line. With no living relatives, the estate will pass to the branch line . . .

Hohenfeld – I had heard Berchta say the Witch's full name: Holda von Hohenfeld.

I sat down heavily. No wonder the Witch had cried.

There was another letter with it, again lined in black, writing of irregularities in the accounts, a daughter from centuries ago whose line could not be traced. The missing daughter was the Witch. It summoned her to Vienna. This was what had taken her away from me.

Perhaps this was it. This was the reason the Witch had kept me at a distance, refused to talk to me of the past companions. They had died on her, one by one, and now her family was gone entirely. Every last person she had ever been connected to.

And yet, I thought of the bones under the earth in my garden.

The bones at the base of the Witch's Tower.

Edgar's unsent letter.

The blood on the clothes.

Wolf's demand for the Witch to *do it now*.

There was some piece I was missing. Like a trick eye

puzzle, the answer was hiding in plain sight, if only I could let myself see.

*

At breakfast the next day, Wolf served nothing. Instead she arrived in a travelling cloak, carrying a small bag.

'Have you changed your mind?' she asked.

The Witch folded her arms. 'No. Have you?'

I looked between them both, unsure and uncomfortable.

'I see.' Wolf's face was a hard line. Her hand tightened around the handle of her bag in the moment before she moved, but then she rounded on me suddenly. 'What is it she sees in you? I do not understand.'

'*Wolf.*' The Witch's voice was as sharp and warning as a blade.

'You are nothing. Just a girl. But you have torn *everything* apart.' Wolf sneered. 'You have no idea what she puts at risk for *you*. I have half a mind to drag you up there myself and—'

In the space of a breath the Witch appeared at Wolf's side, hand around her throat and teeth bared.

'Do not. Threaten. Her.'

Wolf's eyes bulged wide, rolling wildly to see the Witch.

'Stop it.' I stood so abruptly I knocked my chair to the floor. 'What are you doing? Let her go.'

The Witch snarled, and dropped her.

Wolf recoiled, a hand pressed to the red skin of her throat, and said with a hoarse voice, 'You are courting disaster.'

The Witch stalked to the other side of the table, dropped down in her chair and examined her nails in a show of disinterest. 'I am courting acute boredom. You've said your piece, so go if that's what you want to do.'

Wolf pursed her lips, but took up her bag and left without another look at either of us.

The Witch refused my company again that day, but when I pressed my ear to her door I heard the soft sound of sobbing.

∗

At dinner, I was distracted. I did not know where Wolf had gone, and the threat that ran beneath their argument had put me too on edge. The Witch had arrived late, looking more exhausted than usual, and with a wary, hunted look in her red-rimmed eyes. I had visited her in her Tower briefly to deliver lunch and found her hunched over the wheel with her calipers and tape measure, examining the thread wound around the spindle, biting her lip so hard a drop of red blood beaded at her teeth.

In the end, she spoke first. 'What's wrong?'

'Nothing.'

She took a sip of red wine, staining her lips dark. 'You don't have to tell me but I'm not spending my evening like this.'

What could I say?

The Witch loved me, but I knew that love would only stretch so far. She had loved Wolf, in a different way, but that had not saved her. There were things I could do, questions I could ask, that would snap that love entirely. I wanted to stay where it was safe.

What I didn't know had no power to hurt me.

I took a long draught of my own wine, letting it sting down my throat and warm my belly. 'There's nothing wrong.'

When we retired to the study, she took up her viola and stood by the window, skimming the bow lightly over the strings as she learned the fingerings of a new piece of music. May was in full bloom, a low, warm moon hanging above the forest and the smell of jasmine and pine sap drifting in on the breeze. I watched her play, the supple movements of her fingers across the instrument, and felt a flare of that heat again. I wanted to put my mouth on her throat, tongue the delicate skin there, nip at her jaw, grip her waist tightly and keep her pinned like an insect so she could never leave me again.

What had her other companions thought of her? Had any lusted after her? She was beautiful, after all, and to a young man her cruelty may have been no deterrent.

A young man – I thought of all of them as young men; though they must have spent their whole lives here, I had never thought of them as growing old. What was it the Witch had said? *Their lives ran out.*

The Witch played a sour note and the bow screeched on the strings. I frowned.

The puzzle before me was shifting, like a kaleidoscope blurring from one pattern to the next, and soon I would understand what I was looking at.

The Witch threw the viola down in frustration, then dropped into her chair, head in her hands. Today she wore another flimsy dress, black silk cut on the bias with a plunging back and a high neckline like a slash across her throat.

I touched the delicate bones in her wrist. 'Do you want to talk about Wolf?'

She had come down from her spinning increasingly irate lately and I wished I understood enough about her work to help solve whatever problem it was she had.

'Holda, tell me.'

At that she stiffened, raised her head, eyes flashing.

'That is not my name.'

I tried to touch her hair in apology, press a kiss to her cheek but she pushed me away.

'That hasn't been my name for centuries.'

She rose again, pacing before the fire. Her blackened soles, the cracked nails, seemed all the more horrifying paired with her delicate dress, as flimsy as a shift. She looked like a thing of fairy tales, something wild and cunning disguised in silks. I remembered the first time she had come to my family's home, the way she had sat in my father's study like a panther I had seen in the Berlin Tiergarten, all coiled action and whip-sharp reflexes. A predator biding its time.

'Call me what I am. What you have always known me as.'

My mouth was dry. 'Witch?'

She sneered, pleased at my guess. 'As they know and fear me across the land. That is more who I am than that girl. She never got to find out who else she might be.'

I reached for her again, and she drew back sharply. The threads between us were so fine, so fragile I didn't dare test their strength any further.

I let my hand fall. 'Perhaps you could find out now who else you could be. With me.'

'You don't understand.'

'Then tell me.'

'Mina.' She cupped my face in her calloused hands. 'Stop digging. You will not like what you find.'

My cheeks burned too hot and I felt as though she could see my transgression writ plain across my face.

I said nothing more and we salvaged something of the evening, but I spent each moment watching her from the corner of my eye.

I had to know. Whatever it would cost me, I had to know.

XIX

Market day transformed the village into a bustling centre. While I was not welcomed, neither was I driven away; everyone had their own business to attend to. I tacked myself onto the end of the row of sellers, spreading out a piece of tarpaulin on the road and laying out my herbs and barks and teas and powders. I had wondered if I might see Wolf, if she remained in the village – but I saw nothing. Whether she was here or not, I was hardly someone she would want to seek out.

After so long in the isolation of the castle, the market was overwhelming. Everything was on offer: travelling tinsmiths parked their carts to mend pots and cobblers sat outside their shops to patch soles; tailors sewed buttons and haberdashers sold ribbons and reams of lace; butchers skinned glossy rabbits and farmers unloaded crates of potatoes and cabbages and spinach; spinsters came with bags of dyed and raw yarn and chandlers sold bundles of tallow and wax candles. Like pilgrimage to a shrine, people from up and down the valley and beyond, farmers and crofters and foresters, had all made their way into the village perhaps for the first time in a month or more.

Most ignored me. But curiosity or ignorance got the better of more than one, and I had a slow but steady stream of women buying painkillers, fever tonics, teas for colicky infants and infirm elderly relatives. More than one crossed themselves before and after dealing with me, but I sold my wares all the same.

It was an uneventful day, marked only by a goat getting loose from its tether and running through a stand of turnips before being caught – the lesser disaster of the baker burning a batch of loaves – and the dressmaker carrying a vast bolt of velvet through the crowds like the pied piper leading half the townswomen behind her. After my fraught evening with the Witch it was almost a relief to do something so mundane.

By mid-morning, half my goods were gone and I bought fresh kartoffelpuffer and bratwurst to eat for lunch, spending some of the coins I had gathered in a show of goodwill to the rest of the stallholders. I was dipping the sausage into a pot of mustard when a woman came up to me carrying a baby on her hip. I thought she looked familiar, but so many of the women had the same work-hardened aspect, wore the same dark dresses and stiff aprons.

'How much for the snakeroot tea?'

'For fever?'

She nodded, and I gave a price that she only haggled with briefly before digging coins from the purse tied to her belt. The baby wriggled and she dropped them, struggling to bend down and balance the infant.

I reached over a bundle of dried lavender for the coins and had a flash of déjà vu.

No, not déjà vu. This really had happened already. This morning, she had been my first or second customer, asking for snakeroot and dropping her money. I stopped, sat back on my heels.

'Did something happen to the last batch?'

She looked at me blankly.

'You bought snakeroot tea from me already this morning.'

I looked closer and saw the glassiness to her eyes, the way they were focused somewhere behind my head. I thought of the scullery maid scrubbing the pattern from the plates.

I picked up the coins as I had done that morning, counted out her change and gave it back to her along with a twist of tea.

'Thank you.' She put the tea and coins in her pocket and left without another word as the baby began to wail.

Just as it had done a few hours ago.

I put the lid back on the mustard and wrapped up the remains of my meal, a slow dread creeping over me. Did the strangeness of the castle stretch this far?

I thought again of the Witch coming from her spinning wrung out and miserable, the work so delicate and demanding.

Something was wrong with the wheel.

Steadily, the same trickle of customers came to my stall, bought the same things and left in the same order as they had come before. A snag. I considered the possibility of a coincidence, that I was mistaken in recognising the same people. The goat became loose again and even then I tried desperately to find a way that this wasn't happening. The

Witch said the binding spell had conferred a little protection on me, but how long would that last if the tangle grew vast?

The bread got burned, the dressmaker carried her bolt of velvet past the stalls and then the woman was back, baby on her hip.

'How much for the snakeroot tea?'

Just like Hanna, that same vacant expression. I stayed silent and she nodded, reaching for coins I hadn't asked for. They dropped, I picked them up and gave them back to her.

When she left, I packed my goods back into my baskets and walked the length of the market road. If I hadn't known, I would have thought everything was ordinary. Of course everyone was ignoring me: I was the Witch's companion. But they ignored me even if I spoke to them. In desperation I tried wilder and wilder things, clapping my hands right in front of one woman's face, brazenly taking a piece of strudel from the bakery, even slapping one man as my panic grew.

The Witch had told me the dangers of her work not running smoothly but to see the effects in person was more frightening than I could have imagined. The unnaturalness stung like nettles, prickling unease. The need to do something, anything, to stop it.

Like mechanical figures on a clock, the people around me replayed the same moments over and over: the burning of the loaves, the goat, the velvet. At first I had thought myself outside of the snag, immune to its snare, but in a moment of sick realisation, I saw that the Witch's protection had faltered and I had been caught up in it too. Clapping my hands in front of the woman's face, stealing from the bakery, slapping the man, my body like a puppet I couldn't quite control.

I ran faster, breathing harder, a scream building up inside me I couldn't find the way to let out. This couldn't be happening. *Bread*. This couldn't be real. *Goat*. The Witch wouldn't let it, she wouldn't let me drown like this. *Velvet*. My Witch loved me. *Clap*. She would come for me. *Steal*. I had to believe she would come for me. *Slap*.

A soft hand pressed against the side of my face, the scent of juniper and mint, and something gold and shimmering rose up like a veil lifting. The Witch stood over me where I was crouched in the street, arms wrapped around myself like a shield. My face was wet – I had been crying, but I didn't remember. I couldn't remember.

'You're back. You're back.' She stroked my hair, held me as I shook. My body came back to me, the world coalesced into something tangible beneath my feet. A fat fly buzzed past my head and above clouds scudded across the sky.

I whispered, 'Never, ever let that happen again.'

'I won't. I promise.'

The Witch led me to a tree stump and I sat, head between my knees, unwilling to watch her circle the market, weaving time back into shape, rescuing us all from our prisons. After an age, I realised the market sounds had moved on. There were conversations happening around me that I hadn't heard before. I lifted my head in tentative hope, and found no Witch, only a normal day rolling on as though nothing had happened. A man stopped by me and my baskets of herbs.

'Do you have any snakeroot?'

I shuddered, snatched up my things and hurried away, followed by his frustrated voice. The Witch, I found at the far end of the market where the houses gave way to forest and cliff curling up to the castle. She was slumped under a silver birch, as pale as its peeling bark and so still she could have been part of the forest itself. Her eyes were closed, sunk deep into her skull and smudged around with bruises.

I knelt, touched her knee to rouse her. All my anger and fear slipped away. She hadn't meant to hurt us, and she had tried her best to put it right. I helped her up the hill, her arm around my shoulder, mine around her waist to support her home, her weight heavy and warm at my side. I had never thought of her as fragile, but I saw now that she was. She was just a woman, like I was.

With no Wolf to cook for us, I scratched together a meal from the antiquated kitchen, bringing a bowl of salty chicken broth and thick flat noodles up to the study, where I lay the Witch out on a sofa and covered her with a blanket. I helped her spoon it into her mouth until she held up a hand: no more.

I put the soup away and sat with her quietly.

'Tell me what happened.'

She looked at her hands, at the callouses on her fingers from centuries of working the wheel. 'You saw. A loop. The loops are a snag, the most common kind. Imagine a cloth woven from thread: that is the world around us. There can be dropped and twisted stitches, flaws in the warp and weft. Time is everywhere in everything. Not only the passage of your day, but in the passing of the seasons, the ripening of fruit.'

I knew it well. I had seen how time was marked in the rocks beneath our feet and the oil burning in our lamps, the hair growing from my head.

It was everywhere, and so everything could go wrong. Like the human body with a myriad of ways to fail and function.

The horror of the wheel and the Witch's responsibility struck me anew: the scope of disaster that lay waiting.

'I thought your work on the wheel prevented this sort of thing?'

I couldn't help but fear for myself. Whatever magic the Witch had worked to keep me safe had failed.

'I'm spinning the thread too thin. It keeps breaking, snarling.'

I thought of the small tuft of golden fleece left on the distaff.

If the loop in the market was what happened when the thread of time was spun too thin, what would happen when she ran out of fleece to spin at all?

'Can't you get more material?'

The Witch searched my face, a look of anguish making her appear all of her four hundred years. Then she sighed, closed her eyes and sank back into the cushions.

The candles burned down and the moon, a distant, winking disc, took to the sky, but she didn't say a single word.

*

It was as though once she had admitted she was running out of fleece to spin, time slipped its leash entirely.

It became a game the castle played with us.

Walls didn't shift, staircases stayed fixed, but still the

schloss became a labyrinth I was forever racing to learn to navigate before the route changed again. When a section of the kitchens became unstuck from the present, the door to last Tuesday was the only way I could get to the ever-summer room to tend my tomatoes and cucumbers, though it meant always working a week behind where I thought I was. The snowy room I had turned into an icehouse was a little more accessible, but it required a route skirting around the long gallery, which had become stuck in a five-minute loop at midnight, the bells forever chiming in the old grandfather clock. The Witch had snatched my collar and dragged me back just as I had been about to go in and inadvertently trap myself in a frantic five-minute gaol cell. After the Witch had to disentangle three maids in three days, all remaining staff and workmen had been dismissed from the castle. The Witch spent all her time in the Tower, spinning, or holding her calipers to ever-dwindling thread. When I brought her tea or soup, I caught glimpses of ratty, floss-like thread fraying around the spindle, and only the smallest wisp of fleece on the distaff. The Witch hunched in concentration as she fed onto the spindle filigree strands of golden light as fine as dew and cobweb. The warm golden glow had faded and it seemed as though the Witch spun nothing but air and hope. She turned me away when I offered to stay with her. I was no longer forbidden from the Tower, I simply wasn't wanted.

Instead I began to patrol the castle, making note of the more minor snags and putting up signs to warn of the most dangerous sinkholes. I visited the village too, watching for any loops or other indications that the problems were spreading.

There were minor things – fences that wouldn't stay mended, felled trees that regrew overnight – but nothing as horrifying as the loop that had swallowed the market. In the castle, I was frustrated to see the work I had put into the great hall peel away like a discarded rind. Flagstones refractured, dust and dirt accumulated in the corners at a frightening rate, and the newly rehung tapestries unmade themselves, stitches unfurling, thread fraying, the chaos of their bloody battles collapsing into ruins. No matter how hard I had fought to make the castle a home for us, I was never better than King Knute, commanding the tide to turn back. Time was against me, and it was a battle I would always lose.

I thought of Berchta showing the Witch what happened when time unravelled. Of the fine, fragile spiderweb thread the Witch eked out in her Tower.

I couldn't help thinking time was unravelling now.

If anything, my Witch's decline was more rapid than the disintegration of the castle. She wore a dirty shift days in a row, the hem ripped and cuffs stained, her hair was a greasy nest, tangled and wild and her beautiful face was gaunt, hollow-eyed and chapped-lipped. I sent her to bathe, brushed out her hair and washed it, brought fresh clothes from her rooms: a strangely long corset and a sensible skirt and shirt. If she meant to work herself to the bone, she could at least do it clean and suitably dressed.

Before she could disappear into the Tower, I looped her arm with mine and led her from the castle.

'You need fresh air.'

'I *need* to spin. What part of "duty" don't you understand?'

'What part of "exhaustion leads to deadly mistakes" don't *you* understand?'

She grumbled, but let me lead her on a gentle path overlooking the river, leaning on me heavily as though she drew strength from the warmth of my body against hers.

The Witch had insisted on going barefoot, no matter how much I lectured her on the stupidity of such a move. The more I insisted, the more stubborn she became. I loved her for it, and wanted to shake sense into her at the same time. At first the going was easy as we crossed soft, mulchy forest floor where the only thing to prick her comfort were stray pine needles carried down from the mountain top, but then we came to rockier ground and she moved slower and slower, hissing and cursing under her breath.

We stopped to refill our waterskins at a slow-flowing stretch of river. 'I told you to wear shoes.'

'As there is no use in reminding me now, I can only presume you say this to gloat.' The Witch was sat on a flat-topped rock, examining the filthy soles of her feet. I was not sure how she might tell if there had been any damage done given their usual state, but then I saw a flash of red, a single drop welling up before she brushed it hastily away.

'You're hurt.'

'No, I'm not.'

'I can see you bleeding,' I said in exasperation.

'It's a scratch.'

'That can easily become infected. You might be stubborn, but I know you are not stupid. Let me look.'

I knelt before her and examined the rough skin. The Witch

looked away, something stormy in her face. As I had thought, despite the calluses and rough, weathered skin, something had sliced through and a bright trickle of blood stood out.

'We'll need to clean this, and bind it. Moss will do until we can get you home.'

'I'm fine.'

'You should take better care of yourself. I know you have been on your own a long while but that doesn't mean you should neglect yourself. Let me—'

'I said *no*.' She yanked her foot so hard out of my grasp I lost my balance and landed on my behind. 'Stop interfering.'

I lost my temper. 'I try to look after you and you act like I've committed some heinous crime. What is wrong with you?'

'I do not need someone like *you* to look after me.'

'Someone who cares about you?'

That silenced her.

'You're worth caring about,' I said. 'That is what I think, and you cannot change my mind, however nasty you are about it.'

'Stop it. Stop being so nice to me.' She scrubbed at her face with her hands, as though trying to scrub the expression from her features. 'You have no idea who I am or what I have done, so you cannot have the first idea what I do or do not deserve.'

I took a step closer, hands held out and open. 'Then tell me. What did Wolf mean? What is it I'm doing that hurts you?'

She shook her head. 'Nothing. You're not doing anything. It's all me. I make my own misery.'

'If you tell me, maybe I can help.'

The way she looked at me then, I saw all four hundred of her years. 'Mina . . .'

'I mean it. I would do anything for you.'

The Witch looked at me darkly. 'Promise?'

I placed her hand across my heart. 'I promise.'

XX

A blizzard blew in, shocking and wild for June, freezing my pea shoots and smothering my strawberries. The road was quickly swallowed up, a white line snaking from schloss to the village; the forest lasted longer, the rich valley of green slipping leaf by leaf into white.

Time was losing its grip on the seasons.

The Witch watched the snow from the window, a deep line of worry between her brows. I would do anything to take that misery away from her but she would not tell me how. She spent less time spinning now; I wondered if she had run out of fleece on the distaff entirely. I thought of what the Witch had said: time was everywhere, in everything. The loops were only the start of how it could unravel.

I banked the fire and brought us up a hot pot of coffee, a jug of cream and a tray of springerle biscuits and Lübeck marzipan stamped with the towers of the Holstentor city gates. I pulled the Witch from the window and pressed a cup of coffee into her hands, stroked her hair back from her face and kissed her temple.

Dusk came quickly with the snow cloud smothering the

sun. I took my regular route through the castle, noting the shivering ebb and flow of time. I confess I was growing anxious. I had faith that the Witch knew well how to tend the wheel, but the more the world began to fracture the more I felt doubt creep in. I did not understand the problem she faced, and for the first time I began to think that perhaps it was one she could not solve. I bolted doors and closed shutters against the icy wind, then returned to the study, face stinging with the warmth and feet numb in my boots. The coffee was still on the tray, undrunk, the biscuits untouched. A feeling of trepidation came over me.

'Witch?'

I couldn't see her in the study, or through the open doors to her bedroom.

I pulled off my gloves and scarf. 'The coffee's getting cold.'

Slowly, I walked the length of the room, even checking the half-hidden door that corresponded to the door to next Tuesday, but nothing. One window in her bedroom had blown open, and a shower of snow covered her dressing table. I latched it hastily, closing the shutter and brushing as much snow clear of her things as I could. I had only been in her bedroom to wake her when Frieda had set the fire. I had pried into too many things; I had meant to at least leave her this.

Her dressing table was as curious a collection of things as I would have expected. Exquisite modern settings with delicately cut jewels, fat paste gems on thick rings, ornate, baroque necklaces, earrings so heavy I would be afraid they would rip my earlobe, old pieces in desperate need of polishing, dull pearls and fleur-de-lys curls losing their shape. Combs and brushes, empty pots of rouge, creams, eau de toilette. And amongst it, a small box half open, inside a small collection of rings, too large for her hand. Some simple bands, some ornate. Men's pieces.

Rings from the fingers of dead men.

I shut the lid firmly.

A lull fell in the howling wind and I heard the smallest noise, a snuffle: someone crying.

I followed it to another table, this one larger, where a jug and basin were set out with a washcloth. The Witch was under it, curled into a ball. I crawled under with her. Her face was splotchy with tears, knees drawn up to her chin and hair stuck to her cheeks. Gently, I teased them free, tucked the errant strands behind her ear.

'I span and span,' she mumbled.

I dabbed her cheeks dry with the cuff of my dress.

'There's nothing I can do.' She looked at me then, eyes bright with unshed tears. 'Please believe that I tried.'

I smiled because I didn't know what else to do. 'I know you did.'

The moon was poor illumination, so I fetched a taper and lit the candles in the sconces. It still didn't seem enough, so I brought in all the candle holders and candelabras from around the study and lit them, arranged them along the mantelpiece, her dressing table, by her bed, on the washstand, any spare surface I covered with glittering light.

Then I brought in the biscuits, found a jar of preserved cherries, put the coffee to warm over the fire. Her rough hands in mine, I drew her out into the open to see what I had done.

She turned, taking in her bedroom transformed and me at the centre. 'What did you do?'

My face fell. 'You don't like it?'

Her eyes glittered like the candlelight reflected in the mirrors, and I saw she was about to cry again.

'It's beautiful. Thank you.'

We sat cross-legged on the bed, the plate of biscuits between us. I split one up and fed her small pieces.

'Here, you need sugar. My mother always said . . .' I broke off. I hadn't thought about my mother for a long while, how she would sit with me while I ate a stack of lebkuchen at Christmas, asking me questions about myself. I had always thought it was a happy memory, but I saw now that she only needed to ask me all those questions because she didn't know me at all. She had dropped in like a guest, enquired about my progress until her duty was done and then she had drifted away again into her own world, turning back in on herself. 'Never mind what my mother said.'

I let us sit in silence, snapping biscuits in half so we could share the comfort. When the coffee was warm again I poured us two cups, folded her shaking hands around the warm china and wished there was something I could do. But I knew there wasn't. People didn't work that way. You couldn't think their thoughts for them or do the work of healing on their behalf. Whatever she was trapped in, she would have to come through it in her own time. All I could do was stay with her in the darkness, witness her suffering and not turn away; that was one gift I could give.

When the biscuits were gone and the coffee was finished, I

still sat with her until finally, in a small voice she asked, 'Why do you love me? I don't understand it.' Her voice was barely above a whisper, hoarse from crying, but I could hear every word like crystal. 'Why would someone like you want to be with someone like me?'

For a moment I didn't say anything, thinking. Then I left her alone on the bed as I fetched the basin and heated a jug of water on the fire until it was warm enough, poured it into the bowl and brought it and a washcloth to the side of the bed.

'Give me your feet.' I held out my hands.

She licked her lips, pink tongue flickering, then slithered around so her legs slipped out from beneath the cloud of nightgown and those two filthy, dirt-encrusted feet were before me. I had shied away from them so many times, looked at them in disgust from the first moment I met her. I thought they made her animal but I understood it differently now: they were her hurt made manifest. They made her human.

'I don't understand love,' I said, submerging the cloth in the water. 'I don't know how it works or what it is for. I've read poetry and novels and listened to music and viewed art all about love but it was like another language. I thought it must be something that wasn't meant for me. Until I met you.'

There was a soft intake of breath but I didn't look up. Instead I drew one foot towards me and began to run the wet cloth over the sole in long slow strokes.

'I understood what hate was. I hated you at the start; you were rude and cold and cutting and whatever bargain I thought I had made to escape my loneliness turned out to be so much worse than I'd feared. But I also came to understand that loneliness isn't a fixed state. We think rocks don't change, that the mountains around us are eternal and unmoving but it's not true; they are in constant metamorphosis. Worn down by the elements, melted by fire and gouged by ice.'

Slowly, pale, rough skin was showing through, calloused from so long barefoot, and some of the dirt was embedded, like the sole of a shoe. When I was done, I wrapped it in a dry towel and looked up at her.

'Loneliness can be something other people do to us, and something we do to ourselves. Sometimes we don't know anything different; sometimes we've been so hurt, we like the familiar pain of self-inflicted isolation better than the pain of abandonment we've been taught to fear. Sometimes we think it's the only place that will have us.'

She was looking at me with an expression I couldn't begin to read, my baffling, infuriating, lonely Witch. I took her other foot, dipped it in the water then began to scrub a little roughly.

'I hated you because you made me so lonely, when that was what I had been hoping to escape. Until one day, I realised I had got it the wrong way round: I hated you because you meant I *wasn't* alone. At least in isolation the only person I had to deal with was myself. Other people are the most difficult thing in this world; they think and do things you have no control over, want things you can't understand. But other people can also be salvation. You offered me a new idea of myself, if I would let you.'

The water was murky now, the cloth almost too filthy to remove the dirt.

'Around you, I forgot those familiar lonely paths and found

myself four steps towards you, tangled in the undergrowth and yelling.'

She smiled at that, a curl of her lip I would have called a sneer before but I saw it differently now.

'*You* made all that fight worth it. You, who are so clever I want to read through every night to catch up. You, who are kind in the most unsuspecting ways. You, who are the most brave and selfless and resourceful and steel-spined person I have ever known. I am in awe of you. I don't understand love. I don't know what it means, but I think it means some of this, at least. So: I love you. Not for anything you've done for me, but because you see me. You truly see me. And I see you.' I dried her foot, and got up on my knees to kiss her cheeks where they were wet with tears, kiss her eyelids and her hands. 'I love you.'

I held her as she cried a little longer, tangled together on the bed with June snow falling outside the window.

When she was done I took one of the candles, gathered the used plates and let myself out. 'I'll let you sleep.'

'Mina.' She said my name softly, like a prayer. Like an incantation. 'Don't leave.' The Witch was sat in the shadows of her bed, white nightdress and black hair pooled around her, eyes bright in the dark. A flare of heat in my gut.

Desire was not something I had an easy relationship with.

Would I be safe, desiring?

I saw then that the real question was: was I safe with the Witch? Did I trust the Witch?

I pressed the door shut with a soft click and joined her on the bed. We were silent, two figures painted in light and dark.

What had started months ago when a wild beast had stalked into my home and bound me to it, ended here.

'I love you.' I had said it before. I said it because it was true.

I thought she might say it back. There was a moment that hung pregnant between us, her lips parted, my weight poised to move. Then she lifted her nightdress over her head and bared herself to me.

I couldn't breathe.

She was white like snow, white like death save for the filagree of veins and arteries that ran along her inner arms, the fragile skin of her inner thighs, her breasts. My eyes followed the line of her leg up, the branches and roots of her blood until I saw dark hair and I looked away, blushing.

Then I looked back. She had offered herself to me, after all. She wanted me to look.

She reached across the bed and took my hand and placed it on her breast. It was such a small gesture but so utterly, painfully intimate I almost couldn't bear it.

When I didn't do anything, she let my hand drop, softly said, 'We don't have to do this if you don't want to.'

'No.' I shook my head. 'I want to.'

Her mouth curled. 'Oh? Show me.'

So I did.

I had little idea what I was doing but that didn't seem to matter. I took my clothes off and she helped me, unbuttoning and unhooking and untying, until I was only in my corset. She fit her hands around my waist, tracing the sharp inward curve of the boning, then she kissed the tops of my breasts where they spilled over, kissed up to my throat, the vulnerable point beneath my jaw, kissed my mouth as she unlaced the back so I could slip out, my shift going with it, and then I was full flush against her, body to warm body. The kiss grew fiery, she was soft and sharp, the curve of her breast, the jar of her knee against my hip, my hair tangled in her hand.

We lay down in the candlelight, her skin hot and smooth beneath my hand and I let her show me what she liked. My mouth open on her neck, hand between her legs, the soft, wet slick of my fingers rubbing and sliding. She moaned, nails dug into my back, leg hooking around mine. My Witch. I moved my mouth to the crest of her breast and worked my tongue in mirror of my fingers between her legs and she shivered then locked up stiff, keening into my hair and I moved faster, firmer, chased her as she writhed until it was over, and she lay limp, panting, our hearts racing.

When, after a moment, she lay me on my back, my breath caught. When she kissed her way down my chest, my thoughts unravelled. When she parted my thighs and dipped her head between them, my heart stopped.

Desire was falling off a cliff, and trusting you would not die. Desire was walking through fire and being reborn. Desire was an undoing. I was undone.

XXI

I woke with the end of the snow.

As quickly as it had come it vanished again, and soon the summer sun would be sending rivers of snowmelt coursing through the forest and the village. I rose softly, the Witch still sleeping beside me naked in a tangle of sheets and sweaty hair stuck to her back. Heat flared in the pit of my stomach again but I pushed it away; there would be time for that later. We had a lifetime left together, I hoped. I stretched, cracking the bones in my neck and back, squatted over the chamber pot then pulled on a discarded black nightgown of the Witch's and wandered in to the study. I was ravenous for breakfast after the night before. I felt wrung out physically and emotionally. But the Witch and I were together. Whatever was wrong with time, whatever challenge she had to face we would do it side by side and for the first time in months – years – I felt hopeful for the future.

The view from the windows behind the Witch's desk showed the valley, still limned in snow but with summer green flaring up from all directions. Perhaps I would go walking today. Her desk was as messy as ever, papers and letters and memos tossed around like the sea in a storm. On top was a notebook with its spine snapped, falling open at a half-finished page. I had never seen this on her desk before. I recognised the Witch's writing, but it was scrawled like someone in a hurry – or someone chasing too-fast thoughts. I saw the word *time* and the word *broken*. And my name.

Frowning, I sat down, pulling the book towards me to read.

. . . It's running out . . . I have spun thinner and thinner and now there is only a thread as fine as spider's silk, so fragile and yet so much weight upon it . . .

. . . I know what I must do but I cannot I will not I refuse. Please please don't make me do it I beg you oh God please let me keep Mina . . .

I skimmed forward until I found my name again.

. . . Sometimes Mina looks at me and she seems so happy I want to pick up a carving knife and stab her through the heart. How can she be so happy with me? How can she be so happy when I have to choose between her and the world . . .

. . . I span the last of it today. There is only a scrap of thread around the spindle now and no way to make more. Edgar is gone, his life used up like so much fleece become yarn. Now we wait and see what time will do with nothing to spin . . .

I dropped the book with trembling hands.

The companions who left no trace. The bones at the foot of the Tower. The wheel that span something golden and vital.

The kaleidoscope shifted, the pattern coming into shape.

Edgar's *life*.

'What are you looking at?'

The Witch came yawning from the bedroom wearing only a black silk dressing gown, lightly tied so a strip of ice-like skin showed from navel to throat.

'What do you spin on the wheel?' I asked. My voice was something alien to me. Cold, distant.

'I told you: time.'

'But what is the material? The act is to spin the thread of time, but what is that thread made of?' I had stood up, I didn't know when, putting space between myself and the words I could not ignore.

The Witch glanced to the book open before me, a horrified look spreading across her face. 'What were you reading?'

'Your diary. Or maybe your records? I don't know what you call this.'

I expected her to snap at me, but she said nothing, only stood as still and lifeless as a statue.

'I think it is made of a life.' I snatched at my thoughts like darting fish in a pond. 'I found bones in the garden at the bottom of your Tower.'

'Mina.' She said my name, but didn't know what to say next. I saw she was crying.

I paced the room as though I could outrun my thoughts.

I didn't want to look at what was right in front of me. It was too horrifying. I had too much to lose.

I loved her too much.

'Is that what I am to you?' I asked. 'A life for the wheel?'

'No.' The Witch shut her eyes, face crumpled in pain and fear and a deep, crushing despair.

'That is why you take someone every fifty years. Their life only lasts you so long, and then you must replace it. I am such a fool that it took me so long to see it.'

The problems with time, the diminishing fleece on the wheel. It all felt so obvious. I had been summoned to the castle as the wheel's next meal; it was only love that had blinded me from the truth.

I was a fool for love.

'Stop it. Please stop,' said the Witch.

'You don't deny it.'

She slid to the floor, covering her hands with her face.

I didn't know what to do. Even though all the pieces were there, some part of me still refused to believe it was true. I didn't want to lose what I'd thought I had with her.

Beyond the windows, a flush of autumn leaves had swept through the forest canopy. I thought of the wheel in its Tower, the last scraps of thread on the spindle.

'What will you do now?' I asked. 'Were you going to tell me the truth? Or feed me to your wheel unknowing?' In a flare of anger I picked up the book from her desk and threw it. 'Tell me!'

A darkness gathered in the room like the snow had returned, all scent and sight of spring seeping away and a relentless pressure ringed my head.

The truth was out. Her options had narrowed to one.

My Witch opened her eyes.

My Witch was gone.

She rose as her mask slipped into place, the mask of the monster the world thought she was, the wicked witch who held time like a whip she could wield. The cruel curl of her lip, the sharpness of her teeth.

'Oh, Mina. Dear stupid girl. Now you see it. I would say I was surprised it took you this long to work it out, but that would be to call you intelligent. You spent so much time prying into my business, but you had invented a fairy tale for yourself: a lonely witch who would love you if only you broke through her defences. If no one was coming to rescue you from your dismal, small life, then at least you could imagine yourself to be the rescuer.'

I stumbled back, palms sweaty. This was more than the caustic, cold Witch I had first known. For the first time in too long, I remembered why I was frightened of her.

'Stop it,' I said, voice shaky. 'Stop being cruel. This is not who you are. I won't believe it.'

She crossed to the fireplace and rested her hand on the sheath of the hunting knife, ignoring me. 'Do you really think I could love you back? You are a stupid, plain, mortal girl who collects rocks like a child and understands more about trees than people. What is there in you to love, tell me?'

I tried to ignore the sting of the blow. I knew this was a front, the story she had to tell so she could steel herself to do what she had done seven times before. I knew she met pain with anger, lashed out like a cornered animal.

'You don't mean that,' I said. 'I read your journal; I know you don't want to hurt me. You would have done it already if you did.'

I thought, for a moment, I saw her falter. A look of pain flashing across her face.

Then she snarled, 'You don't know the first thing about what I want. You think I haven't tried to find another way? You think I haven't spent four hundred years in this castle *desperate* to find a way out? The world doesn't care what we *want*. You're stupid and trusting and you still haven't learned the truth of the world. It is cold and brutal and love is a word that is hollow.'

The knife hummed as she pulled it free.

'What will it take?' Her voice broke. 'Do I have to kill you for you to believe me a monster?'

It might have been a trick of the light, but for a moment I thought I saw her eyes glimmer, wet with tears.

'Let me help,' I whispered.

'The only way you can help is by feeding yourself to the wheel and saving me a fight,' she sobbed. 'I am the evil Witch in the castle. Your mistake was forgetting that.'

'Please. Holda. I love you.'

Blade flashing, she raised her arm and bared her teeth. I stumbled towards the door, keeping a chair, a sofa, a cabinet between us, and she mirrored my movements, circling me like prey.

'You are *nothing*. You are meat and I am the butcher.'

She bounded forward, hurdling a couch and I scrambled back, wrenching the doorknob and flying into the hall. Behind me the Witch gave a yell of frustration.

I ran full pelt, feet slapping on the boards, going nowhere but down, down, towards the great hall and the grand doors to the courtyard and the gatehouse and the bridge over the chasm into the forest, waiting every moment for that knife to bite into my side, her breath as hot on the back of my neck as it had been last night.

I knew she didn't mean a word of her cruelty, but I also knew she had faced the same dilemma seven times before and there was only one choice she could make. She could love me, and it would not be enough.

But no hand closed around my nightdress. I reached fresh air, bare feet on flagstones and the last of the sudden snow; I stopped only once, on the other side of the bridge to look back at the schloss. It was as cold and bleak as it had seemed the first day I arrived. The Witch's Tower loomed above it all, and squinting, I saw something move in the window. The flutter of dark hair around a pale face.

My stomach lurched and I threw myself headlong down the winding road to the village.

As frightened as I was, a thought lodged in me and I carried it away: she had let me go. The world hung in the balance, and she had let me go.

SUMMER

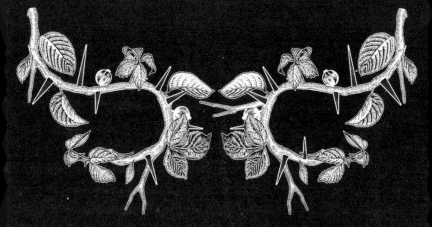

XXII

Something, somewhere, crunched, and I opened my eyes.

A hedgerow blocked out the sun, behind its leaves a brilliant blue June sky. Cursing, I heaved myself out of the ditch I had bedded down in for the night. The noise had been an approaching cart rolling over a dead branch on the valley road to Blumwald.

I ached. I ached all over as though I had been beaten with a poker, and now was stiff with too many hours asleep in the wrong position. My stolen clogs had rubbed a blister down the sides of both feet, and my stolen dress pinched under the arms. I fled in only a nightdress, and had to make do with whatever I could steal from laundry lines.

In the village, everyone turned from me. They would not help the Witch's companion.

I wondered then, if they knew. I thought of my father's fear when I had returned to visit.

He had known the Witch would kill me, and sent me to my fate anyway.

There was no one coming to help me, and no one I could ask for aid.

All I had was myself.

As always, I was alone.

I walked as hard and as fast as I could to start, still feeling the ghost of the Witch's fingers closing around my arm at any moment. I walked through the night, blessed by a full moon that followed me along the cart tracks. I walked three nights and days before I came to anything like civilisation and I wondered how I would ever find my way back to Blumwald.

Did I mean to go back?

I knew what I risked by leaving the castle.

Without another life fed to the wheel, the Witch would have nothing to spin. Time would collapse, then stop altogether.

It would be the end of the world, and I had left her to face it alone.

I shook the thought off and kept walking.

When I had finally broken out of the Witch's valley it had been like rain after the baking heat. Broad fields planted with barley and hops spread across the valley floor, between it the silver ribbon of the river and the meandering path of the road. From the shape of the mountains and the position of the sun, I knew the way to Blumwald. I walked, numb to the pain in my limbs. I knew this: the swing of my arms, the ache of my thighs, the rise and fall of my chest. *This* was home.

Any hope of a life with the Witch had been a delusion. There was only one way it could ever end.

Cracking my joints, I levered myself out of the ditch and chased after the cart to flag it down. I bartered the earrings I still wore for a ride in the back with its cargo of beets and goat fleece heading for Blumwald. In my bedraggled, dirt-stained state no one would recognise me as the duke's daughter; I was just another road-worn girl working her way to the capital. I was nothing.

You are nothing. You are meat and I am the butcher.

I shuddered and buried my face in my hands. I could not let myself think about it. I was miles from home and there was no space to break yet. I pinched the insides of my arms, pressed my fingers against my eyes until the tears stopped. All around me the smell of beet and earth and goat was overpowering. At the front of the cart, sitting beside the farmer was a girl, no more than ten or eleven, who had a hank of wool in her lap and a drop spindle that she worked like a toy. My mother's drop spindle still lay among my things in the castle, lost to me forever.

I lay down on a sack of fleece, head pillowed on my hands and watched the thread grow between her fingers, the spindle twisting at the flick of her fingers, as we bumped our slow way towards the old home I had fled.

'Good God!'

My father dropped the blueprints he was holding up to the sun. He wore his summer linen, muddy boots set firm in the foundation trench that had been dug for the new railway station.

'Mina? What are you doing?' He climbed the ladder out, followed by a retinue of servants.

Halfway to Blumwald I had seen the cuttings for the new

railway track begin, a wide swathe of land stripped bare and dug out in preparation for the laying of sleepers and steel rails. I had hopped off the cart before we got to the city walls and walked through the shantytown that huddled around the edges. Half the clapboard houses had been torn down already to make way for a new road from the gates to the station, and the dig was racing ahead in the fine weather.

'Hello, Papa.' My voice was hoarse from lack of use. How long had I been walking now? A week?

I heard the whispers starting already, like they had before:

. . . escaped the Witch a second time . . .

. . . companion returned . . .

Let them talk.

They had all sent me to my death without a moment's hesitation.

My father stopped an arm's length away, still too awkward to cross the boundary to intimacy, even now.

'You're back again,' he said.

'I am.'

'Well, then.' He glanced around his advisors and servants then back at me. 'Let's get you home.'

I followed him to the carriage and allowed the seat to be covered with a travelling rug before I sat on it with my dirty clothes, and was driven all the way to the Summer Palace, dazed and silent. I thought of the Witch. Was she in her study now? Did she look out at this summer sky as I did? Or had summer been lost to the chaos of time unravelling where she was?

It was a short journey to the palace over cobbles that shook the carriage.

My father pulled down the blinds over both windows.

'It's time to tell me what happened,' he said, and it was the softest I had heard his voice towards me for a long while.

I looked at my hands, scored with dirt and sunburned. My fingers were long and slender like his, but squared off at the tip like my mother's. Pianist's hands, she had said when I was little and my father had loved to listen to us play together.

What *had* happened?

'I found out the truth,' I said simply.

He sighed. Leaned back on his seat and pinched the bridge of his nose. 'I had hoped you wouldn't.'

I felt strangely calm. I knew I should be angry with him, or upset, but I felt neither. Only this muted, heavy sensation. Too much had happened and I felt sapped of my ability to feel any more.

'It is a secret passed between each duke. A solemn duty. One you must not share, do you understand? If the people knew what the Witch truly had power over . . .'

That was why he had been so frightened of the Witch when she came. Why he had been ready to let me go.

'You knew, and you sent me with her anyway.'

'Yes. I am prepared to do whatever I must do for my duty.' The line of his jaw was set tight, no warmth or gentleness in him.

I looked him in the eye. 'You let me go to my death.'

He held my gaze; the duke sat opposite me, not my father. For the first time, we sat together as equals.

'Would you think differently if I had married you to a

distant prince, sent you alone to a strange land and seen you perhaps only once more in my lifetime? Every parent sends their child out into a life they cannot guarantee will not be short and difficult.'

I thought of him that day in his office, concerned with his conference and Bismarck and making this *problem* go away. So he had. Me, and the Witch, out of the way.

This was not home.

We stopped outside the city walls, traffic halted in either direction as a path was cleared for the royal escort.

He had told me before what he thought my duty was. My oath to the Witch.

'You think I should have let her use me.'

His silence gave his answer.

Then, with a small shake of his head, he said, 'What's done is done. She will find someone else.' His finger tapped against the window frame in an uneasy beat.

The thought of it made me sick, but it was all we could both hope for. The wheel needed a soul or it would be the end for our world. All I had done was exchange my death for another's.

We reached the palace and the carriage crunched over gravel as it pulled up to the steps.

'Tell me one thing. One thing, and I won't ask again.'

He nodded for me to proceed.

'Do you ever think of my mother?'

For the second time that day I had surprised him. The carriage felt too small, we were folded in together in a way neither of us had ever been comfortable with.

'I see a lot of your mother in you,' he said. 'Less of myself.'

I thought of my mother withering in the palace under the weight of her own complex moods. I thought of her days in bed, her flares of passion and her slow, miserable death.

'She was like you. Content with books, a small, quiet life. Her reading glasses, the armchair by the fire. That is how I still think of her.'

'My mother never wore glasses,' I said.

He frowned. 'Did she not?'

'*I* do. She didn't.' She was never content. She never liked her small, quiet life.

He had never known either of us.

'Did you want me? After Mother died, did you still want me here?'

There, I had said it. The question that had plagued me for years. It lay between us like a fish caught from the river, slick and squirming and grotesque.

And I realised it didn't matter what he said. Whether he had wanted me or not, it would not change the way he had treated me.

'No. Don't answer.'

When I moved to leave, he stopped me.

'I loved you and your mother.'

'Loved,' I repeated. 'Not love.'

'That is not what I meant.'

I unlatched the door. 'Yes, it was.'

He held up his palms in a gesture of surrender. 'I'm sorry that's how you feel.'

I was tired. I was so, so tired.

He didn't follow me out of the carriage, and I knew, now, never to expect anything from him again.

✳

The rumours worked fast, expanding like a river with snowmelt as I was passed through the palace, greeted by Klara shrieking and pointing and hugging, my stepmother looking close enough to faint, before being plunged into baths, hair combed, clothes stripped, body scrubbed. By the time I was clean, all the city knew what had happened to me better than I did.

Wrapped in a dressing gown, my feet took me to my old room, unthinking. Inside it was empty. No, that wasn't right – it was full of furniture, a bed, clothes press, washstand and desk – but everything of mine had been stripped out.

My stepmother appeared with a pair of maids carrying a storage chest.

'We redecorated,' she said, pointing to the mint green wallpaper in a modern Aesthetic style. 'Do you like it?'

I stared around at the alien space. It was like I had been scrubbed out of existence. Just as after my mother died, and she had been cleaned away like a layer of dirt.

'Of course you can stay here,' she said indulgently. 'I haven't finished hanging the paintings, but if you like you can decide where they go.'

'Thank you,' I said mechanically. 'Where are my clothes?'

The maids opened the trunk and I saw my dresses stuffed in with their skirts crumpled and lace crushed.

'I'm sure you understand we did not expect you to return – again,' she corrected herself.

If my father had told her the truth about the Witch, and the fate he had sent me to, I didn't care. I had been betrayed too many times to feel it.

'It was the only sensible thing,' she said. 'We needed the space.'

I thought of the vast palace and all its unused rooms. I thought of the women I knew of who had lost children, and left their rooms untouched in memorial.

I wondered what mark I had left here. If any.

I was dressed and my hair dried and put up, and the world moved around me like I wasn't really there. There was to be a dinner tonight to celebrate the miracle of my return. I had tea with my stepsisters, went out onto the balcony to be witnessed by the city, was checked by a doctor.

My visit before had been brief, but enough to reignite the town's unease. Now I was back for good, fear raged like wildfire.

I had been a sacrifice to keep the rest safe. What now?

No one was safe.

If only they understood just how much danger I had placed us all in, they would have tied me up and carried me back to the Witch themselves.

Perhaps my father was not so uncaring, in that light. He could have done much worse than simply treat me with dispassion.

The dinner was large and lavish. The best part of a year had passed since I had last sat at this table. A year since I had lived as the daughter of the duke. The building of the railway station was toasted alongside my safety, a sea of red faces and sideburns and silk gloves all drinking to a girl they didn't know.

I was the centre of attention for a short while. Curiosity about my escape overcame their trepidation; was she *truly* a witch? What dark magic did she weave? What horrors had I seen? I could have told them countless things that satisfied their want for darkness, but I clammed up. The story, good and bad, was mine. The *Witch* was mine. Sharing it with these carrion birds was like pouring water into a leaking bucket; no matter how much I gave, it would drain away and I would be left empty. So I fed them drips, never enough to satisfy. They turned away from me in the end and I excused myself from the table as soon as the last plates had been removed. My route took me past my stepmother's chair, and I heard a snatch of what she was saying to the Generaloberst seated next to her.

'. . . Of course now there's the matter of role here. My girls have made such good matches, I'm quite at a loss what to do with a girl like *that* . . .'

I was a miracle no one wanted.

✳

I went to bed for a week, and nobody stopped me.

After my triumphant return, no one seemed to know what to do with me. The novelty of my escape had worn off rapidly, and increasingly I was greeted by outright hostility. Klara's wedding was only a few weeks away and my stepmother seemed to occupy every space with preparations; dressmakers and cooks and florists and an army of servants being marshalled for the celebrations. Else would travel back for the wedding, and Johanna had already returned, pregnant again as the emerging matriarch of a dynasty.

I slept in the ugly shell of my old room that my stepmother had put her stamp all over, like a dog marking its territory against a tree. With me gone, the family she wanted had been complete. I had always thought of my stepmother as benignly negligent, more dispassionate than wishing me ill; now, seeing myself scrubbed from the palace like a bad memory, I was starting to change my mind.

The me who had lived with the Witch would have done something about it. The me who had tried to turn a haunted, miserable castle into a home. The me who had tried to love a beast.

You are nothing. You are meat and I am the butcher.

So I slept, and slept, and no one bothered me about it. Sometimes when I woke there was a tray of food on a console table, sometimes there wasn't. The long summer days stretched out in a glowing, warm-washed eternity of birdsong and sweet-scented breeze. I hated it. After everything that had happened, I had expected to cry, to wake from nightmares. Instead, I was numb. A lump of fat and bone and hair lying in sweaty, ripe-smelling sheets staring blankly at the canopy of the four-poster bed.

I heard my stepmother tell the maids I was resting after my ordeal, but I knew what I was really doing there: hiding. Like I had been when I had first met the Witch in the stables. I was hiding from the choices I had made and the life I could not seem to escape. I had risked everything to go with the Witch, yet here I was less than a year gone past and nothing changed.

And I hid from the truth: I missed the Witch.

I rolled over and pressed my face into the pillow and all I smelled was soap and feathers and sweat.

After everything she had done. After everything I now knew, I still missed her.

But it was over. She was gone.

I left my bed eventually because if I didn't get up of my own accord no one else would make me.

I called for a bath, scrubbed myself clean and spent an hour washing my hair and combing all the tangles out of it, then sat in a sunny window with my hair spread out around my shoulders to dry. While I waited, I cut my nails with a tiny pair of scissors and worked cream into my hands. Then, I dug through the chest of my old things the servants had brought down from the attic to find something appropriate for the weather. It was hot and sticky, and I had eaten well with the Witch and spent less time hiking so my body had changed. My thighs were perhaps a little slimmer and my waist thicker, but I didn't care. It was the body that the Witch had held on that last night we spent together. It was the only thing I had left with any memory of her. Her, who I had loved, not the monster I had seen at the end.

The black nightdress I had fled in had been ruined by the time I got halfway home; I'd walked in it, slept in it, used it as a cloth to carry food once I'd found other clothes, mopped away sweat and mud, stemmed bloody scratches and torn it in half to wrap around my blistered feet in their clogs. It had been taken off me at some point when I'd been brought back to the palace, and burned, I assumed. I had nothing left, not even a scrap of lace. The last link to my Witch, gone.

My books and papers and walking gear had all been packed away as well, so I took myself up to the attic to hunt them out. Rafters arced above broken furniture, smoke-damaged paintings and the clutter of generations. For a moment I thought of the castle, of the seven trunks lined up from each of the men before me, and of my things still scattered throughout my room.

I found my old things thrown in to a crate haphazardly, books under water canteens and a knapsack. Beneath a too-small pair of walking boots, I found a doll my mother had given me, its porcelain face cracked and muddied.

I had forgotten about this gift. I was too old for dolls when I unwrapped it one Christmas Eve, and I hid my disappointment as my mother looked on in hope; it had only been another sign she didn't know me. Now, all I saw was her love. She had tried. She had missed the mark, but still she had tried. That mattered. I carried the doll back to my room and did what I could to repair it. The dress could be washed and sewn up, but I wasn't sure how to repair the crack in its face.

It was the height of summer, but I felt cold. It was the coldness of an empty room, a grate long lacking a fire. I longed to walk again, to climb to the crest of the mountain and breathe large, touch soft leaves and coarse rocks, but I couldn't find the energy to go. The forest reminded me of the Witch now, and if I climbed to a summit, I would only be looking for her valley.

So I went to my mother's grave, doll tucked into my pocket. Weeds had grown across the stone casket and a winter's worth of moss caked the lettering. I plucked wildflowers to lay by her head and tidied the creeping dandelions and grasses.

All the while I cleaned, I kept my back to the trees, and the memory of the Witch.

XXIII

In the approach to Klara's wedding a July heatwave was in full force, bearing down on fields to wither crops, browning grass and drying up streams to a trickle. The church was to be dressed with flowers, but they were crisping in their beds, draining of colour before my stepmother had a chance to order them cut and arranged. There were hothouse flowers still in bloom, at least, watered and tended by her gardeners, and the menu was swiftly changed to a chilled soup, ices and sherbets swapped in for stewed fruit.

I welcomed it. The turn of the seasons was the only proof I had that the Witch still eked out the last of the golden thread. She would take another victim, I told myself. Another soul would feed the wheel now. The guilt that troubled my sleep was no more than I owed.

Klara grew more fretful; all of us were impatient and bad-tempered from lack of sleep. The heat that made thinking foggy turned night time into a battle for at least a moment's rest. I took to sleeping naked by the open window on a bed made up on the floor. I didn't care any more if the maids came in and found me. Everyone knew me as Witch-touched now, tainted with the madness of seasons spent in the presence of magic. It would be no stranger that I slept naked than it would be if I began to howl at the moon.

But when we woke the week of the wedding, the heat had vanished. A pale sky, fuzzy with cirrostratus, looked over a world fresh with dew so cold it was almost frost. It wasn't completely strange for July to turn cool, but there had been no break in the heat, no thunderstorm as we had all expected.

The crops that had struggled in the drought had no respite, freezing in the soil before any rain came. I watched the farmers' carts roll into the market only half-full; negotiations over sacks of grain turned sharp, and water butts around the town were at a low ebb.

I thought of the sudden snowstorm that final night in the castle, how time let slip its grasp on the seasons, and shivered.

I had seen Frau Hässler only once, when I shopped for new gloves for the wedding and passed at the far end of their street where it met the cathedral square. Her house was dark, shutters barred tight and no smoke at the chimney. A young woman, her blonde hair in a long braid down her back, stepped out from the dark of the cathedral, helping Frau Hässler, smaller and more bent over than before, across the threshold. For a moment, I considered going to her. Frieda had been right about everything. If I had listened to her, I could have saved myself so much pain. I owed Frau Hässler an apology. No – far more than that. But I didn't want to see what my actions had done; I didn't want to see how her grief had doubled. I asked amongst the servants later and found that her grandniece had taken her in after Frieda disappeared. Frau Hässler hadn't spoken another word since.

The wedding rolled forward with guests arriving from all over the newly formed German Empire, Prussia in the north and Bavaria in the south, from the Austro-Hungarian Empire to the East, Bohemia and Slavonia, and even one duke from Denmark whose lands had been swallowed up by the Empire and was keen to prove himself German.

I kept to the margins, knowing the best place for me was where no one had to notice me. A smart dress had been retrieved from storage and with a little tight lacing I still fit into it. Klara looked beautiful, as she always did, her shining chestnut hair pinned up with diamond stars in the style of Empress Elisabeth of Austria, and her bridal gown was sewn from white silk embroidered with silver. I didn't often envy my stepsisters, but I let myself sit with the feeling as the service continued, the thought of how it might feel to be loved so widely, to know everyone had come together for you.

I covered my eyes with my handkerchief.

It was a pleasant service, the church packed with guests from both sides of the match and at the wedding breakfast after it was easy to seem present while hovering at the edge of conversations. I drifted along the surface like a pond skater, smiling and making polite small talk, while any part that was truly *me* was very far away.

I was brought back to myself when the crowd parted for a moment and I saw Klaus, tall and a little stooped over and talking animatedly to someone. My father's secretary that he had hired instead of letting me help him.

Klaus spotted me too, and joined me.

'Your Highness. I am glad to see you safely home. I am not

sure I understand where it was you went – witches are not a thing I believe we still have in Berlin.' There was a note of amusement in his voice. 'But it seems a good thing you have returned.'

'Thank you. It is . . . pleasant to see you too.'

He was as I remembered. A little dishevelled, a little earnest. I assumed my father found him a useful aid if he was still here. I considered him again, a year older and my heart a year more battered. If I was to find a place here, then I could do worse than Klaus. Perhaps if my stepmother pressed me on my plans, I could mention his name. It would be marrying beneath my station, if I were any of her daughters, but I'm sure no one would mind me tidying myself away.

'We were all so thrilled to learn someone had escaped that awful place in once piece!' A woman had joined us, petite and pink and yellow, her blonde hair braided in a crown around her head and her cheeks rosy from wine. 'Klaus, do introduce us.'

He pulled her to his side. She was short enough to tuck neatly under his arm, like they were a paired set. 'May I introduce my wife, Maria?'

Of course. A wife. It had been a long time after all. 'How do you do?'

She took my hand and curtseyed and I remembered I was the duke's daughter still, someone to be deferred to and held at a distance.

I took all my sick, cold feelings and swallowed them. 'Thank you. If you will excuse me,' I said and slid away while I could still stay polite.

I made it all of ten paces before my stepmother swept me up with a sly smile and a firm hand on my shoulder.

'Mina, there's someone I'd like you to meet.'

I was led across the hall and presented to a wizened woman in the heavy petticoats of early in the century, before the crinoline had taken on the work of spreading skirts wide; her grey hair was in tight ringlets on either side of her face, a lace cap tied under her chin and an ear trumpet in her hand.

'Here we are, Gertrude,' said my stepmother loudly. 'This is the girl.'

I was pushed forward so her rheumy eyes could assess me.

'She's a good girl, aren't you, Mina?'

I didn't know what else to do so I nodded.

Gertrude squinted at me again. 'Oh, very well then,' she said and my stepmother drew me to one side.

'That went well!'

'I'm sorry, I don't follow.'

She folded her hands. 'We thought this might be more . . . to your inclination,' she said delicately and my cheeks burned.

There was no way she could suspect what I had felt for the Witch, what I had done with another woman, but the images flashed through my mind all the same. The curve of her bare shoulder, the Witch's hair in my mouth as I kissed her neck, the weight of her breast against my hand. I coughed and lowered my face.

My stepmother continued, 'I don't want you to think we have forgotten about you, your father and I. We've spoken on it and thought you might like to return to the position of a lady's companion, as you volunteered for it previously.'

Volunteered for – she meant being sacrificed as the Witch's companion. Was she still telling herself I had been away as a lady's companion? I looked past her to Gertrude, who was now clutching a crystal glass of sherry.

'I . . . will think about it.'

I couldn't bring myself to ask if she and my father could make a match for me. I had no desire to marry some strange man, but it was something else to be given up on entirely.

My stepmother patted my shoulder. 'Good girl. Now I know you won't give your father any bother. He works hard enough as it is, he doesn't need a flock of women giving him more to worry about.'

I gave her a bland smile, and said, 'Of course.'

The party continued without me. I walked through the French windows onto the rolling lawn behind the palace. The moon was showing pallid in the daytime sky, a tissue-thin disc behind the clouds and sun like an uninvited guest. But night would fall, and the moon would have its time. Over the edge of the palace wall, I could see the clock tower of the church, its face as broad and blank as the moon above.

I frowned. The hands were frozen at twelve. I looked around uneasily. Had they been moving that morning?

I stayed outside, watching the shadows shift over the terrace like a sundial, hunting for the passage of time in any place I could find.

I thought of the night I had spent on the palace roof between the Witch binding us and my departure with her the next morning. If time was to snag up like a pulled stitch, it

SUMMER

could do worse than holding me there forever, to always be on the cusp of escape, and never disappointed.

✳

The next morning, Klaus had vanished.

I had slept uneasily, waking more than once to fumble for my watch to check whether it had stopped. At one moment, I thought I heard a cry, the sound of a scuffle, but my watch ticked on and no doubt there were many revellers abroad. Somewhere before dawn I slipped under too deep and woke groggy and disorientated.

My watch had slipped from my hand and its face was cracked. The hands were still.

Swallowing a wave of fear, I rose and dressed and left to join breakfast, for once urgently desiring the company of my stepfamily.

That was how I found Maria.

My route down passed her and Klaus' room; the door was open and I saw her inside still in her frothing white nightdress, hair hanging over her shoulder in a thick plait and her face splotchy with tears.

'What happened, tell me.' I took her hands and drew her to sit on a velvet footstool in her bedroom but she resisted me, continuing to pace before the window.

'It took him . . . It took him . . .' She kept saying the same words over and over, as though a thought started that she could not bear to finish.

'It took him what?' I could not understand her meaning.

Only half the bed had been slept in, but his top hat was dangling from the back of a chair and his shoes were all lined up by his case. If he had gone somewhere, it would have been barefoot.

The window sash hung at an odd angle, as though it had been wrenched within its frame, and one pane was cracked. The rug by it was scuffed up, and an unlit lamp was overturned from the bedside table.

I frowned, thinking of the cry I had heard in the night. 'Does he have any friends he might visit or business to attend to?'

Maria didn't reply to me, only pacing, muttering to herself. The girl was in shock. I rang the bell for someone to bring tea, but there was no response to that either.

Anxiety swelled into fear.

I took myself to the kitchens to see why no one had responded to the bell. It was as though a hush had fallen over the palace. No birds sang outside, no breeze stirred the curtains. The kitchen was steaming hot with breakfast preparations, moving like gears and cogs in a machine, a great repetitive working of kettles hissing, knives chopping, plates clattering. The cook stood at the range, stirring a pot that had long since boiled dry. A scullery maid stacked and restacked the same dish. Another wiped a mop over the same shining flagstone.

I knew what I was looking at: a loop.

I stumbled into the scullery and vomited into a sink.

No. Please, no.

This was my fault.

I had fled from the wheel, and the Witch had no life to

spin. Again I had shut my eyes to the truth: the Witch must have a sacrifice and I had denied her one. She had not been able to take another. I was the one she had bound, it was my life destined to feed the wheel.

Time was unravelling, and it was my fault.

I scrubbed my eyes dry, took long slow breaths until I felt like my arms and legs were my own again, my body something I could move, and then I set to.

Klaus was the piece here that didn't fit, but I had a suspicion.

It took him.

I had heard it as the start of a sentence, but it was complete.

It took him.

She took him.

Maria still paced the bedroom, unseeing. The loop had caught her entirely. I studied the room, the windowsill, the doorknob, the carpet, his shoes. And I found what I was looking for. Dirty footprints beneath the rucked-up rug could have many owners, but these came from bare feet, not shoes. By the windowsill where a nail stood proud of the casement, a snag of black lace.

She had been here. The Witch.

I wondered if she had come here to take me back, and changed her mind. Or perhaps she wanted me to know what I had made her do. My heart felt like a stone, a heavy, jagged lump of basalt pinning me down. I could not let someone else go in my place. Not Klaus with his bright future and distraught young wife.

And not my Witch.

I would not let her stain her hands with blood again. She had been a child tricked into this duty, shackled to the wheel alone for too long.

If there was a chance I could save her, I would take it.

I sat another moment more, working the scrap of lace between my fingers, reckoning with my fear. Something of her to hold on to. I was alone here at the palace, but that was not new. That loneliness I feared, the meaninglessness, the unwantedness, it had already happened. I could try to fight and hold it away forever, or I could grieve what my life had been, see it for what it was, and stop being controlled by the fear of it.

The Witch had given me good memories to hold alongside the bad.

She was worth saving.

I felt light. Certain.

The worst had already happened. Nothing I did now could undo everything that had come to pass. All that I had felt – all there was, was to accept it. Mourn it.

And leave it behind.

I was not afraid.

XXIV

From my father's stables I took his strongest, fastest horse, threw some food and money into a knapsack and walked to the edge of the city.

I rode as fast as I dared: it could be a long journey ahead and I didn't want to risk tiring or injuring my mount. Following the river-road, I worked along the valley, marking the days as I slept in hedgerows and bought oats and hay from passing farms for the horse. It had taken Frieda months of wandering through the forest to find us; if the Witch didn't want me there, I knew the castle would make it fiendishly difficult for me to reach it.

In the end, it proved easier than I had thought; all I needed to do was follow the glitches in time – the women drawing bucket after bucket from the well, great trees shrivelling into saplings, a stream running backwards. Like poison spreading from a wound, the tears in the fabric of time branched out from the Witch and the wheel.

Where they clustered, I turned off the main road, and into the forest.

Night fell like a finger snap: one step I rode in the sweltering summer sun that burned my forehead and the back of my neck, then next in cool, balmy night. The forest was transformed into a palette of black and grey and blue smudges, leaves and vines and undergrowth losing their definition. I rode between flowing black river and rustling black trees, the moon swallowed up into a slim crescent. It had been full a few nights ago at Klara's wedding.

I slept bundled up in a travelling cloak at the base of a tree and when I woke, we were in autumn. Drifts of crisp leaves had smothered me in the night and across the mountainside the green of summer was transformed into a fire of red and orange and yellow, ebbing against the evergreen pine trees around the peaks. I rode through autumn and into winter, snow starting as abruptly as night had fallen. A blizzard whipped through only to be replaced by hail and then a bright, windy spring day. I shook the snow off my cloak and set my head down, thinking only of moving forward.

I rode through sleet and sunshine, spring and summer, midnight and midday, hailstones bouncing off my shoulders and rain soaking my hair. I worried time had collapsed so thoroughly I would never reach the castle. Perhaps this was another kind of loop and I was doomed to ride through the seasons like some figure in ancient myth, trapped forever in my quest. I had lost all track of how long I had been travelling, sleeping when I was weary and rising when I had energy again. Days had stopped meaning anything. But slowly, the road began to slope up and away from the river, switchbacking up the mountainside until it reached the village.

The village was frozen in the day I had left; I recognised

the same people sweeping their doorsteps or carrying firewood, and small banks of snow were still piled up, forever melting in the July sun. Time had all but stopped, trapping all the townsfolk in a juddering half second of action, twitching their hands, jerking their heads like a puppet show. The Witch's binding magic had protected me from the loops for only so long before – I would have to move quickly. I led my horse between them, careful not to brush against any of the figures. I wondered how long they could survive like this, not eating or drinking or sleeping. But then if time had stopped flowing, could age or hunger even touch them? I stabled the horse behind the inn with a full nosebag of oats and only a naive hope the loop would leave him untouched.

I turned towards the castle. It rose over the village like a painting, picked out in grey and white and black, a cold monolith of stone and timber and slate. A mist wreathed the forest, smudging the castle's outline and casting a milky pall over the trees. But it couldn't hide the vast blackthorn hedge that had sprung up around the schloss like a wall, twelve feet in height and as impenetrable as the stone foundations of the castle itself. I walked its perimeter, taking in the sharp thorns as long as my finger, the gnarled branches twisting back in on themselves, weaving together as tight as if they'd been worked on a loom. It had been a narrow hedge when I had first come, only another tangled part of the wildwood. Now, it was a moat, a mountain range.

I stood, hands on my hips, and peered up at its height. My Witch lay on one side and I on the other.

At the bridge across the chasm, the blackthorn was

especially thick, so dense I could see nothing of the other side. I could hack my way through and find myself tumbling into the raging torrent below. So instead, I returned to the village to cross the river there, then wove a path through wild forest up the mountainside to the foot of the castle. My apothecary garden was consumed somewhere inside; I knew I had found it when I came to a section shorter than most, where little fat blue and purple berries hung heavy on the branches – sloes fit enough to make a cupboard full of jam – and amongst the roots mint and rosemary and kale and peas still grew.

Nestled in the heart of the hedge, one branch growing through an eye socket, was a skull. A living memento mori: rosemary for remembrance, strung round with bones.

It was my garden all right.

And on the other side, the door at the bottom of the Tower – my way in. I had my pocketknife, but it would be about as effective as digging a grave with a thimble. Running my fingers over the thorns I felt an energy humming inside, the raw power of time run amok. I broke off one thorn and between one blink and the next it had regrown. No, this wasn't a challenge that could be beaten by brute force.

I settled down on the remains of the cabbage patch, now grown so lush and wild I couldn't tell where one head ended and the next began, and contemplated my options. The path I had lined with flints still showed through the foliage, and I picked up a piece to have something to move between my hands as I thought. This task required patience, and consideration, and commitment.

The memory came to me of the Witch that first morning

we had eaten breakfast together. Stubborn and prickly and reluctant to bend – I hadn't been that much different. I had been determined to make things work the way I wanted them to; I'd wanted to shape the Witch to my will, and had learned how futile and selfish that was. Only when the two of us learned to bend together, to grow around each other like ivy around the trunk of an oak had we been able to build anything that could last.

There was no point forcing something that did not want to be. You could only build on what was.

I weighed the flint in my hand and threw it at the hedge. It didn't quite bounce, but it wasn't far off. I could not tear this wall down – but perhaps I could build over it.

Using my skirts as a basket, I began to gather the flints from the paths and piled them up by the hedge. It was shorter here, only just reaching above my head. I soon realised I wouldn't have enough rocks with the flint alone, so I fetched every stone I could find, fallen branches, anything to pile against the hedge. At the edge of the village, I took stacks of firewood, dragged trestle tables and chairs painstakingly up the hillside to pile at the blackthorn like an offering. Night never fell, only blazing July sunshine hour after hour, burning my neck and wetting my face with sweat. I rested briefly, arm thrown over my eyes, then worked again, building with the most solid and heavy things at the bottom of the pile, and shaping the rest into something resembling a flight of stairs. Once it was high enough I fetched a horse blanket from the stables, then paused to drink from my canteen and steady my nerves.

Slowly, arms out for balance, I climbed the pile of rubble. A handful of stones sheared off in a rockslide and I went down on my knees hard; the motion subsided and I kept climbing. I was perhaps only two metres up in the air, but it felt like I was balanced at the crest of the mountain. Gingerly, I pulled the horse blanket up behind me and slid it over the top of the hedge so I could crawl across its width without impaling myself like a shrike dropping its prey onto the thorns.

At last, I could see to the other side of the hedge; my garden was there, wild and riotous, and beyond, the base of the Tower. The door was like new, shining with polish.

I hadn't thought this far ahead. With no makeshift staircase on this side it was a sharp drop to the ground, but there was nothing else for it: I would have to jump to clear the spikes that protruded from the side of the hedge. I crouched, gathering my nerve again.

Love was a leap of faith.

I launched myself into the air.

I was prepared for the climb this time round.

My hands were sweaty from exertion and nerves as I followed the stairs in their tight spiral, impatient to reach the top and frightened of what I might find. My feet and knees ached from the heavy landing off the bitterthorn hedge. I had fought so hard to get this far; now the final stretch lay ahead of me and it felt like the longest of all.

Whatever happened next, I would know one way or another what was to become of me.

The door at the top of the Tower lay open and I stepped inside.

Klaus stood in the middle of the room, beside the great unmoving wheel, eyes glassy and body strangely slack. A golden glow hovered above the surface of his skin, just as it had around my hand that day the Witch had bound us. It was his life being drawn from him, the raw stuff of time ready for the Witch to spin through her wheel.

But the distaff was empty. No new thread had been spun.

On the spindle, only the barest suggestion of something: dandelion haze, smoke from a snuffed candle. Insubstantial. All but gone.

I wondered how long I had before time stopped completely.

I found my Witch curled on the floor under the window, as I had seen her the day she had rescued me from the wheel, arms wrapped around her knees and expression desolate. It took me a moment to realise she wasn't wearing black, but white. I recognised it as one of my shifts, perhaps the one she had lifted over my head in the dark of her room, the last moment that we were close.

Time had stripped her back to the girl she had been, lost and frightened and trapped.

I saw her, and I knew what I was going to do was right.

Travel-stained and sweaty and trembling from lack of sleep, I went to her, crouched beside her and took her face in my hands.

'Hello, Witch.'

When she saw me, she didn't move at first, blinking her large dark eyes slowly. 'Are you real?'

'Yes.'

'Liar.' A tear splashed on the front of her shift. 'My Mina wouldn't be that stupid.'

I stroked a tangled lock of hair behind her ear, brushed my thumb over her temple. 'You think too highly of me. I am a fool for you.'

I kissed her softly and she leaned up into my lips like I was water in the desert. We hung there, consumed in the nearness of each other, the flutter of her pulse under my fingers, the blazing heat of her skin, the soft give of her flesh as she drew me close.

Then, like thunder breaking in a summer sky, she pushed me away with enough force I fell back on my elbows.

She rose, wraithlike. 'You should not have come here. You cannot stop me from doing what I must.'

I felt suddenly too aware of Klaus standing by the wheel, the golden shimmer of his life ready to be shorn from him like fleece.

'I didn't come here to stop you.'

She arched a brow, and I felt a shiver of familiar anticipation; I knew that look so well. She could be scathing and brilliant at once, her tongue cutting in one breath and kissing me so softly in the next. I wanted it. I wanted all of it.

For all that the fate of the world lay on my shoulders, some simple part of me was glad just to be with her again.

'Then tell me, what did you think you could do here?' she said. 'You see I have the boy. I have no need of you now.'

I stood, a little shaky from my days of travelling, and steadied myself on the window frame. 'Perhaps I need you.'

She snorted. 'You think to save me with love? You come too late. There is nothing left in me to save.'

I smiled at that. 'We can never truly see ourselves,' I said, moving myself between Klaus and the Witch. 'Because I see in you someone who deserves saving. Someone who should have been saved countless times over. I see someone who has endured so much hardship, and stayed human through it.'

'Stop it,' she snapped. 'Stop lying to me.'

I saw her resolve tremble, the bud of hope that maybe she could let herself believe what I said was true. That she deserved more than what she had been condemned to.

'You are no monster. You take no pleasure in what you do. You have lived an impossible situation and many would have dealt with it far worse.'

'Don't.' She covered her face with her hands, drew shuddering breaths.

'You have been through centuries of hurt, and yet you still let me in. You opened yourself to me, let me share your life. You gave me somewhere to belong. Somewhere to love and be loved. *You* gave all that to me.'

The longer we spoke, the more the golden glow around Klaus faded, sinking back into his skin. Whatever she had done to draw his life out to ready him for the wheel was wearing off. The glassy look slipped from his eyes and then he was blinking, as though rising from sleep, and he took me in.

'Your Highness?' He looked around the room, seeing the wheel, the Witch, and not seeing them, the strangeness too much to accept.

'Downstairs, now,' I said, gesturing to the door. 'Quickly.'

He seemed too dazed to question me, and descended the stairs with a dreamy lightness to his limbs.

The Witch was distraught. 'What have you done? The wheel must be fed. I must spin. Fool,' said the Witch, with no sting in her voice. 'Hopeful idiot.'

I smiled. 'Always, for you.'

I knew there were more important things to do but none of them seemed to matter as much right now as pulling her into my arms and kissing her again. So I did it, feeling her tense, then sink into me, kissing me with earnest need.

'I thought you would hate me,' she whispered against my neck.

'If you are a monster it is only because they have made you one.'

Her lashes were stuck together and glossy, and she looked at me with such naked hope. I kissed her softly, slowly, savouring the salt of her lips, the line of her waist beneath my hand. 'You know I love you, don't you?' She nodded but I pressed her. 'Say it.'

'You love me. I love you, too, Mina, I love you. I should have said it before.'

I stroked my thumb across her cheek, heart full and warm to hear it. She rested her head against my shoulder and we breathed together, the slow rise and fall of her chest with mine. The world felt heavy, like syrup. Behind her, I saw the last spindly smoke-like thread around the spindle fade.

It was time.

I held her face for one last moment, took in the specks of

grey in her irises, the curve of her brows, the arch of her lip, the filigree of lines at the corners of her eyes.

'Tell me everything will be well,' she whispered. 'Lie to me.'

I smiled, tears spilling down my cheeks. I loved her so, so much.

'Everything will be well,' I said. I smiled, a soft, fragile thing. 'By oak, by ash, by bitterthorn, I swore an oath to you. I mean to keep it.'

And I reached for the wheel.

'No!'

It was too late.

I placed my hand on the distaff this time, not the spindle; the distaff where I had seen that hazy cloud of golden light dwindle each day. I felt it hunger for me; like a river dammed, it longed to break, the weight of time bearing down upon the wheel. The same shimmering halo rose from my skin all along my body; the world turned golden and I saw my life pour down my arm to spool around the distaff.

I was dying.

My hand went cold, then numb, then my arm and my shoulder and neck and chest.

And then I was gone.

XXV

Time stood still.

The last of the spun thread faded, and the steady flow of time wound to a halt.

Above a strange, hidden valley nestled between mountains, a castle lay under perpetual winter. Around it had grown a vast bitterthorn hedge, as tall as a house and so thick little light passed through. The village below was a silent tableau; no birds sang, no voice broke the air. No tree swayed in the wind, and no breeze carried the smell of snow from the mountaintops. The sun sat at the cusp of the horizon, split in half by the sharp ridges and peaks, forever poised to rise again, or slip into darkness. Across the valley night lay suspended in the sky, reaching shadows that would never recede.

The castle stood alone. Still, unending and immediate. All of eternity in a moment, and one moment for all of eternity.

The Witch stood by the wheel at the top of the high Tower.

A thick tangle of something golden and light and warm was wrapped around the distaff, ready to be spun.

But no hands worked the fibre.

At the base of the wheel lay a body, pale and deathly. Like

scraps thrown onto the discard pile, only a collection of flesh and limbs. Her life hung around the wheel, stripped back to raw material ready to be fashioned into something else: time. The fabric of a life stretched out like thread to be woven in a pattern of loss and joy, creation and sorrow.

But the Witch did not spin.

It was her duty, but what did it matter, without her. Without Mina.

The weight lay on her shoulders, and for the first time in four hundred years, it was too heavy.

She would let the world die, frozen in an unmoving moment like an insect in amber, like a body in a peat bog. She would let the world come to an end, rather than let her hand be the one that took Mina's life.

She would not spin. Even if it meant her own death, the death of all life, she would not spin.

With the very last scraps of time left to her, the Witch sunk to the floor, tangled her fingers in Mina's hair. Lay down beside her love, wrapped her arms around her to keep her lifeless body warm, and let time stop.

XXVI

I was everything and nothing. Everywhere and nowhere. I felt myself light, like a cloud, like the vaporous mist from a kettle, or a hunt's kill in winter, side ripped open and organs steaming against the snow. I was light and darkness, tomorrow and yesterday, never and always.

I saw the Witch lie down with my empty body. I knew I had sacrificed myself to the wheel for a reason, and some distant part of me despaired. My plan had not worked. I should have known she would not spin if it were my life to be used. I looked on her face for a long time, and I thought, somewhere, my heart was breaking.

It was not the first heart that had broken in this Tower.

Just as when I had touched the wheel before, I was dragged into the twist of time's thread. I saw all four hundred years of the Witch's life with the wheel spread before me.

I saw the Witch again, young and desperate, pacing the Tower for days alone. She span and span as the golden fleece on the distaff dwindled; a servant came at last, drawn by the weeping in the Tower. The moment she touched the wheel in curiosity, her life flowed out of her body just as mine had, and wrapped itself around the distaff, ready to spin. The Witch recoiled in shock. Then, in hideous comprehension, she searched for some way to reverse it.

I saw her fail.

Spinning on, though she had to stop to retch, hands shaking so badly the thread was lumpen and ropey and time snagged around the castle in loops she didn't understand how to untangle.

I saw her roll the body down the stairs and out of the Tower door into my garden where the bones sank into the earth and flowers grew from eye sockets and rib bones.

I saw it happen seven more times. Each time the Witch fed the wheel, it lasted for the span of life the victim had remaining: a half-century, sometimes more, sometimes less.

It broke my heart to watch her learn it.

At first the Witch brought someone to the castle for help. She was lonely and scared and thought with assistance, she could study magic well enough to find some other way to spin, to break her curse. He was a kind-hearted scholar who loved learning and taught her to play the viola. With his help, the Witch mastered a little magic, but when they tried to harness the complexity of the wheel's powers as Berchta had done, that power was old and unfamiliar and evaded her grasp. When the news came that her father had passed away of old age, the scholar stroked her hair while she sobbed, and told her she still had him for family.

But the thread grew thin, and the wheel needed a life.

The life of someone she had grown to love, to trust, to lean on when she was scared or exhausted or hopeless.

The Witch fed him to the wheel at knife-point, blood staining the doublet and hose I had seen locked away in his trunk, because what other choice was left.

I watched her break, then.

I watched her bawl until her voice wore out because no one was coming to save her. The curse was true: she would spin alone until her fingers withered and her back bent double, until the end of time.

My Witch didn't make the mistake of loving again.

She learned to measure out her attention, to tidy away her heart. Love wasn't worth the grief it brought.

I saw six more companions come.

I saw none leave.

Sometimes the arrangement was purely mercenary, a stipend paid to a family, a man kept prisoner like food stored for winter.

Sometimes, early on, she would try to make them happy. Books or music or food, whatever they called for.

More often, in her darkest years, when it felt as though her soul was a corroded, twisted thing long burned out of her like wood turned to charcoal, she let her anger and despair rule, and she reigned terror on whatever human sacrifice had been flung into her path.

In the end, it became routine.

The years sloughed away like the mountaintops wearing down or rivers gouging deeper into the earth.

A life was spun, it wore out, she summoned another companion with the threat of wrath and dark magic.

She learned better than to grow attached; when one life ran out, a new one must take its place.

Finally, I saw Edgar. Sat at his bureau, paused in the act of writing when a much younger Wolf interrupted him.

'She will see you now.'

Edgar stood abruptly, dropping his quill.

'But—'

'All will be explained. She waits for you in the Tower.'

I watched him go, curious and unthinking.

At the top of the Tower, the Witch stood wreathed in shadows. The light from the wheel had ebbed to a glimmer, but it was enough to ensnare Edgar, just as it had me when I had broken in. He reached a hand toward one spoke, and the Witch interrupted.

'No. Not there. The distaff. Can you see for me whether it is damaged?' Her voice was as low and dark as the night beyond the window.

Edgar nodded in his trance, and put his hand to the distaff instead.

The Witch turned her head away in that moment, hiding her face from what she did. So well-practised after so many years that she could kill with a word.

When it was done, Wolf returned; together they rolled the body down the stairs and into my garden.

I saw his body rot, the soil welcoming him home.

I had found them after all, my previous companions.

I watched the Witch grow cold and hard and lonely. I watched weeks pass where she didn't speak a word. Months where she saw no living thing.

Piece by piece, she lost herself.

Better to be a monster that didn't care about the people

snuffed out, than a frightened girl trapped in a responsibility no one had taught her how to bear.

The Witch's family died, one by one. Unknown half-siblings, and cousins, and aunts. Her nieces and nephews died in turn, and their children, and their children, until the threads of anything like family or home were dust, remembered by no one but her. With every death, she died too. If there was no one else to bear witness, had those memories of her family ever been real?

Her legend swallowed the truth, but who was to say what was truth any more. She was the monstrous witch on the high hill, the beast in the castle that spirited away one man each generation.

The final letter came, the one I had seen her read: banded in black, bringing the news that her line had died out. She was completely alone on this earth.

I saw it all like the pages of a book closed firm together, each small tragedy nestled up against the next until I lived it with her. I had loved her, whether she wanted me to or not; that was our tragedy. I loved her so much I went willingly to the wheel.

Something snagged. Some ripple of confusion.

The pages pulled apart as the curse buckled.

Spin alone until the end of time.

Something was different.

Something had changed.

In that cold, silent tower, time had stopped.

And the Witch did not spin alone.

XXVII

The light behind my eyelids was golden.

I was warm, like a cat curled in a patch of sunshine, like a winter's night beside a roaring fire.

I felt strong.

Unthinking, I stretched out my arms, my legs, cracking my knuckles and rolling my head – and found the Witch curled cold around me.

Something important had happened and I didn't quite remember what.

But my Witch was there, her brows knitted together in an expression of such sadness it seemed obvious that I should kiss her. So I did.

She stirred, making a soft mewling sound, then roused at the press of my lips, eyes flying open wide.

There was something important and I couldn't grasp my stiff fingers around its threads.

The Witch was slower to rise, reaching for my hand and studying it, turning it over. 'You're not dead,' she said in wonder.

That was it.

I had sacrificed myself to the wheel. I wouldn't let my Witch bear the weight of another death at her hands, so I had offered myself willingly.

Together, we turned to look at the wheel. Something golden was snagged around the distaff, but into it was woven silver threads, and copper, and white and pale blue and rosy pink – it was like sun on water, light refracting into its thousand component parts.

A little me, a little her. The love we had for each other, the life we had built together.

Still gripping my hand tight, she looked at me with such emotion, such wonder, I thought she was going to cry again.

'I could not bear to use your life on the wheel, so I let time stop. It was the *end of time*,' she whispered. 'And I didn't spin alone. I had you.'

Tentatively, she rose and began to work the wheel again, feeling the fibres of this strange new fleece, its radiant, cool glow. Thread built on the spindle at a steady pace, even and strong.

I looked at my hands, still half expecting to see a haze of gold rising from them again, my life being drained.

But they were just hands, calloused from work and dirt caught under the nails.

Love made a life rich, I thought, a little given could build into something strong and new. Enough to grow on its own.

Beyond the window, wispy clouds scudded across the blue July sky and the chatter of birdsong was raucous. In the distance: voices, the strike of hammer on anvil. The river thundered past and the treetops danced in the breeze. Summer was warm and bountiful and in the earth things grew.

When enough new thread had been wound around the spindle, the Witch drew back, eyes prickled with tears. I drew her to sit with me, stroked her face, tucked a stray strand of hair behind her ear and it struck me how easily I did it. The gap between us seemed shrunk to nothing.

I knew it would take work to keep it that way, but it was work I was willing to do, and I saw she would do it too.

She rested her head against my shoulder and I twined our hands together.

'You saved me,' she said. Her voice was so soft I barely caught the words.

I thought about it for a while. I thought about the first time I had met her in the stables, then in my father's study when we had been formally bound. The cold winter months when she was sharp and I was brittle. Our tentative truce, and the ember of something that had grown between us that had led me to come back to her from visiting my father in Blumwald. To choose to believe her over Frieda.

I thought of the ways I had hurt her, betrayed her trust. I thought of the way she had lied to me and closed me out.

This should never have worked.

And yet, somehow, it had.

Because both of us wanted it, and both of us worked for it.

'You saved me too.'

My heart was full, I understood what that meant now.

I would go to sleep at night and get up in the morning, and

even if I was the only one in the bed I would not be alone. There was someone to remember me when I was not there and think of me when I did not think of myself.

Loneliness had lost its power over me, and all that was left, was love.

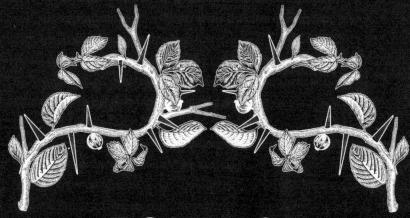

EQUINOX

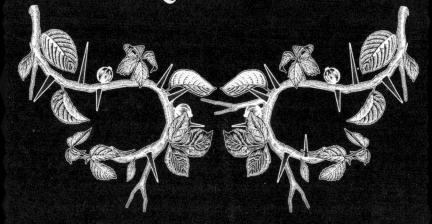

XXVIII

There is not much more to tell, only that we were together, and we were happy.

I wrote to my family, telling them I had changed my mind and would stay with the Witch after all, and invited them to visit whenever they wanted.

It took a few months but eventually Klara came with her new husband, nervous and curious. I had not expected myself to be glad to see her, but I was. She had taken a step towards me, and I would take one towards her in return. For the first time, I thought perhaps I could have a relationship with my stepsisters on our own terms, without my father or stepmother involved.

The Witch was cautious at first, as spiky and awkward as I had ever known her, but I held her hand under the table all through dinner, and over coffee she asked Klara what her travels to Venice were like and my heart swelled with pride.

The blackthorn still grew wild, but no worse than any hedge, and I had picked a ripe harvest of sloe berries the autumn before. They were bitter, but I knew so many ways to make them sweet.

Life began to take shape.

Wolf arrived one day carrying the same travelling cloak and carpetbag she had left with. She still eyed me disapprovingly, but after she and the Witch disappeared into her study for a few hours, she emerged with a slightly softened expression and even deigned to speak with me occasionally.

We remained half-tethered to the castle; time still had to be spun, but now that life flowed freely, bountifully through its walls the wheel seemed content enough to let time grow fat and many-hued on the spindle, ever replenishing and rich. The Witch began to teach others to spin. Me, at first, though I had no knack for it, then Wolf, who was quickly competent and worked up great spools of thread.

I would never travel. I would never see the new German Empire, or Paris, or the ocean or any of the things I had once imagined. There was a cost to my life with the Witch, but I was willing to pay it.

If we could not go to the world, the world could come to us.

We flung open the doors to everyone, the hall roaring with fires in all four fireplaces and the great spur of limestone glowing. My father and stepmother never came but I understood him better now, and needed him less. He knew he had not done right by me, and it was easier for him to avoid that shame by avoiding me.

When I felt ready, I wrote a long letter for Frau Hässler about her children. I told as much of the truth as I could, but sweetened the story. It was the only kindness I could offer.

After several months I had a letter in return from her grandniece to arrange the return of Frieda's remains; she shared the news that my father now paid them a generous stipend.

The only true regret I had was that I could not visit my mother's grave.

The darkness would cross my Witch's face sometimes, the deep marks of sadness and grief that never quite left her. 'I should have thought of it before,' she would say, and all I could do was pull her close and remind her that she had done everything she could.

Sometimes she would turn away, push me off her lap because her legs were going numb.

But sometimes she would hold my face in her hands, thumb brushing my lip, and say, 'I would never have broken the curse without you.'

However many years I loved the Witch, I didn't think I would ever get used to her looking at me like that.

She surprised me with a gift one autumn. A carriage waiting at the door, packed with flowers.

'Go,' she said softly, kissing my hand. 'See your mother.'

I had never told her the exact date of her death, but somehow the Witch had found out, and she would bear the weight of the wheel alone for whatever time I needed.

'I promised,' I said, too full of love and grief, 'I promised I would not let you spin alone again.'

'And I won't.' She pushed me towards the carriage. 'Because you will come back to me.'

'I will.'

It became a yearly pilgrimage to Blumwald to my mother's grave.

I wondered what she would have thought of the Witch. I wanted to think she would have liked her, but the honest truth was that I didn't know. She had died when I was too young, my memories of her were those of a child. I would never know her as a woman, just as she would never know me.

*

A bright June morning a year after the curse had been broken, I swept into the study in my bare feet and light summer skirts, and pulled the Witch from behind her desk. She still mostly wore black, but now and then she would raid my wardrobe and I would discover her wrapped in a peacock shawl or flashing a red petticoat. Today, she wore the grey socks I had knitted for her.

'Come with me.'

'I'm in the middle of my correspondence,' she protested. 'The Elector of Bavaria is still enquiring about damaged watermills when the rivers ran backwards—'

'I want to show you my courgette flowers,' I said. 'I'm going to stuff them with cream cheese and fry them and then you will love me more than yesterday.'

I used to think time was a river, flowing ever onwards but now I knew better. Time is a thread in cloth, woven backwards and forwards through warp and weft. The pattern is something we can only see once the fabric is finished.

Summer lay heavily over the castle with the promise of another year. The beginning of something new.

The Witch cast a last longing look at her desk heaped with letters and papers and ledgers. 'Oh, very well.'

I kissed her cheek. 'We have all the time in the world.'

Acknowledgements

This book has been a labour of pain as much as a labour of love. In the spring of 2020 my mother died. It had been a long time coming, but however a death comes, it is always a shock. Until that moment the person you love has been there in the world, a beating heart and breathing lungs, a location to hold them fixed. Death is an undoing. It unravels reality, unpicking the stitches of a lifetime of relationships, and leaving something unmade, something alien and ugly. I was a stranger in a strange land, and I did not know how to find my way.

So I wrote.

My mother was an Arthurian scholar, a voracious reader, an intellectual. The worlds of fiction, culture, history, art, were one of the few places she came alive. It was the only place I could still meet her. That's not what I thought I was doing at the time, but I can see it now. A reaching out into the turned earth of death and shaping it into something real.

In the spring and summer of 2020 I wrote because it was the only thing left to me. London moved in and out of harsh lockdowns, I was too grief-stricken to work and I lived alone, far from the family I had left. I was overwhelmed by feelings of loneliness, a barren, cold despair that threatened to capsize me. This story was my refuge, my heartwood, the vital core that was left after the world stripped me bare.

I hope I have conveyed something of what I wanted to: that loneliness makes monsters of us all. And that there is hope, and space to change. Always.

There are people I must thank.

First, my agent Hellie Ogden, worked tirelessly to help me write and rewrite this story to bring it to full bloom. To Paul Lucas for his invaluable input, and Emily Randle and Ma'suma Amiri for looking after me so well.

To Chloe Sackur for your wise editorial vision, and your encouragement when I didn't think I could work on this book any longer. Thank you to everyone at Andersen, Kate Grove, Eloise Wilson, Charlie Sheppard, Paul Black, Sarah Kimmelman, Robert Farrimond, and to the cover artist Andrew Davis, and the Walker Books sales team.

Thank you to Chelsey Pippin for being the other half of my brain, for the space that's always held open between us, for your constant companionship and compassion. I do not know what I would do without you.

To Kiran, my sister-pal. By the time you read this it will have been twenty-three years, four books, two dead mothers, and one baby between us. Here's to the next twenty-three years.

To Kate Dylan and Sarah Underwood for being there week by week, for listening to countless meltdowns and crises of confidence, for your cheerleading and your faith in me. I cannot wait until I can put all our books together on my shelves.

To Saara El-Arifi, Tasha Suri and Tori Bovalino for your kind words, your understanding and your patience. You've seen me at my absolute worst, and I hope, occasionally at my best. I am lucky to count you as friends.

To Daphne Lao Tonge, Samantha Shannon, CL Clark, and all the London regulars, thank you for all the dinners and drinks, having writing friends makes things so much less lonely and I appreciate you so much.

Thank you, Ava Reid, for your friendship and support, and for giving me a place to find understanding and solidarity as I've begun to come to terms with some of the most difficult things that have happened in my life.

To Maddy Beresford for letting me unhinge my skull and dump the contents of my brain at your feet over and over. You make me a better writer, and your friendship means the world.

To all my writing friends in person and online for your company, your empathy, your encouragement, and your talent. A particular thanks to my early readers, and blurbers, who were the first inkling I had that maybe this book wasn't a total failure. Helen Corcoran, Lex Croucher, LD Lapinski, Kiran Millwood Hargrave, Kylie Schacte, Emma Theriault, Lizzie Huxley-Jones, Shelley Parker-Chan, Xiran Jay Zhao, Yasmin Rahman, Sophie Cameron, Judy Lin, Francesca May, LR Lam, Laura Stevens, Amber Chen, Pascale Lacelle, Bex Hogan, Charlie Morris, Catherine Johnson, Katie Webber, Hannah Kaner, Laura Sebastian, Alwyn Hamilton, Allison Saft, Lyndall Clipstone, Kat Delacorte.

To my non-books and books-adjacent friends, sorry this is

all I talk about. Kiran, Kirstin, Allison, Jenny, Jane, Tasha, Kate, Harry. If we've lasted this long, I think that's it, I'm in your lives forever. That's a threat.

To my family. My dad, and to Tim, Saskia, Coco, Tony, Jack, Lottie, Kai, Sula, and Lorca, though I have not met you yet. Thank you for all your support and love during some truly awful years. I don't have much to say because luckily I've said most of it to your faces already.

To anyone who's read or supported my books, you make this all worth it. I only hope I get to keep doing this for as long as I'm able.

And to the lonely: I hope you see me, and I see you.